THE ORCHID LOVER

THE ORCHID LOVER

Mary de Laszlo

CHIVERS
THORNDIKE

This Large Print book is published by BBC Audiobooks Ltd, Bath, England and by Thorndike Press®, Waterville, Maine, USA.

Published in 2005 in the U.K. by arrangement with Robert Hale Limited

Published in 2005 in the U.S. by arrangement with Robert Hale Limited

U.K. Hardcover ISBN 1–4056–3107–4 (Chivers Large Print)
U.K. Softcover   ISBN 1–4056–3108–2 (Camden Large Print)
U.S. Softcover   ISBN 0–7862–6981–2 (General)

The text of this Large Print edition is unabridged.
Other aspects of the book may vary from the original edition.

Set in 16 pt. New Times Roman.

Printed in Great Britain on acid-free paper.

British Library Cataloguing in Publication Data available

Library of Congress Control Number: 2004110553

CHAPTER ONE

'Smile please. Say sex.' The photographer smiled himself to show them what to do, his tombstone teeth flashing in his too pink face.

Sarah smiled obediently. She must appear cheerful, not have the people seeing this group photograph later remark on how miserable she looked. Looking miserable always added years to your face anyway.

Matthew Lawrence Bingham, the newly christened member of the Anglican Church, screamed loudly. Evie, his mother, vainly tried to soothe him. He was far too young to know that you had to put on a show for the outside world. This christening party was almost the same size as their wedding two years ago, but the Binghams were rich, liked to flash it about a bit, and Evie, Sarah's god-daughter, had married Larry, their only son.

Sarah studied Larry's parents. His father had plump roving hands that were as much nuisance as an attentive wasp to any young woman. He was well polished by wealth. He had a shiny face, shiny hair and a shiny Italian suit. Larry's mother was expensively dressed in some designer creation better suited to a film première, not to mention someone younger. Under her impeccable make-up lurked a careworn anxiety.

1

Despite all their money, they are middle-aged like the rest of us, Sarah thought savagely. Too young to be old, too old to be young.

Kate, Evie's mother and her friend since childhood, came over to her.

'Bit over-the-top,' she said, in an undertone. 'Not really us at all.'

'A touch of Florida meeting Notting Hill, I'd say,' Sarah whispered back making Kate giggle.

'I'm sorry Dan can't be here; he would have had some choice remarks to make,' Kate said. 'Does he really work on a Saturday?'

'No, he had just made plans to—' What *had* he made plans to do? If she couldn't find a quick, plausible answer, Kate would suspect something was wrong and interrogate her. To her relief, another friend approached them and Sarah was saved from having to answer.

Daniel, her husband of twenty-four years, had changed. It was nothing earth-shattering; he probably did just have too much work, which made him so preoccupied. Times were difficult in the financial world, with the recent birth of the Euro and the indecision of the British Government over whether to join or not.

Dan used to love parties, believing that one needed to have a good time with friends to alleviate the tensions of the office. But recently he'd made excuses not to go out so often, saying there was something on at the office, or he had a client to see.

'Christenings are not really my scene,' he'd said with a deprecating laugh, seemingly forgetting how they had enjoyed themselves at three last year. 'Especially something the Binghams would put on.'

She wanted him here with her in this over-decorated house—everything that could be was tasselled, frilled or gilded. She wanted to share it with him, joke about it on the way home. Hearing it second-hand wouldn't be half so funny, if he'd listen to her description of it at all.

A toast was drunk and there was loud laughter, faces turned towards the child. Mechanically, Sarah lifted her glass, aching with misery. Dan didn't listen to her any more. He was always watching an important programme on television, or reading some vital article in the newspaper. When she talked to him—however cheerfully and lovingly—his face took on an expression of irritation, edged with boredom.

'Great to see you, Sarah! Dan not here?' Colin, an old friend, came up and kissed her.

'No, he's tied up with something else.' She smiled, hoping she looked relaxed, happy, not worried out of her wits at the way Dan had changed over these last months.

Naturally, she'd thought of everything, her imagination charging along in overdrive.

3

Another woman, a mortal illness, depression, imminent bankruptcy, even redundancy and him pretending to go to work each day, as Gina's husband had done. But when she'd asked him if something was wrong at work or at home, he'd become offended, as if she had insulted him; angry, as if she'd accused him of a crime. She had asked him again last week, when he had said he couldn't come today.

'Why should anything be wrong, just because I don't want to come to a christening?'

Why, indeed? After all, they weren't joined at the hip.

When she got home some hours later, bursting to tell him about the whole charade in glorious technicolor detail, he was not there. Where was he? He always used to ring and tell her where he was, leave loving, jokey messages on her mobile. The answerphone sat dead and silent in the empty house, no little red light winking to tell her someone had called. Hideous pictures of twisted metal and his broken body loomed up to frighten her. It was past eight o'clock—if he had met up with friends, wouldn't he have let her know?

When she heard him open the front door an hour later, she jumped up to greet him, all anxiety gone, words almost falling over each other in her relief.

'And you should have seen the cake, Dan, big enough to skate on! And they had satin boxes of sugared almonds, like the French do, and a quartet playing discreetly in the background.' Then she stopped. He looked awful, his back bowed, deep lines biting into that once boyish face. He could not meet her eyes.

'What is it, darling?' She held on to him. 'Whatever it is I'm here for you. We'll face it together.' She pulled all her reserves of energy around her, making a mental list of all the disasters that could have struck him.

'It's nothing, really. I'm just tired.' He extricated himself from her grasp as if she were a stranger who had accosted him on the street. He went straight up to bed, leaving her bleating foolishly in the hall about getting him a drink, a hot-water bottle, anything he wanted.

'Just leave me alone.' His voice wavered on the edge of panic.

'All right,' she whispered, not knowing what to do with this new man, this new direction their life was taking.

*   *   *

She should have guessed. How true that cliché was, the wife being the last to know. Was it because they burrowed their heads in the comfort of their homes, assuring themselves frantically that everything was really all right? Or had she been too smug with their relationship, imagining that he would always love her, would never stray?

Sarah could not watch Dan go as he left the house—the home they had built together—for the last time. She heard the now familiar throb of the car, the little cough it had as it paused at the junction then picked up and spun away. He had driven away with her dreams, the very essence of her being, leaving the remnants of their family scattered like broken treasures at her feet.

She did not cry. She imagined her tear-ducts as dried-up river-beds; deep grooves cut in the earth, where water had once run. There were surely no more tears left in her, only the empty husk of pain deep in her chest. Twenty-four years of marriage gone in a moment.

She had not seen it coming. Dan had been different recently, she acknowledged; bad-tempered, late for meals, and coming home from the office tired and needing hours of sleep. But she had not seriously thought he wanted to finish their marriage, walk away from it as if it were some tumour or bad habit he wanted to be rid of.

'Not you and Dan, surely you'd be the last people . . .' was repeated again and again by their friends and family, like a hideous refrain.

Was she guilty of being too busy with the children, the house, the garden and her job? But if she had left it all to run itself, given all her waking moments to Dan, would he have loved her better? Or, would he, as she suspected, have been irritated by her molly-coddling? Should she have taken more time to question him, winkle out his fears? But every time she had tried to coax him into confiding in her, he had snapped at her, angry she should suggest that he had anything to say.

Perhaps a wife could never win, for a middle-aged man, she'd learnt from him in these last weeks, didn't seem to feel loved whatever you did for him. They could not see that the meals you lovingly prepared, the home you kept warm and clean, the way you put yourself out for them, was love.

Love was not just having sex round the clock; love was not even a taut young body with pert breasts to stir the ageing loins. But they didn't know that. Their wives' battle-scarred bodies, the slightly drooping breasts, the flabby stomachs that once held their children, reminded them of their own ageing bodies. This physical preoccupation seemed to eclipse other important things, such as shared tastes and interests over the years, loyalty and honour. Such qualities seemed almost extinct these days. It had ever been thus, ageing men seeking to relight their fires with ever-younger women. They searched for lust, not love, but she had not thought Dan—sensible, solid Dan—would throw away twenty-four years of a successful marriage merely for lust.

The room was filled with photographs. Laughing babies, held by her and Dan when they were young and happy. Small children extra-polished in school uniforms for the school photograph. Dan at his fiftieth birthday party, grinning in a silly hat. Tim tanned and glowing on a skiing holiday. Polly unnaturally serious on her horse. One of them all, taken last June, happy and windswept on the beach in Portugal. Pictures of a life, her life, their life, now destroyed by Dan's roller-coasting libido and his will to 'live while he had the chance'.

He'd looked so foolish, she couldn't help thinking that; might even have said it, anyway she showed it in her expression. This had made him furious, got him shouting about how dull she was, how she wanted to stay cocooned in her domestic rut while the whole world rolled on outside without them. Only recently had she noticed that age seemed to have caught up with him. He was a few years older than she was, but he was still attractive—had his own teeth and hair, as he used to joke. But a man nearing sixty, with a slight paunch and grey hair, does not look good in tight chinos and bright shirts which his own son would rather die than wear. As for the sports car— these older men might seem youthful driving them, but getting in and out of them with their bad backs and creaking knees destroys this youthful image. Bent half double on the pavement, slowly and painfully straightening up, knocks all the glamour into the gutter. Dan wasn't the only man who'd done it. Philip and Garth, two of their friends, had done the same thing, leaving behind bewildered, shattered families.

'I won't leave you penniless. I know my responsibilities,' he said piously. 'You can keep the house for the moment. I'll give you enough for the bills. Of course, if you sell the house to buy something smaller,' he'd smiled, as if he were being reasonable, 'then we'll share the proceeds. Property has gone up enormously over the years.' Guilt money, paying her off to make him feel better.

'Where will you live?' Why had she asked that, put herself out for more pain?

He had the grace to look uncomfortable. 'I, well . . . we have a flat. It belongs to Nina.'

Nina. Now she had a name, it was worse. When it was just 'a woman I've met in the office, we've fallen in love', it had been easier, as if he had contracted chicken-pox and it would soon be over and the real Dan would emerge again from this frightening chrysalis, and they would go on as before. Knowing her name made it final.

He couldn't kiss her goodbye, even on her cheek, not even shake her hand. He, who had known her body more intimately than anyone else, through all their youth and middle age. He, who had shared the birth of their children, had laughed and cried with her, now treated her as an awkward stranger.

She was like a ship that had been cast aside in a vast and troubled sea, bereft of the tugs that had been attached to her for so long. The children, Dan, his office colleagues, their lifestyle, the friends they had made together, who might now take sides and not stay with her. All this had gone with his leaving. Last month she had known who she was; who was she now?

The telephone rang, harsh in the lonely house. It was Linda, who lived two doors down.

'I saw him go. You must be feeling dreadful. Shall I come round?'

'Oh, no, thanks . . . I've things to do.' She didn't want Linda with her round cheerful face, her questing eyes, searching out her reactions. Her bracing 'You're bound to find someone else, you're still quite young and attractive.' Why did people always assume you could recover from the loss of one person by finding another?

'You mustn't be alone to brood, that's fatal. I'll come round, make you a coffee—or something stronger—and we'll work out things to do. You said you always wanted to learn bridge, and I need help with Save the Children and—'

'No, thanks. I . . .' She felt bulldozed by Linda's manic cheerfulness. She didn't want to learn bridge, help with a charity, even sit down at the kitchen table with Linda over a mug of coffee, or start drinking wine mid-morning. She wanted to creep off out of sight to lick her wounds. She felt alienated from normal life, the life of men coming home, of discussing the day's events, planning holidays and social activities, going to the supermarket, cooking dinner for more than one. Even going to work felt impossible now, as if she had lost half of herself and could not function alone.

'Now, Sarah, we're all with you. Men are shits, they bleed you dry when you're useful to them, and the minute they no longer need you they're off making fools of themselves with younger women.'

'I'm sorry, I've got to go.' Sarah put down the receiver gingerly, as if Linda had wired it up to an explosive device and it would go off in her hand. She didn't want to go down that road, littered with shitty men who'd hurt women, though somehow the once decent Dan had become a shit. She hated him for the destruction he had caused, but she was not a man-hater.

She drifted into the living-room, a square, delphinium-blue room with muted yellow sofa and chairs, one chair rather daringly done up in bright yellow with blue cornflowers scattered across it. She'd chosen the material herself, trawling through the square blocks of safe colours first, then suddenly seeing this one in a display on the wall. It had called to her like a summer's day, like the heady scent of flowers in a Mediterranean market, dazzling, and rich, lifting her up from her usual classical taste. Dan hadn't liked it; too brash, he'd said. He preferred beige, or old gold.

Funny, that. She laid her hand on the back of the chair. He had accused her of being dull, and yet when she had broken out in this tiny way, he hadn't liked it at all.

The telephone rang again, making her jump. Not Linda again, she couldn't stand it. She was weary of her friends' and neighbours' kindness, their knowing looks, their sympathy. How much did they know that she didn't? Had they seen the cracks widen to chasms in their marriage before she had? Had they seen Dan frolicking with this girl not much older than his own daughter?

The ring was strident, demanding as a baby's cry. Bracing herself, she picked it up.

'Mum, it's me. How are you?'

'Polly. I'm fine. What are you up to?'

'Lots. Look, will you mind dreadfully if I don't come home this weekend? There's a party and someone—well, a bloke, of course—who's going and . . .'

Her heart smote in two as if battered on an anvil. 'Of course not, darling. You have fun. Might you manage next weekend?'

' 'Fraid not, a gang of us are going over to Boulogne to buy some booze for Emma's party, then there's exams, but maybe after that. No, *definitely* after that.'

12

'When you can, darling.' She hoped she sounded as if she hadn't a care in the world. Held back that yawning terror of being alone for so long. There would be no one to shop for, to cook for, no heaps of dirty laundry to transform into neat, fresh-smelling piles. She, who'd always grumbled at such tasks, now longed for the stability of them.

'So, how are you, Mum? Is Dad there?'

She knew from her daughter's voice how she longed for her to say yes, it was nothing, we are staying together. The house is a home again. Dad is chasing the snails in the garden, or looking up his stocks and shares in his favourite chair, (not the cornflower one).

She said, 'No, love, he's not. Things haven't changed; he wants his space, he's worked hard all his life and—' Why was she making excuses for him? He was of sound mind as far as she knew, and had made this brutal decision to end their marriage himself. She didn't want him back, not the man he had become.

'So you're all alone, Oh, Mum . . . I . . .'

She forced herself to laugh; it sounded more like a cry for help. 'Of course I'm not alone; no one's alone in the Crescent you know that. Linda rang just before you, wants me to join the Bridge Club. There's lots for me to do, people around. I'll be able to get out more now I'm . . .' she cursed the wobble in her voice, 'now I haven't got to cook dinner every night.' How she longed to cook dinner, sit with Dan in comfortable apathy with a glass of wine, indulging in what he used to call 'Tesco talk'.

'I can't bear to think of you alone.' She heard the tears in Polly's voice.

'I've often been here alone when Daddy was away on business,' she reminded her. But she hadn't felt lonely then, glad sometimes of a few days to herself to catch up on things, busy with preparations for his return. 'I have my job, and anyway, I too need a new life. You and Tim have your own lives, just as it should be and—'

'Yes, but you and Dad should have your own life *together.* You have time and money now to do more exciting things now that we are gone.'

'Pol, things don't always work out as we want them to.' If only she could take her own advice.

'I hate Daddy for just going like that. It's disgusting. Why, this girl is only ten years older than me. How could he love her better than you? She's not even pretty.' Her voice was that of a small, hurt child.

There was no answer. When Tim and Polly had both gone to university within a year of each other, Sarah had thought Dan would be pleased that they now had some time and peace together without their constant demands. At first they had gone out together a bit more, gone on little trips abroad with their friends. Later, he had become quieter, sunk into himself snarling like an old dog when she questioned him. He began to buy clothes more suited to their son, telling her they were for 'dress-down Fridays'. He had his hair cut *en brosse*, giving him a taut, more ageless appearance. He told her not to bother to cook him dinner, as they were too frantic at the office, he would have a sandwich or an omelette when he got home. Then there was the sports car, just two seats, and no room for a family.

'I want a bit of fun,' he'd said. 'I've worked so hard all my life. We couldn't afford it when we first married, it's time I spent something on myself.' She had understood, smiled with indulgence. Even said what fun it would be to go on jaunts in it, just the two of them. But it was not her he had bought it for. He did not want *her* squashed in beside him.

Then, two weeks ago, he had confessed to an affair with a young woman, this 'Nina' in his office. He'd stood right there in the middle of the carpet, angry, defiant, as if it was certainly not his fault, most probably hers.

'What do you mean, Dan?' The words had seemed so inadequate. As the hammer-blows pulverized her heart, sick cramps demolished her insides.

'I'm in love with her, it just happened. It's different than with you; I'm fond of you, immensely fond, but this is so exciting.' His face had shone as if he wanted her to share in his joy, while she stood foolishly there, wanting this scene to stop and yet watching it roll on relentlessly.

'I think it better that I leave. Don't worry, I'll see you're all right financially.' He flung these weapons at her, each word cutting into the very core of her being.

'We needn't get divorced—it will give us more money between us. You know how the lawyers are the ones who come out best in such situations.' He'd said it reasonably, as if he was doing her a favour.

On he'd gone about the spark having gone from their marriage, how it was time to move on. They were both young enough to start again.

Perhaps she was, being in her late forties, though she didn't feel like it. How could it have happened to her and Dan? Dan, who had been her first serious boyfriend, who had loved and nurtured her all these years. Why, only a couple of weeks before he'd told her he loved someone else, they had made love, comfortably and contentedly as before.

She had cried, begged, implored him to stay. She felt hot now with embarrassment, remembering how she had clung to him, saying she would even put up with the girlfriend, sure it was just a phase that would soon burn out. But the hard truth was, he didn't want her any more. She had seen the guilt in his eyes, known that the cruel words he threw at her about being dull, stuck in a rut, were made to justify himself, clear his conscience at his defection, but it had not helped her.

Polly and Tim had come home bewildered at this sudden change to their comfortable, stable lives. Tim, in his last year at Edinburgh, hardly ever came home these days, but she knew he liked the bolster of knowing his home and parents were safely tucked up in the background of his life. Polly, at Durham, felt the same, and now Dan in his selfish stupidity had torn out their security by the roots.

'I'll be fine, darling,' Sarah said now, with a certainty she did not feel. 'Now, tell me about this new bloke. What's he like?'

He sounded like most blokes, but yet he must be different to the others, as Daniel had been for her.

'You're still young, Mum, and look great. You too might meet someone new,' Polly said, with false cheerfulness.

'I think it's too late for that.' She tried to sound jokey. She did not want anyone else. Could not go through this tearing rejection again. Before this, she always tried to look good, even felt that her body was not bad for a woman her age who'd had two children, but now she recognized that it was no longer taut with youth. There were grey hairs on her head that the hairdresser skilfully covered.

How would she dare undress in front of another man? How could she bear to see the revulsion in his eyes when he saw her ageing flesh? That is what Dan must have felt that last night he'd made love to her, though it was in the dark, so she could not see his eyes. Had he had to psyche himself up, thinking of this other girl, before he could perform with her? Had he shuddered while his hands touched her familiar body, imagining the fresh young skin of this girl?

Her own husband had rejected her; how could she ever uncover herself for another man and risk his revulsion?

CHAPTER TWO

'Does this suit me?' The middle-aged woman with the bulging thighs and bottle-blonde hair tugged at the delicate silk round her hips. She looked like a packet of meat straining from its plastic skin in the supermarket.

Sarah couldn't tell Mrs Bradshaw the truth. She must tactfully suggest something else, to play along with the illusion that this woman had in her mind. Traces of beauty clung to her like a fading rose, but every time she came into the shop she wildly underestimated her dress-size. In her imagination did she still see the thin woman she once used to be?

'I think the green suits you better.' She held up the green embroidered dress. It was a size bigger, and would not hug those hips quite so tightly.

'But I love this blue, so rich . . .' Mrs Bradshaw trilled, turning herself again, as if to hide the offending bulges.

Sarah had worked here six years now, designing the clothes for this boutique. They were often short-staffed, so she had to double up as a salesperson, or help pack up the clothes to take them to sell at charity fairs. Celine, an old friend from art school, who owned the shop, bought the materials from India. Wonderful glowing silks embroidered with birds and flowers and butterflies, inspiring Sarah to design exotic trouser suits, dazzling embroidered coats. Two girls in the sewing-room at the back of the shop made them up.

She caught Celine's eye and she came over.

'Now, Mrs Bradshaw, I'd like to see you in the green, or even this raspberry pink.' She took the dress off the rack. 'That blue drains your colour a little.'

She was hopeless at her work now, hopeless at everything. Celine had been wonderful when she'd heard of Dan's leaving. She was so much easier to cope with than Linda was.

'God, I'm sorry, Sarah. What a pig,' she'd said, when she told her. 'What can I do? Do you want time off?'

'I don't know,' she'd sniffed; tears she had once thought dried up came too easily now, like rain in the monsoon, especially when people were kind. They both got in early, quite an hour before the shop opened and before the girls who did the sewing. It was the best time to discuss the sales, the materials and the staff, while they were on their own.

'I don't want you to have time off, Sarah. It will soon be getting into the time of Ascot, Henley, and summer weddings, when people buy the most. Anyway, what will you do with time off, apart from mope, and that will kill you?'

'I know. I want to work, I'll have to anyway, and I only come in three days a week. I can manage that.'

'Do you want to come in more?' Celine jabbed out her cigarette, regarding her intently with her calm grey eyes.

'No. I don't want to change.' She'd meant she didn't want her life to change at all. She wanted Dan back where he belonged so she could sink back in comfy relief into the niche she'd spent so much time and energy creating.

'I'm glad now I never married,' Celine said. 'I know I wanted to when I was younger, but really only because everyone else was and I felt a sort of misfit not to have done it myself. But now I treasure my independence, and the feeling that no one can mess me about, hurt me as Dan has hurt you.'

The pain was as bitter as a bereavement, yet Dan was not dead. He was careering around in a red sports car with a girl young enough to be his daughter. It was hell thinking of that, thinking of him in bed with someone else. That was her trouble; she felt the act of sex was something special, something you shared only with someone you loved, someone who loved you. But it wasn't like that today. Sex was the same as a game of tennis, or a round of golf. You did it as a 'need', as your right to a normal life. Sex was used as a selling-point for everything, from jazzing up Jane Austen on the television to selling chocolate bars. Seemingly everyone but her was at it. Had Dan felt left out too, felt he ought to join this libidinous bandwagon before he needed a prescription for Viagra?

'I'm not the only one who's been dumped,' she said, wondering now if she'd been kind enough to other women she'd known who had been through the same shattering experience. In the general gossip after such an event, blame had often been laid on the deserted wives. 'She never really bothered with her looks after the children were born' or 'he worked far too hard, and she just spent all his money'. Various other failings were trotted out as if it were entirely the wife's duty to keep the relationship going. What were they saying about her in the Crescent now?

Mrs Bradshaw was persuaded into the raspberry dress and then into a matching coat. Delightedly she turned herself about, this way

21

and that, in front of the mirror. Sarah envied her confidence, or was it her blindness? Did Mr Bradshaw still love her? Did he pay her dress bill?

When she'd gone, Celine said, 'So, what will you do about money? Will you have to sell the house?'

'Dan is still giving me just enough to pay the bills. It makes him feel less guilty, and he doesn't want a divorce—we all know how much that can cost.'

'Cost who?' Celine broke in. 'It sounds to me as if he's having his cake and gobbling it up, too. If you went to court, it would all be tied up properly. You must go for a lump sum, though. If he pays you in instalments and drops dead before he can pay it all, you lose out. And if he really does love this other woman, why doesn't he want to marry her?' she asked, in the abrupt way she had.

Celine thought Sarah was foolish agreeing with Dan over this—or at least going along with it. It was hard to explain that she felt numb, too apathetic with grief and bewilderment to fight him over this. Divorce was too final. Keeping things as they were at least left a tiny path open between them.

'This way I get to keep the house. I don't want to move,' she said, ignoring the painful thought that Dan had done it as a bribe to keep his payments to her low. 'The house is my only emotional security. It reminds me that once we were a happy family.'

'Then I'd sell it, move to something smaller and pocket the difference. You've got to move on, love. You've done your bit, bringing up the children and all. Look on this as a new freedom. Think,' Celine threw her an encouraging smile, 'now you can do whatever you like.'

Sarah tried to smile back. That was what was so terrifying; she knew what she wanted, a rewind of her life. Things to be safely back as they used to be. Celine guessed this and gave her a hug.

'There's no going back,' she said. 'There never is, for any of us. Now, why don't we do a new collection? I've been thinking about it for ages, fabulous sexy underwear to go under these clothes. I can get masses of that lovely soft silk, in all sorts of colours. What do you think?'

Sarah laughed. 'Bras are more complicated to design than a suspension bridge!'

'You could learn, and anyway, they would be designed especially for the evening, to wear under these clothes. Not for all day, or going to the gym. Imagine,' Celine's eyes sparkled mischievously, 'Mrs Bradshaw in her raspberry embroidered coat, then her raspberry silk dress, then,' she giggled, 'a raspberry silk bra, pants and petticoat. Perhaps even with a little embroidered butterfly or flower somewhere strategic, to match up on the coat.'

'You'd need an awful lot of silk to cover her boobs.'

'Tow ropes to hold them up!' Celine giggled. 'But if we did just a few sizes; smaller sizes, for women who don't need quite so much coverage.'

'Petticoats would be easy, can't we just try with them?'

'No, I want to try all of it, suspender-belts, too. We want to get more men in here, buying for their girlfriends,' Celine said with enthusiasm.

Girlfriends, Sarah thought bitterly. Could men not buy them for their wives? Did becoming a wife make a woman so dull, so lacking in sex appeal, that sexy underwear would be wasted on her? But Dan wasn't that sexy, not any more. His legs had become thin and pale, his bottom all but disappeared, or anyway gone round to his stomach. He stooped a little, reminding her of an ageing heron. Yet only a few weeks ago she had loved him, felt comfort curled up against his body in the night. It was loving him that made this hurt so much.

*   *   *

At lunch-time, a pretty young girl came in with an older man. She had long blonde hair and a baby mouth. She wore a tight velvet top that finished just above her flat tanned stomach, and skinny black trousers. A silver stud winked from her tummy-button. The man was about fifty, with steel-grey hair and a blue pinstriped suit. Her father? Her lover? Before Dan left her, Sarah wouldn't have cared a bit, live and let live, but now she hated this unsuspecting man for preying on this young girl.

'Can I help you?' she addressed the girl.

'I want to try on one of those trouser suits.' The girl meandered over to the rack where they hung. They were made of velvet or silk, with wide bright cuffs embroidered with flowers, tiny birds or butterflies.

Sarah sized her up; unlike Mrs Bradshaw, this girl was far too thin, she could be a six. She handed her a dark-blue suit and a pearl-grey one.

'This is all we have in your size at the moment, but we can make something up to order.'

'I wanted black,' the girl pouted, a spoilt baby with a spoilt voice.

'We can make you one,' Sarah repeated. 'Silk or velvet, and whichever pattern of cuff you like best.'

The girl looked bored as she listlessly rifled though the rest of the clothes on the rack. The man hovered uncomfortably by the door.

Sarah moved away from her, letting her look. She wouldn't buy anything. She knew the type; they liked to shop, they wanted to buy something now, this minute. They could not be bothered to wait for it.

She must have given the man a more severe look than she intended, for he blushed and looked awkward, said to the girl, 'Is there nothing you like, pet?'

Pet. Was that what she was, his little pet to play with? Did Dan call his new girl that? The bitterness bit into her and she glowered at the man. Had he got a discarded wife somewhere, suffering as she was, while he made a fool of himself over this spoilt child?

The man's lips tightened and a wave of despair crossed his face. 'Why not have a dress? There's a pretty black one over there, on that rail,' he said reasonably, going over to the dress, which, as Sarah knew, was at least three sizes too big for her.

'No,' the girl sighed. 'I don't see anything I want. Perhaps we could go to Harvey Nicks.'

Celine, who had been discussing her new idea for underwear in the sewing-room, came back into the shop and caught this remark.

'You've got a lovely figure,' she gushed. 'Now I'm not quite sure what you are looking for, but this dress would look wonderful on you.' She pounced on a pale-blue one in the middle of the rack. It was a sample. Sarah knew it was not one of her best designs, and it had not sold very well, but in a moment Celine had the dress on the girl and it looked as if it had been made for her.

'That looks wonderful,' the man enthused,

catching the girl's eyes in the mirror and smiling at her.

'I don't know. I wanted a trouser suit.' The girl pirouetted in front of the mirror.

Sarah left them to this ridiculous charade, silently cursing all middle-aged men who chased after these young girls. They had had their turn when they were young; couldn't they leave these girls to find boys of their own age? But then, she supposed young men often didn't have the money or the savoir-faire that the older men possessed.

Did Dan parade his little chick in shops like this? Buy her all sorts of clothes to please her? To please him?

When they had first met, Dan was still studying and he did not have the money to indulge her so. Once, he'd saved up all his bus fares, walking to college in the wind and rain, to buy her a silk shirt. That was real love. A lump grew in her throat like an expanding balloon. When they'd got money, like this man—and Daniel now—they were only buying something for themselves. It was a form of bribery, keeping these girls sweet with presents so they would disregard their failing bodies. After all, you never saw a *poor* old man with a pretty young girl on his arm, did you?

She looked at this man with pity now. Did he really have to demean himself so? Could he not find a woman nearer his own age? Perhaps that was the truth of it. His self-esteem was such that he couldn't compete with one. He needed a foolish child to look up to him, to be impressed by him.

Catching her look, the man regarded her with concern. He had kind eyes, she thought suddenly, and he was attractive, well dressed and obviously intelligent. Why had he been hit by this destructive madness? She wanted to ask him, demand even, if he had a wife and children discarded somewhere.

Then she caught Celine's anxious glance. She must not take out her misery on the customers. She had no right to. Perhaps she should stop work for a while until she'd got over this ridiculous hatred for middle-aged men with young females.

The girl took the dress and the man paid for it, as she knew he would. Sarah packed it up in tissue paper, all the while making polite noises about how pretty it was.

The man took out his credit card, platinum no less, and she swiped it through the machine, reading off his name before she did so. C.N. Harrington. Casper? Charles?

He signed the bill with an exaggerated squiggle, and when she looked at it she could not read it.

He smiled. 'Christian. Christian Harrington.'

She said nothing, handed him back his receipt and his card, and gave the dress in its glossy bag to the girl. Just another middle-aged fool, she said to herself, and did not watch them leave.

CHAPTER THREE

'*Supersexy stud seeks lively companion,*' Linda read out, laughing. 'What a choice. How about this one? *Handsome, articulate, young 50-something, loves music, the theatre, good food and having fun. Seeks slim, stylish, sensuously attractive lady to share enjoyment of life.*'

'If they are all so attractive and fun-loving, why are they alone?' Sarah remarked, but she laughed, too.

'All these men want slim women. No wonder they are alone, if they are so fussy. I bet most of them are no oil-painting themselves; at least, not one you'd want to hang on your wall.' Having a passion for chocolate, Linda had given up on the battle to stay slim.

'I'd much rather enjoy the pleasures of life than be a thin, crotchety old stick impaling men on my hip-bones' was one of Linda's favourite remarks, though the only man she had to impale was her husband, Gerry.

Sarah had spent the evening here with Linda. Gerry wasn't there, which was unusual. He'd been sent suddenly to some hot spot concerning his business, taking over from someone who was ill.

Sarah liked Gerry. He was large and amiable, comforting like an old teddy bear. The four of them had often done things together before Dan had left. Going to films, trying new restaurants, even going on holiday together. She took another gulp of wine. Really she'd drunk too much this evening. She'd regret it tomorrow.

Negative thoughts began to push themselves into her fuddled mind.

She must not allow herself to think that Linda had only asked her to supper tonight because Gerry was not here.

Linda had been very kind these last few torturous weeks, asking her to lunch or coffee when Gerry was at the office, but she had never asked her over in the evenings. It was then she would have liked to have gone out. The days were almost bearable, the desperate ache of her loss containable. She worked in the shop three days a week and had designs to work on at home. But the evenings were long, and she hated being alone night after night in that huge double bed. Weekends were torture when she saw other couples her age pottering around contentedly together, just as she and Dan used to do. Now, she felt like a pariah. Linda didn't trust her near Gerry. Did her other girlfriends feel the same?

How could she tell them that she didn't want their husbands? If she had, she would have grabbed them when they were younger, more attractive.

Linda flicked through the dating columns again. '*Encounters.* These people must be all right, from *The Times.* They sound far more exciting than Dan. Gerry, too, for that matter.'

'What if one of them was Gerry or Dan?' Sarah attempted a laugh. 'Imagine turning up for a hot date and seeing one of them sitting there.'

'Oh, Gerry wouldn't do anything like that.' Linda's smile was awkward. 'He's not the slightest bit interested in . . .' she paused, flushed, 'well, you know . . . bed. Anyway there's more to life than sex, isn't there, and it's a little undignified at our age don't you think? After all, we know we love each other and we have lots of cuddles.'

Linda would never have confided such a thing if she hadn't drunk too much. Sarah didn't think sex was at all undignified; well, not between people around the same age, anyway. Dan had a dodgy back, which had sometimes interrupted their lovemaking by going into spasm. How was it holding up with this new, younger woman? She had a sudden image of him contorted like one of those ancient figures after the volcano at Pompeii, stiff and immovable, encased in larva. To her amazement, it made her giggle.

Linda misinterpreted this and shot her a pained look.

'We had a very active sex life until last year.

Then it became rather boring, and neither of us can be bothered with it now. I bet yours and Dan's was the same.'

Sarah was not going to discuss their sex life with Linda. It would be all round the Crescent by lunch-time. It had been very exciting at the beginning, but these last years it had become comfy, not especially ambitious. Was he up to all sorts now? Would his spasmodic back stand up to it?

'It depends,' she said, in answer to Linda's question on sex being undignified, 'but I do agree there is more to love than sex.'

'Of course there is, though you'd never think so nowadays. All these young girls popping into bed with anyone they fancy, then bleating about commitment. They all say they are having such fun with their drink and sex binges, but I think they are a cry for help not a cry of joy.' Linda poured herself out some more wine.

Sarah wondered if Polly popped into bed with anyone she fancied. She'd been engaged to Dan at her age and hadn't had the chance, though of course morals were different then.

'I think it's threatening people's relationships. I mean take Dan.' Linda sat back self-righteously, as if she were an expert on such matters. 'Middle-aged men can be so influenced by such things. No doubt he felt he was missing out on some tacky other life, quite forgetting that there were so many more important things that he'd worked so hard for and succeeded at. Now he's thrown them all away, looking rather ridiculous while he does so. I mean, why do men put so much importance on what they can do with a few inches of gristle?' She laughed sourly. 'Surely their brains are more important?'

Sarah got up. It was time to go home.

* * *

When she opened her front door, the light was on and music was playing. Polly rushed into the hall to greet her.

'There you are, Mum! Where were you? I've been so worried.'

'Pol.' She kissed her, her heart contracting with fright. 'Are you all right? Why are you home today?'

Polly frowned, her pretty mouth sulky. 'Why should anything be wrong? I said I'd be here for the weekend.'

'Of course you did, darling, and it's wonderful to see you.' She hugged her again, relishing her warm body in her arms. How she'd missed this close contact with a living person. 'It's just that it's Thursday and I wasn't expecting you today. I'd have stayed in if I'd known you were coming. When did you arrive?'

'About an hour ago. Where have you been?' Polly demanded again.

Sarah refrained from saying, 'Now you know what it's like, worrying bout someone being late home.'

'I had supper with Linda, that's all.' Reading the unspoken question in Polly's eyes, Sarah knew she had been worried that she'd been out with a man. Funny, that; both she and Tim had urged her to find someone else, as if it was only a matter of going to some shop and picking out the right size, colour and shape, as you might a dress, but in reality they did not like the idea that she might find someone new.

'Sorry, love, no hot date. Just Linda. Not even Gerry was there.'

'You were there ages, it's midnight.'

Sarah put her arm round her. 'So? What's so special about midnight? Will my clothes turn to rags, my coach to a pumpkin?'

Polly laughed. 'Oh Mum, it's good to see you laugh. I'm sorry. I just came home early to surprise you, and you weren't here.'

'And I'm thrilled to see you. Have you eaten?'

'I found some dusty cereal at the bottom of the box. There's nothing much in the fridge,' Polly said reproachfully.

At once Sarah felt guilty. She should have been here, kept the fridge filled with pasta, cheese and eggs, as she had in the old days. Steady on, she scolded herself, don't go down that road again. You are being independent now. Polly doesn't look as if she's starving and no doubt she manages to eat well enough when she is not at home.

She sensed that Polly had come home to find reassurance. Finding the house empty and hardly any food in the fridge had unnerved her. She hugged her. They all needed propping up now.

Polly sat on her bed and told her about Joe, the new man in her life. Occasionally she saw Polly glance at the space in the bed which Dan used to occupy. Sarah had moved herself into the middle of the bed now, piling up the pillows to make herself a sort of nest. Though neither remarked upon it, she knew that both of them felt hurt and betrayed at his absence.

*   *   *

The following Saturday, Sarah took the bus up to Bond Street to buy a present for her godson's eighteenth birthday. She wandered up the street, browsing at the lavish windows as she went. Everything seemed very expensive. She'd end up going to the jeweller in Walton Street; they always had things she liked, but it was fun looking here first.

The throb of a car engine distracted her. A red sports car juddered to a halt. She was overwhelmed by a dizzy sickness. It was the same make of car that Dan had bought; she couldn't remember the registration number. It resembled a monstrous frog, squatting there at the kerb. The driver's door opened and a man got out. It took her a moment to realize that it was Dan. He got out slowly, his back bent over, his bottom out as if he was about to sit down again. Slowly, he straightened up. To her surprise, she felt a pang of sympathy for him. Had he really looked as old as this before?

He went round and opened the passenger door, and a young woman sprang out. So, this was Nina. The jealous pain almost stopped her breathing. Nina was dressed in black and had red hair, not bright red, more a sort of subdued copper. Her face was long, rather pale; she was certainly not a beauty.

Dan looked up and saw her. Sarah stood rooted like a tree on the pavement. He looked surprised, a little guilty; he gave her a hesitant smile.

'Sarah—how are you?'

Nina stared at her, glanced enquiringly at Dan before scrutinizing her again. The familiar look Nina threw Dan unleashed the anger that lurked inside her. This man had been her husband, the father of her children, and he had given it all up for this nondescript woman.

'How do you think?' she retorted, coming closer to them.

Dan's mouth twitched with a nervous smile, his hand fluttered feebly in her direction as if he wanted to placate her. She went on,

'I needn't ask how you are, Dan. You look

terrible, so ill.' Fear flashed in his eyes and she felt a pang of guilty triumph. Dan was a hypochondriac—you only had to remark that he looked unwell and he was round at the doctor's surgery at once.

'He's very well,' Nina retorted, glaring at her.

'Well, he doesn't look it. Perhaps I should have gift-wrapped him for you, all glitzy paper and sparkly ribbon,' Sarah said spitefully.

'What a bitchy remark, Sarah. Not like you at all,' Dan said, looking at her reproachfully.

'Who's the bitch?' Sarah retorted.

'You're very unkind,' Nina bleated.

The anger at his destruction of their lives was as hard as a shield inside Sarah.

'Really?' she said. 'And I suppose he has told you what a terrible wife I was to him? How I didn't understand him, made his life so miserable he had to escape to you?' As she said this, she saw from Dan's shameful expression that she had hit the mark. This betrayal hurt her more than anything that had gone before.

'Sarah, this isn't solving anything,' he said desperately.

She felt as if she were on a stage and must perform. People hurried by, but she thought that some lingered, sensing an exhibition.

'That,' she said, loudly and clearly, 'is a sign of your guilty conscience. By telling lies about me, you feel you can excuse your selfish, ridiculous behaviour. You know we had a good marriage, but you threw it away for the trappings of adolescence and you are making a fool of yourself.'

'Give it to him, girl!' a man passing them quipped.

Sarah came to her senses then. Dan had his arm round Nina. He looked white and anxious. Nina's face was hard, pointed like a little mouse. What honestly did he see in her? She supposed it was bed, but she didn't even look sexy.

'You know what they say about old fools, Dan.' Her voice was quieter now. It held a note of regret. She left them, walking quickly away back to Piccadilly, down to Hyde Park Corner, down half of Knightsbridge, until she reached her jeweller in Walton Street. She saw nothing as she walked, but she felt that if she stopped she would fall apart. Had she really said those things? She meant every one of them, though the deep pain of his loss still seared through her.

What were they doing in Bond Street? Visiting jewellers, too? Was he going to marry her, or buy her some bauble to cement their love? She must not think about it, she must seal her mind from such thoughts.

She wondered what their friends thought of Dan and Nina. Did they ask them round together? But what an insignificant little mouse she seemed. Was that why he had gone with her? So he could rule over her, get her to do what he wanted? Did that make him feel good? Had she made him feel bad?

She strode down the street alongside Harrods. Was *that* it? Had she become too bossy?

She reached her jeweller's. The man on the door opened it for her and welcomed her in. This courtesy pricked the old tear-ducts, but she controlled herself enough to ask to see some cuff-links.

She'd never seen her godson wear anything smart; no doubt Nick would really like an inexhaustible supply of beer and cigarettes. But perhaps one day he'd grow up and get a job that occasionally warranted wearing a pair of nice cuff-links.

Sarah chose a simple silver knot design, with the understanding that Nick could change them if he wanted to. But knowing Jenny, his mother, she would put them away until he became respectable.

She left the jeweller's with her package neatly wrapped. Once, the shop used to have glossy bags to carry things home in, but now they advised her to put her purchase in her handbag so as not to draw attention to it.

'A sad reflection of the times, madam,' the door man remarked to her as she left.

'It is,' she agreed, but in the mood she was in she'd be a match for any mugger. The anger at Dan and Nina—the mouse and that frog-like car—the description sounded like the title for a children's book—still squirmed and bubbled inside her. She marched down the street and turned sharply in the curve of the road leading to Fulham Road, and walked smack into somebody. He trod on her toe most painfully.

'Watch where you're going!' she barked at the jerseyed chest of the man she'd collided with. He put out his hands to steady her, to steady himself.

'I'm so sorry,' he said, holding her a little away from him.

She looked up into his face, frowning with annoyance and pain. He had swept-back grey hair, light brown eyes that looked at her in concern. She'd seen him before, and she saw the flash of recognition in his expression.

'I'm really sorry. I do hope I didn't hurt you,' he said, one hand still under her elbow.

Her big toe throbbed like mad. She longed to pull off her boot and rub it, but the boots were too long and the whole action would be too complicated, too undignified, to perform in the middle of the street.

This was the man who had brought that silly little girl into the shop. She had lumped him in with Dan, as a pathetic ageing man destroying all that was good in his life for a selfish whim.

She glowered at him. 'Yes, you did.' She forgot this man and thought of Dan. 'You hurt

40

me dreadfully, now let me go,' she tore her arm from his grip, 'and watch your step in future.'

He started as if she had slapped him across the face. 'I'm so sorry, where did I hurt you? Shall we sit down somewhere? Have a drink?'

She did not want him to be nice to her, this man who preferred little girls to grown-up women.

'No, thank you. I don't want to have anything to do with you.' She took a step away from him, but the movement hurt her toe and she winced.

'Can I call you a taxi to take you to hospital, or home?'

'No, you cannot. Just leave me alone.' She bit her lip against the pain and pushed past him.

She hobbled up the road as fast she could. To her relief, a number 14 bus stopped at the lights and she got on it. Whatever was wrong with today's middle-aged men? In her mother's day, it used to be middle-aged women who were so miserable with their empty nests and their 'nerves'. She didn't know a single woman like that today. It was the *men* who had gone completely to pieces.

41

CHAPTER FOUR

The charity lunch party, held in aid of breast cancer, was in full voice. Sarah knew quite a few of the women there. It was a stand-up do, and people were shovelling food into their mouths, balancing a glass and trying to talk at the same time.

'I'm so sorry about you and Dan,' Gail, one of her neighbours blurted in her ear, as if she felt she had to get it out. 'It gave me such a shock; after all, you seemed so . . . solid.'

Sarah, who had been quite enjoying the lunch, now felt as though a damp blanket had been thrown over her. She hated the gleam of prurient curiosity that appeared in some people's eyes, as if they longed to know the dirt so they could smear it round in some superior way.

Seeing Dan and the mouse-woman, as she now thought of her, in the street had knocked her hard. It was bad enough knowing her name, but seeing her in the flesh was the final stab. She wasn't that pretty, and ironically this made her feel worse. If Dan had dumped her for some luscious, beautiful young woman, she'd be some way to understanding him, but had he disliked her so much he had to leave her for that nondescript little mouse?

She was not too ashamed at her outburst,

42

though it was rather out of character—but it was shaming to have shouted at that unfortunate man she'd bumped into. It would be very embarrassing if he ever came into the shop again with his 'pet'.

'It must be so upsetting after being together for so long,' Gail went on.

'It is.' Sarah turned to the woman on her other side. She didn't know her, but she was talking with Linda.

'And suddenly we've found the house of our dreams! Exactly where we've always wanted to be, near Aix, but we can't afford it unless we sell our house here. We've got to do that fast, before someone else snaps it up.'

Linda asked her why they couldn't take out a loan on the house in France, but the answer was complicated. Sarah, not much interested, but only asking because she wanted to prevent Gail from wheedling out any more gossip about her and Dan, said:

'Where is your house?'

'Just off the New Kings Road. It's very sweet, we love it, but this one came up and Paul says we ought to grab it while we can. Those houses are like gold-dust in that part of France.' She went on at length to describe her house. Linda, who couldn't face a rerun, wandered off, leaving Sarah alone with her.

'There are two of them at the end of the street, so it has a bigger garden than the rest. Four bedrooms and nicely done up, though we were going to re-do it this autumn.'

Sarah knew where the house was. It was in a short, pretty road off Parsons Green. The houses were all painted in ice-cream colours. She suddenly heard herself saying,

'Which agent is it with?'

'Oh, are you interested?' The woman turned to her, as eager as a terrier.

'N—no, I'm not looking, actually,' Sarah confessed, realizing that this woman would jump on any possible buyer, however remote, and she had raised her hopes without meaning to.

'Oh.' The woman looked disappointed, said wistfully, 'Of course, it would be wonderful to sell it privately. Then we could do our own deal on it, make it advantageous for all of us. Where do you live now?'

'I live round here, too.' Sarah described the house she loved. But now, with its heart torn out of it, it no longer felt like a home. The cost of it was becoming a serious worry—the money Dan gave her and her salary did not seem to stretch very far. Would it not be nice to have a new, smaller house? Do it up, make it her own?

But she hated house-hunting. It was such an emotional roller-coaster. The house you liked was too expensive, or falling down, or you were gazumped, or the dreaded 'house chain' broke somewhere along the line and you lost out that way. She certainly would not want to deal with all of that on her own.

The woman seemed to sense her thoughts. She said, almost pleadingly, 'You could come and look at it, if you like. But we need to sell it at once. I'm going to see some estate agents on my way home from here.'

'I'd have to sell my house first, and really it won't do me.' Seeing the woman's crestfallen face, she said as an offer of comfort, 'Give me your telephone number. I might hear of someone who'd like it.'

'Thanks. My name's Annie Blake. Here's my card.' She thrust it into Sarah's hand. 'In fact, I'd better go now, get it on someone's books. Bye.'

'Bye,' Sarah said, thinking she would leave, too.

*　　　*　　　*

That evening, as she sat at the dining-room table, working on her designs, the doorbell rang. She glanced at her watch; it was half-past eight. She got up and opened the door. Gerry Squires, Linda's husband, stood on her doorstep, swaying slightly.

'Gerry,' she smiled, pleased to see him. He looked as if he'd been tossed about in a whirlwind, mussed-up hair, bursting out of his city suit, his blue shirt creased and his tie askew. But then he always looked like this.

He bent forward to kiss her. 'Can I

come in?'

'Lost your key?' she joked. 'Have you time for a drink?' She led the way into the living-room. 'What will you drink? I think Dan left some whisky.'

'Bloody fool, Dan,' Gerry said, 'leaving a lovely woman like you.' She was touched at his sentiments. They had, all four of them, shared some good times together.

'It's done now,' she said, 'but I do find it very hard.'

'You must do.' He stood in the middle of the room, regarding her intently. She asked again what he would like to drink. He made a sudden lunge at her, crushing her in his arms, raining kisses on her face, her neck, her breasts, anywhere he could reach with his large, red lips.

'Gerry, stop it!' The more she struggled, the more excited he became. He was panting, kissing, slurping; arousing nausea and revulsion in her instead of passion. With a superhuman effort, she pulled at his hair with one hand and whacked him on the back with the other. 'Stop it!' she screamed in his ear. 'Stop it at once!'

He loosened his hold on her; his eyes had a crazed look.

'Sarah, you must be so lonely, in that huge bed all by yourself. I've always fancied you, you must know that.'

'Gerry, you must be mad.' She jumped away

from his grabbing hands and ran into the hall to open the front door.

'I'm lonely, too,' he said, following her. 'I thought we'd be able to help each other.'

'But Gerry . . .' He thought she wanted sex from him. She used to value his friendship, look on him with affection; now he had ruined it.

'What about Linda? You can't just come round and expect—' She shuddered.

He caught the movement and she saw how it wounded him. She felt degraded, furious, and immensely sad that sex was all he was offering. A quick tumble to slake his lust. He would have been far more useful if he had offered to look at the washing-machine, which was making dubious noises.

'On your way, Gerry.' She opened the door.

'You know how much I care for you, Sarah.' He had a silly grin on his face, as if he must humour her.

'Not in that way,' she said. Linda had confided that Gerry was not interested in bed. Well, she'd got that wrong. He was rampant, leaping on her like that the minute he came into the house. Would Gerry be the next one to roar off in a sports car with a mousy girl by his side?

'But aren't you lonely in bed?' he tried again, as if he could not believe that she did not want to sleep with him.

'Not enough to sleep with . . .' She would

have said 'you', but despite it all she couldn't bring herself to hurt him further. She suspected that underneath his jovial manner lurked a small, hurt boy. Instead she said, 'Someone else's husband. Especially as you live in the same street. Now go,' she said sternly, 'and never, ever do this sort of thing again.'

He slouched out of the house into the street.

'You won't mention this to the old girl, will you?'

'Just go!'

'If you are ever lonely . . .' he repeated before she shut the door behind him.

She stood in the hall, shaking. Gerry, of all people! How could he have shamed her so? But is that how men saw her? A lonely, unrequited woman, desperate for sex?

The empty house seemed to stand judgement on her, accusing her of some unconscious behaviour that had brought him here. She no longer fitted here, a single discarded woman among the other couples. What if the other people in the Crescent had seen that charade? They would soon pass it on to Linda, cause untold trouble by their remarks, shame her even more.

She felt unclean, as if she had been violated. Then she remembered Annie Blake, who wanted to sell her house. She snatched up her bag, trawling through it until she found her

48

card. She wouldn't want the house, but it might be worth looking at, as practice.

*   *   *

Sarah arrived at Annie's house just after nine. It was as she described, two houses side by side at the end of the street. They were both painted the same shade of Wedgwood blue, which gave the illusion that they were one house with two front doors.

Annie appeared nervous. 'You're the first person I've shown round. I was going to fill the house with flowers and the smell of freshly brewed coffee to make it more desirable, but I haven't got round to it. An estate agent is coming later today. I'm dreading that. They see all the faults, don't they?'

'I think they often overpraise the house to get it on their books, then, if they can't sell it, they start picking it to pieces, saying no one wants small houses, large houses—whatever yours is—at the moment,' Sarah said, looking around her.

The house was a different shape to the other houses in the street. It was wider and lower. The small hall was at one end, then the living room, then a large kitchen/dining-room. This opened out into the garden. The sun streamed into the house, lifting Sarah's spirits.

As she went round, she could feel the house slowly attaching itself to her. A sense of excitement crept through her. How much easier it would be to live here. It was more compact than her house, but there was still room for Tim and Polly. It was in the area she loved and knew well, but far enough away from the Crescent and Gerry and the neighbours who had known her as Dan's wife. Here, it would be different. Here, she could start again as herself.

'Who lives on the other side of you?' she asked Annie, wanting there to be a difficulty—people who partied all night, something to put her off.

'Robert Maynard, but he's hardly ever here now. He's recently inherited a business up north, but he's nice, you won't have any trouble with him. So . . .' Annie waited expectantly. 'Do you like it?'

'Very much, only,' Sarah braced herself to tell her story, 'my marriage has broken up and I'm in limbo at the moment. I don't know . . .' She tailed off, feeling foolish that she couldn't cope with this on her own. Dan had been so good at everything like that. He just got on without involving her at all.

'If you really like it, Paul, my husband, could help you. Can you come to supper tonight and discuss it with him?' She was so eager, Sarah couldn't help but get caught up in her enthusiasm. Having supper with them wouldn't hold her to anything.

'What do you think about it?' she asked Celine, when she got to the shop later and told her about everything, including Gerry.

'If you like it, go for it. A new house will help you come to terms with Dan's defection, establish your independence. As long as the money side works out.'

'I've got to sell mine first, but it should be worth more. Goodness, when I think of when we first bought it, it was almost falling down and Fulham was unknown. We could barely afford it. I think it cost twenty-five thousand. We had to have a huge mortgage.'

'Frightening how inflation has rocketed in our lifetime. You couldn't buy much for that anywhere now. What's it worth now? Seven hundred thousand? Eight?'

'I think so, but then the new one will not be cheap. But, oh, the children!' She gasped in horror. 'I'd forgotten them, they'd hate to move.'

'Tough.' Celine, who had no children, said firmly. 'You've given them years of your life, now it's your turn. Do you need a solicitor? If so, use Rebecca. She'll sort out everything for you.'

Rebecca was their company solicitor. She would certainly see to everything.

That night, at supper with the Blakes, Sarah found herself agreeing to buy the house. Paul,

Annie's husband, was a jovial man whom she took to at once. What clinched matters even more was that he had friends who were looking for a family house in the Crescent and might like hers.

'It is obviously meant to be,' Annie said piously.

'If I can persuade Tim and Polly,' Sarah said.

She rang them when she got back that evening.

'But, Mum, you can't!' Tim cried out in agony. 'It's our home.'

'But you are hardly ever here, and anyway this new house will be a home.' She tried to ignore the guilt clutching at her heart.

'It won't be the same,' he went on.

'Life is not the same any more, darling, remember that.' She refrained from bursting out, 'Your father has ruined it for us, blame him, not me.'

'Oh, Mum, we've lived in our house all our lives. Nowhere else will ever be the same,' Polly wailed.

'Come home and see it before I make the final decision. Tim said he would. Tomorrow's Thursday; come for the weekend. I have to make a quick decision or I'll lose it,' Sarah said then added as a softener, 'You can do up your own room just as you like it.'

*   *   *

Tim and Polly came home that weekend. Saturday also produced a letter from Dan. One of them must have told him about the move.

Are you sure you are making the right decision? After all, I don't think you are in the right frame of mind for something of such importance. Wait a while.

Sarah recognized his words as a stab at getting his own back after her scene in the street. This only fuelled her determination to make her own decision.

Paul Blake's friends came round to see her house on the Friday. She arranged for them to come early, before Tim and Polly arrived home. Her children might well be sullen and difficult if they saw prospective buyers poking round their home, but as she waited for Paul's friends, she suddenly had cold feet herself and wished she'd put them off. It was all going too fast, perhaps next week she'd wake up and realize it had all been a huge mistake.

Paul's friends were a young couple, with three small children, and they loved her house at once. They had been looking for a family house in the Crescent for ages, and they told her terrible stories of how they had lost houses elsewhere at the last minute. They kept looking at each other delightedly as she led them from room to room, and she had not the heart to say she'd changed her mind. This house needed a family; it no longer made her welcome.

Linda came round early on Saturday morning. Tim and Polly were still in bed. She said with indignation, 'I think you are mad to move, Sarah. You're happy here, and we all know and like you.'

It was difficult to feel relaxed with Linda now. She'd managed to avoid her these last few days. What would she say if she knew that it was thanks to Gerry that she no longer felt she could live here?

'I need a change, a fresh start, and I'm not far away,' she said lamely, not able to meet her eyes.

'Gerry thinks it is a bad idea, too,' Linda went on. 'You know what they say, after a bereavement you shouldn't make any major decisions for at least a year.'

'This is not a real bereavement.' Doubt grabbed her again. Perhaps she was mad to move; perhaps Gerry would feel less threatened if she moved to another street, and would become a real nuisance. She'd see what Tim and Polly made of it.

When at last they emerged from their bedrooms, they all went round to the new house. The Blakes tactfully went out, leaving them to it.

Polly grudgingly admitted that she liked it.

'You could make that cupboard place into a shower-room, then it would be ensuite to my bedroom. And the garden's great; pity we can't have the other side of it, too. But we can have barbecues and things, have our friends over, can't we, Tim?'

'We had barbecues in our old house when Dad was here,' Tim answered sulkily.

'Look, you two,' Sarah said firmly, 'I've got to live my own life now. You've both got yours, but because of your father's potty behaviour, I'm on my own now. This is what I want to do. You are hardly ever here, Tim, but you will still have your own room in this house.'

'Come on, Tim, don't make it difficult,' Polly said, turning excitedly to Sarah. 'I've seen some great wallpaper in the Designers Guild.'

Tim slumped on a chair. Like Dan, he did not talk about his feelings. Sarah suspected that their break-up had hurt him more than he would admit to. He would see selling the house he thought of as home as yet another betrayal. But he would have to come round, accept that things had changed for ever.

They went back to their universities on Monday morning. Polly was cautiously excited about the move, while Tim was resigned.

Paul Blake drove the whole thing forward at breakneck speed, which at least stopped her dithering away and not making any concrete decisions. She was sleepwalking through life, had been ever since Dan had left, drifting along with the flow of it, too apathetic to protest.

She wrote a note to Dan asking him to come and collect his last bits of furniture. He lived in Pimlico now.

'I want you to come alone, arrange for Tim and Polly to be here if you need some help. I shall be out,' she wrote. Even though she was leaving the house, she did not want that mousy creature poking and peering round the place they had created with such love together.

Dan rang her one evening. 'I'll be round on Saturday with a van,' he said tersely. 'Gerry said he'd give me a hand.'

'Fine, I'll be out all day.' She put the phone down. 'Two-headed creep Gerry,' she muttered.

When Dan's things had gone, the house felt even more denuded. It reminded her of a holiday resort out of season, with deserted leaves blowing in the empty streets, loud with the silence of loneliness.

There seemed to be so much to pack up and sort through. Things for the charity shop, things for the dump, things to take with them.

University had broken up for the summer. Tim and Polly came to help her before they went off again on some projects of their own.

It was a bittersweet time for the three of them. Possessions, especially childhood ones, evoked memories—memories of the good times now gone.

'If Daddy had died, we would have a better feeling about looking back,' Polly said suddenly, tossing a couple of books into the bag for the charity shop. 'He used to read me these, over and over, but now I don't want to think about it.'

'He's still your father,' Sarah said, hating Dan for hurting them so.

'He's not the same man at all, all stupid with that woman. He can hardly talk to us any more—she gets jealous,' Tim said morosely.

Sarah stayed silent. Tim and Polly usually met up with Dan for lunch when he was on his own, but they had gone over to Nina's flat a couple of times for supper. She did not ask questions, too afraid to hear how happy Dan was, what fun they had without her.

'You can chuck all this out. I don't know why I kept them anyway,' Tim said, kicking the bag of Lego aimlessly with his foot and discarding a very expensive steam engine, which belched out real steam, that he used to love.

Sarah resisted the temptation to pack up all his old toys, books and tapes, and keep them. She had to let go of the old life, as they had. Later, though, she compromised and retrieved some of the better things, telling herself if she ever had grandchildren, they would enjoy them.

The two houses were valued, and to her delight Sarah made quite a profit from the sale. Dan must have heard of this, too, for he rang her again.

'I know I said you could keep the house, but I didn't know you were going to sell it so soon. I'm entitled to some of the cash, we agreed on that.'

The way he said it chilled her. She had always shared anything she had with him, but now he would share it with that mouse and she did not feel so generous.

'I'll let you know what's left over. It needs a lot doing to it, and they weren't giving it away,' she said, and put the telephone down.

Later, he sent her a letter explaining in long and complicated detail how fair he was being. The price of property had shot up and he deserved his share of the profit. She tore the letter up and sent it back to him, saying if he wanted a divorce it could be dealt with then.

Suddenly, all the frantic packing was over. It was her last night in the Crescent. They had bought the house when she was pregnant with Tim, and Dan had been left a little money by his grandfather. The house had been grubby and shabby, made up as bed-sits. Every room held a riot of coloured wallpaper, with a different-patterned clashing carpet. They'd seen through the dirt and the crudely divided rooms to the family house it had become. This was the linchpin of their world; now she must let it go and move on.

Tim and Polly had somehow slipped away,

not able to bear 'a last night'. She understood that, wished she could avoid it, too. She wandered from room to room, seeing the ghosts of a happier life. The marks on the laundry-room door, where she'd measured the children as they grew; the bright patches of clean wallpaper on the parts of wall that had been covered by furniture or pictures they had chosen together. Once, her marriage had been bright like that, before it had faded and died.

She slept with the agitation of someone with an early plane to catch, afraid not to wake. When the morning came she struggled up with relief, wanting the move over.

In the new house, her days became a round of builders, and searching for wallpapers and colours. She put in a new kitchen; the old one had warped cupboard doors. She took Polly's advice and turned the cupboard into a shower-room. She juggled work between it all, until she was so stressed and tired she didn't know how she kept going.

Dan rang her again, he always rang while she was in the shop knowing she usually answered the telephone there. He told her to stop being childish over the money and give him what was left over as the difference between the old house and the new. He would stop the money he gave her for the bills if she wouldn't be fair.

'Don't you talk about being fair to me!' she snapped. 'Because of you, I had to move, and while the builders were there I got them to do everything, once and for all. So, please stop ringing me here. I want to get on with my own life.'

After all the bills to do with the move, there was nearly £120,000 left over. With bad grace she had sent him £70,000, and spent the rest on doing up her house. This did not please him, as he had wanted it all but she no longer had it, so that was too bad. She offered to pay it back at the rate of one pound a week, adding to his anger. She could imagine him grumbling to the mouse in the evenings about her.

Polly took a great interest in the decorating, and between them they turned a serviceable house into a very pretty one. Even Tim became enthusiastic and chose some red paper for his room, though it made it resemble a nightclub more than a bedroom.

*   *   *

For the first time since Dan had left her, Sarah felt happy, pleased with her achievement. She was filled with a new energy; even with less money, she would get by. This energy showed in her work.

'That dress and long jacket is great,' Celine enthused. 'I've tons of orders for it. It suits everyone, young, old and assorted shapes. The underwear is not bad, either. We'll get the bras right in the end.'

*　　*　　*

Early one evening, about a month after she'd moved in, Sarah was relaxing with the newspaper when she was disturbed by a sharp knock on her door followed by a ring on the bell.

Gerry! Her mind shrieked. She had not seen him since she had moved—she hadn't seen anyone, she'd been so busy. But if it was him, he would be sorry.

The bell rang again, urgently. She tiptoed to the front door to peer through the spy-hole to check that it wasn't Gerry. It was not.

A man of about her own age stood frowning on the doorstep. His brown hair was ruffled. It was obvious from his sharp eyes and the tight lines round his mouth that he was extremely annoyed.

'Is it true,' he addressed her firmly, 'that the Blakes have sold this house to you?'

'Yes, they have. I've only recently moved in.'

'I'm afraid that they had no right to sell it to you,' he said, and she saw he was fighting to control his anger. 'They promised it to me. I'll be seeing my solicitor in the morning.'

61

CHAPTER FIVE

Sarah shut the front door in his face in panic. What right had this man to accost her like that on her own doorstep? Was he some maniac who'd called on her at random? Some unfortunate mental patient who had forgotten to take his medication? There had been a man wandering round the Crescent some years ago who'd terrorized the elderly by denouncing them as Communist spies whom he had just reported to the authorities.

If only she could control the underlying fear that spawned like an invasive weed through her determination to start a new life. Was she to be plagued for the rest of her life by barmy middle-aged men?

The bell rang again, sharp and strident, making her jump. She fled into the dining-room at the back of the house, her hands balled into fists, as if ready to defend herself. She stared defiantly out into the garden, forcing herself to breathe deeply and rhythmically. She would not answer the bell again.

It was the word 'solicitor' that caused the fear. Had the Blakes done something dishonest? Sold her a house that didn't belong to them? A house that belonged to this man who had come back—perhaps from some long trip abroad—to claim it?

Whatever would she do if they had? Everything had been done so quickly; she had just gone along with it in a sea of panic, desperately wanting to escape the pain of the collapse of her old life. She couldn't move back to the Crescent. That was sold now. If only Dan had stayed, none of this would have happened, but he had not, and she cursed him roundly. She would have to cope with this herself; it made her feel immeasurably lonely. She'd ring Celine to ask for Rebecca's home number and get her to deal with it.

*   *   *

'She's away in Spain until next week, but don't worry, he sounds like a nutter. Shall I come round and chase him off?' Celine said cheerfully.

She wanted her to come, but she didn't want to become a needy bore to her; after all, Celine had been coping with her life alone forever.

'No, don't bother. He didn't look too bad, well dressed, quite a pleasant face when he wasn't scowling.'

'That doesn't mean that he's safe. I'll come round. I'll bring my long scissors with me, snap them at his groin. That will shift him!' She laughed.

Her cheerfulness made Sarah laugh, too. 'I

felt very pleased with myself for moving and all, but just one thing like this can upset me. I hope he really is mad and that there isn't a genuine problem with me owning the house.'

'I'll come round, and we'll call the police if he's dangerous. I suppose he might have mistaken the house. Was he drunk?'

'No, well, I don't know. I slammed the door in his face.'

Celine was round in ten minutes, but rather to her disappointment the man had gone.

'You should have brought your scissors round when Gerry came,' Sarah said. Celine was the only person she could tell about Gerry without it being built into a leaning tower of gossip and innuendo, until it finally collapsed on top of her.

'I'd have enjoyed that.' Celine snapped her scissors in the air. 'Done some radical cutting out.'

'He said something like "they promised it to me",' Sarah said, wishing the sudden shock of his statement had not made her forget exactly what he had said. 'What if it wasn't theirs to sell, or they had already sold it to him?'

'Don't panic until you have to,' Celine advised. 'Now I'm here I'll stay a bit. He might come back.'

He did not, but the next evening, when Sarah returned from work feeling scratchy and tired from a troubled night, the door of the house beside hers whipped open and out he came.

'Good evening,' he said coldly, standing on the pavement beside her, slightly barring her way to her own front door. 'Before you shut the door in my face again, I would like to talk to you.'

She regarded him with disdain. He was dressed in a cream shirt and pale jeans. His face was lean, with a well-shaped mouth and slate-blue eyes. He did not look threatening, but he looked cross. He must be the man (whose name she had forgotten) whom Annie had said she'd have no trouble with.

He said, 'My name is Robert Maynard. I live next door, as you see. Would you come in for a drink? I've something important to discuss with you.'

'No, thank you, I will not. What is it you want to say?' Fear crawled like ants over her body.

His face was creased with annoyance; drawstrings of lines tightened his mouth. He relaxed it a moment and it improved his looks. She wanted to get away from him, but was afraid to open her own door in case he pushed himself inside the house and trapped her there.

'I've been working all day and I'm tired. I didn't sleep well last night, either.' She glared at him. 'Can't you put whatever it is in a letter?'

'No, I think it better to talk it through. The

thing is . . .' He glanced up the street, and Sarah guessed he wondered if he was being watched. Well, that was neighbours for you; they always wanted to know what was going on. She didn't know any of them yet; one or two had welcomed her, but she had no one to call on for protection if she needed it, but she would not go into his house or let him into hers without someone else being there with her. She needed Celine with her scissors.

She said, to bring an end to it, 'We'll meet on mutual ground. I'll see you at that coffee place on the corner in ten minutes.'

'All right, but tell me your name first.' He looked at her as if he would only deign to sit with her if he approved of her name.

'Sarah Haywood,' she snapped.

He nodded, turned sharply from her and marched back into his own house, shutting the door with a defiant thump. Sarah let herself in and dropped her bag in the hall. She was overcome with exhaustion. The last thing she wanted was to join him and no doubt be bullied by him.

She caught sight of her reflection in the oval mirror that hung in the hall. She needed more lipstick and her hair was anyhow. Though why should she mind? After all, this was not a date. It was her next-door neighbour, who would no doubt see her at her worst, putting out the rubbish or blindly feeling for the milk in the early morning.

She brushed her hair just a little bit and put the slightest smear of lipstick on her mouth. She waited in the kitchen for a full fifteen minutes until she left her house to go to the coffee shop on the corner. She envisaged a foolish charade of them both leaving their houses at the same time. Perhaps even colliding on the doorstep. Would they walk down the street together, or on opposite sides of the road?

He was there at a table by the window. He jumped up when she arrived, relief chasing the irritation from his face.

'You said ten minutes.'

'I'm here now.' She was hit by shyness. This was the first time she had sat alone with a man she didn't know since Dan had left her. She felt like a gauche teenager and had a terrible temptation to giggle foolishly.

'What can I get you?' he demanded briskly, as if he did not want to waste time getting her anything.

'Cappuccino, please.' She wondered if she should pay for her own.

She watched him queue at the counter, saw the impatience bunch his face. He was obviously not a man who liked to be kept waiting. She found herself wondering what he would be like as a lover, then seeing him look at her she blushed and glanced away, as though her thoughts were dancing all over her face.

He came back with the cappuccinos, pushing a foaming cup speckled with chocolate towards her.

He said at once, 'I've lived next to the Blakes for ten years. They always promised me that if they sold their house, they would offer it to me first.'

'I didn't know that.' She sipped her cappuccino to hide her nerves, almost scalding herself.

'Well, they did. Now I come back to find that they have disappeared and that you have bought it.' He sounded aggrieved, as if she had done it on purpose to annoy him.

'They offered it to me,' she said. 'I met Annie at a lunch. She told me they wanted to sell it urgently to buy a house they had always wanted in France which had just come on to the market.'

'But they promised it to me. I have the money. I would have bought it immediately. They should have let me know about it,' he insisted.

The cappuccino left a small moustache on his upper lip. He had a nice mouth, soft and full. She must stop thinking like this; *she* was the mad one. He was her enemy. He wanted her house and she sensed that he usually got what he wanted. He was bad tempered and would no doubt be the neighbour from hell. She must not be so foolish and weak as to fancy him. It was only because she was without

Dan that she was suffering from the 'little woman' syndrome, needing a man to protect her. She'd been used to a man in her life for too long.

She said firmly, 'I'm sorry about that. But I bought it in good faith. My solicitor's away for a few days, but I'll get her to confirm it as soon as she is back.'

'I very much want the house for my orchids,' he said, as if he was telling her of some world-changing reason which would make her feel obliged to give in to him.

'In the house?' she asked stupidly.

'No. I was going to knock the two houses together and put a conservatory in your garden.'

'Wouldn't it be better to do that sort of thing in the country? You'd get more space for your money there.'

'I don't want to live in the country. I want to live here, in my house. It was in a terrible state when I bought it. It had to be completely gutted and started again. I spent ages, not to mention a lot of money, making it just as I want it.' His eyes appeared to go darker with intensity.

'So did I,' she retorted. Fear and that stupid guilt that somehow it was her fault that he hadn't got the house added to her agitation. 'I bought the house in good faith, and did it up. I want to stay in it.'

He tried another tack. 'Perhaps I could talk

to your husband?'

'I have not got a husband.' The old panic and anger that Dan no longer cared about what happened to her assailed her. It was that he no longer cared for her after all these years together that hurt the most. 'I did this on my own, and I'm not giving it up now.' To her humiliation, she felt tears rise in her throat. She took a savage sip from her cup, scalding her mouth again.

His voice became more gentle. 'I don't mean to upset you.'

'Well, you have,' she said, getting up before she disgraced herself by bursting into tears in front of him. 'It is *my* house, bought with *my* money and I will not let it go.' She swept out of the coffee bar, but he followed her.

'Surely we can come to some agreement?' he said. 'I'll help you find another house. Just as nice, nicer even.'

She was aware that people were watching them and she wondered what they would make of it. She imagined them taking sides when they knew the details, no doubt confirming Robert's story, siding with him, as he was a familiar face in this area.

She wanted to go home, shut her door and be safe in her house, but now this man had upset everything. He lived next door; they shared the same internal wall, the same garden fence.

She whirled round to face him.

70

'I want you to go away. I want to go home alone. I want to live in peace. You haven't been here for weeks, so go back to wherever that was and leave me alone.'

'I was away working. I don't need to go away in the near future.'

'Well, keep away from me. I simply detest middle-aged men.' Her temper broke loose. 'I am tired of the selfish way they think they can have whatever they want, no matter who they hurt.'

'Is that what your husband did?'

'None of your business. Now, go back to your orchids and leave me in peace.' She stormed away from him and turned into their street. She wondered if he was following her, and braced herself with more verbal missiles to throw at him, but he did not come.

She went into her house and double-locked the front door behind her. Catching sight of her angry face in the hall mirror, she felt ashamed at her rudeness. She had not meant it for him, but for Dan—she needed to take her anger out on *him*, not any other man who annoyed her.

Orchids; sinister, beastly things, she thought childishly. Was her neighbour like that, too? *Oh, Dan,* she sobbed into the curtain. *How could you do this to me? Turn me into such a dragon?*

71

CHAPTER SIX

It was a warm afternoon in July. The morning had been frantic, and Celine had been held up at a meeting and had only just arrived in. Sarah stared lethargically out of the shop window at the people passing by. She needed a caffeine fix to revive her, but she felt too lazy to get up and make one.

Since her confrontation a few days ago with Robert Maynard, her fragile optimism in her future was severely splintered. She had not seen him since their meeting at the coffee shop, but she was painfully aware that he was next door.

The houses had been built about a hundred years ago. They were solid Edwardian, with thick walls, but they let through some sounds—the hum of the Hoover, faint strands of music, the ping of the burglar alarm being put on and turned off. But the worst place was the garden in the evening, when they were both at home. They could not see each other through the wall and the high trellis that separated them. The plants were dense, winding their way through the slats of the trellis covering all the gaps. But what would it be like in the winter when the plants died down? Would she be plagued by seeing him each time she went outside?

The weather had been marvellous recently, and it was lovely to sit in the garden when she got home. But for the last two evenings she had felt uncomfortable sitting there and had instead sat inside, near to the open French windows, inanely thinking that if she went outside he would watch her from an upstairs window. She refused to look towards his house, not wanting him to have the satisfaction of knowing that he bothered her. When she left for work in the morning and returned at night, she prayed that he would not be there outside his house at the same time as she was outside hers. His presence, real or imagined, overwhelmed her. She hated to think of him there, plotting his next move to seize the house from her.

She became aware that a man was staring at her from the street. He lifted his hand in a small salute and came into the shop.

Her heart gave an alarming lurch. It was the man who'd bought that dress for his baby girlfriend, the man to whom she'd been so rude when she'd knocked into him in Walton Street. Was he coming back to buy more clothes for that dratted 'pet'? She would have to be polite and not put him off.

'Good afternoon.' She hoped Celine, hearing the door, would come out of the sewing-room and deal with him herself.

'I suddenly saw you sitting there,' he said, with a shy smile. 'We parted rather badly last time we met.'

Was he going to complain about her rudeness? If he was going to buy lots of clothes for his 'pet', she'd better grit her teeth and be nice to him.

'It gave me such a fright the way we knocked into each other like that. You stood on my foot. That's why I was so cross.'

'I'm really sorry if I hurt you.' He smiled again. He had a nice smile, which glowed in his light-brown eyes. Pity he wasted it on a spoilt schoolgirl.

He glanced round at the brilliant silk and velvet clothes hanging on the racks, as if searching for inspiration.

'I suppose you wouldn't like to come out for a drink to make up for it?' His words tumbled out in a rush.

'Good afternoon.' Celine bustled out of the sewing-room, a red silk trouser suit over her arm. She threw one of her radiant smiles in his direction.

'Good afternoon,' he said, looking rather self-conscious. He glanced at Sarah, as if gauging her answer to his invitation.

Celine said, 'Can I help you with anything? That dress you bought earlier in the year was so pretty. We've got some new stock in, if you are interested.'

'The dress was pretty, but I don't want anything else just now, thank you.' He looked out of place in this sumptuous, silken den.

A tinge of sympathy for him touched Sarah, but she couldn't go out with him for a drink. He preferred young girls, like Dan did. She'd only feel older and more wrinkly and flabby just by knowing that.

'I'll pack that suit for Mrs Mattock,' she said, as a way of escape. Celine handed it to her. She hung it on the rack beside her as she took out wodges of tissue paper and lay them on the counter.

Seeing he was not leaving or wanting anything Celine still hovered, occupying herself tidying through the rack of clothes, doing up the buttons of a shirt, checking a pair of trousers would not get creased by the way they were placed on the hanger.

'So?' he said softly to Sarah.

Sarah busied herself with the paper and the trouser suit. What harm could a drink do? It was hardly an invitation to bed, or anything else for that matter. No doubt he thought she was a motherly type and wanted someone to talk over his affair with. Well, he'd chosen the wrong person in her!

'When were you thinking of?' She felt she had to say something.

'After you finish here today?'

Today? Now? She needed time to think, but she supposed it would be better to do it now, not dither away wondering whether she would or wouldn't go. It meant she wouldn't have to go straight home, risk Robert jumping out of his front door, armed with some other proposal to seize her house.

'Thanks.' Then, thinking she sounded ungracious, she added, 'I'd love to.'

'Good.' He looked relieved. He named the wine bar just down the road, and left the shop.

Celine rolled her eyes with exaggeration 'My, I think he fancies you.'

'I don't. Remember that young girl he brought in? Probably got her pregnant or something, and wants my advice,' Sarah remarked gloomily. 'Bet he starts with, "as a mother, what would you do?".'

'I'm sure that's not true. How does he know you're a mother anyway?' Celine looked out into the street at his fast-retreating back.

'I might change my mind and not go; though it is something to do. Good practice for my new life,' Sarah said, putting the tissue-wrapped trouser suit into a bag. 'There, shall I call a taxi to deliver it?'

'Yes, the housekeeper should still be there.'

When she'd done that, Celine said, 'I've been asked to spend a week with the Fieldings in Italy at their huge villa; you know I go there most years. It's in the last week of August, running into September. They suggested I brought a friend, and as I've no particular man in tow at the moment, I wondered if you'd like to come? You'd only have to pay for the air ticket, and there's plenty of good deals around.'

'Oh, Celine, but what about the shop?'

'I'll get Maggie to run it for a week. August is dead, anyway. Just a thought, you might like to get away.'

'I would.' She thought longingly of the russet light of Italy, the familiar landscapes mirrored in Renaissance pictures. She hadn't planned a holiday at all this year, put it out of her mind each time it nudged at her. Usually every summer she and Dan, and any children that wanted to, went somewhere together. Where would he take that mouse? The thought filled her with bitter jealousy.

'Yes,' she said, hugging Celine, 'I'd love to come, thanks so much for asking me.'

'Good. You'll like it there; it's very laid-back. All sorts of people come in and out. I spend most of my time lying in the sun, reading—you can do what you like.'

Excitement buzzed through her. It was something to look forward to. Being a single woman, Celine often went away on her own—though staying with friends was hardly on her own, but it was something Sarah was going to have to get used to.

Three customers came into the shop one after another and Sarah, her mind filled with thoughts of Italy, almost forgot her drink ahead. She'd forgotten the man's name, which was highly embarrassing. She wouldn't go. Then it was half-past six and they closed the shop.

77

'I think he's called Charles,' Celine said as she left, going down the street in the opposite way to the wine bar. 'Have fun.'

Somehow it seemed more complicated not to go. He seemed nice enough and would 'do for practice'. She remembered the hideous insult girls at school had used to describe some hapless youth: 'I wouldn't even use him for practice.'

None of this helped her nerves as she approached the wine bar. He can't eat you, she told herself. That was the sort of thing her mother had said to her when she first began to go out on dates. Teenage nerves in a middle-aged body, she thought wryly, taking a deep breath before going in.

The bar was one of those modern plate-glass places. It was like being in a goldfish bowl, with the whole street watching her.

'Good to see you.' He was sitting at the bar, a huge thick glass curve, its bevelled edges water-green. A large glass vase filled with shells and strange curly twigs stood at the end of it.

'Hello, Charles,' she said shyly.

'Christian, my name is Christian.'

'Oh!' She blushed. 'Sorry, I'm hopeless with names.'

'I don't even know yours,' he said.

'Sarah Haywood.'

'So, Sarah, what will you have to drink? Champagne?'

'Yes, please.' She sounded like some gauche creature that hardly ever drank champagne. Well, she hadn't for ages, and never on a date —except with Dan.

She sat down with Christian at a small table by the window. The sun shone in on them, no doubt showing off every bit of baggy skin and wrinkle that she possessed. 'Pet' would have looked marvellous in this light, with her springy young skin. Sarah decided she had got to the age that needed soft candlelight, even pitch darkness on a bad day.

'Don't you love the sun?' he asked, basking in it like a lizard.

'Shows up too many defects.' She moved out of the way of it. She drank her champagne, savouring it on her tongue. It was cold and delicious. This was the life, drinking champagne with an attractive man. It would be ruined in a minute, when he asked her advice about that child. He'd say he felt safe to confide in her. How dreary. If only she had the guts and the grace to dance on the table. Show him she was still young and exciting under her sagging skin.

He said, 'How long have you worked in that shop?'

'Ages. I design the clothes. Celine and I were at art school together a hundred years ago. We met up again by chance, she was looking for a designer and there I was.'

'That dress was very pretty,' he said.

'I expect she looks marvellous in it.' Sarah hoped she didn't sound crabby.

'I don't know. She probably never wears it.'

'But surely she wears it for you, when you go out together?'

He laughed. 'We don't go out together. She's my god-daughter. It was a present for her eighteenth.'

'God-daughter?'

'Yes. You didn't think,' his face slumped, he looked offended, 'you couldn't think I was going out with a *child*? A spoilt one at that, I don't mind saying.' Then, seeing her expression, his darkened. 'So you *did* think that. You must have thought I was on some sort of Lolita trip. Why did you think that?'

'I'm sorry,' she said. 'I don't know why I thought that.' She did, but she wouldn't say.

'Did I look like that? Some pathetic creep who can't get a woman of his own age, has to baby-snatch?'

'No,' she said, 'you did not. I just thought when you called her Pet and . . .'

'Pet is short for Petronella. Her mother's choice. Her father, James, is one of my greatest friends. He got carried away by Gloria, her mother. We all knew it wouldn't last, and it didn't. But as I am her godfather, I do buy her presents from time to time.'

A surge of happiness followed the champagne bubbles. But he still looked offended by her supposition. She said lamely,

'The thing is, my husband ran off with a younger woman. Not quite as young as . . . Pet, but enough to make a fool of himself. I just feel so angry and hurt that I take it out on any middle-aged man who bosses me about or, like you,' she gave him a contrite smile, 'appears with a young girl in tow. I'm really sorry I jumped to the wrong conclusion.'

'I should think you did,' he said, a little mollified.

How could she be so prejudiced? As well as grinding her confidence into the ground, Dan's behaviour had addled her wits. What could she say to Christian now to make up for it?

But why had he asked her for a drink, if he didn't want her motherly advice? Surely not because he had stepped on her toe all those weeks ago?

Her mobile phone played its merry tune in her bag.

'Oh, sorry,' she said, relieved at the diversion. 'Please excuse me a moment.' She checked who was calling, said to him, 'It's my daughter, Polly.'

'Go ahead,' he said, affecting a sudden interest in the goings-on in the street through the window.

'Mum!' Polly shrieked down the line. 'Dad's having a baby. Isn't that *sooo* disgusting?'

CHAPTER SEVEN

She lost control. Tears welled up and gushed from her eyes, running down her face as though a tap had been turned on and she couldn't stop it.

Christian looked horrified. 'Has someone died?'

Sarah shook her head, managed to tell Polly she'd ring her back. Christian thrust a handkerchief at her and she buried her face in it. Of course she knew that Dan was sleeping with the girl, that was why he was with her, but now that she was pregnant it somehow confirmed it—and it hurt like hell.

She had to hide somewhere. Here in this bar she was like someone on screen. Glass everywhere, showing her distress from a hundred different angles. She got up and fled to the loo. She went into one of the cubicles and sat on the seat and howled.

A baby, how could he? He'd got two grown-up ones already. All the memories of his joy at her pregnancy and birth of the children flooded back relentlessly to torture her. How could he share this precious intimacy with someone else? And the children—how would they feel having a half-brother or sister, perhaps many half-siblings?

Someone knocked on the door, a female

voice said, 'There's a bloke outside, asking if you are all right.'

With superhuman effort she pulled herself together. 'I'm fine. I'll be out in a minute.'

She took a few deep, shuddering breaths. Her chest felt tight, bound in anger and pain. What a time to be told this, when she was on her first date since Dan had left her. She couldn't stay here, she must get home and ring Polly and ask her for more details.

She washed her face. She looked ghastly, all red and blotchy. Christian would take fright and run off, and she wouldn't blame him. She dreaded walking through the wine bar again in full view of everyone, but she had to do it. The longer she waited, the more embarrassing it would be. If only she had her sunglasses with her, they would hide the worst of it.

To her surprise, Christian was waiting outside the ladies' room. He took her arm.

'Let me take you home.' His face was so concerned, it nearly made her burst into tears again.

'I'm fine. I'm so sorry. I've just had bad news. Thank you for the champagne.' She moved to leave him. She must get away. Get home.

'I insist on taking you home.' He came out in the street with her. He hailed a passing taxi and opened the door for her.

'I'll be fine now, thanks,' she said. But he got in after her and sat down on the back seat beside her. She had not the strength to refuse him, and sat biting her lip, forcing herself to concentrate on doing silly sums in her head. Ninety-four and seventy-two, add it, divide it, multiply it. When this didn't work, she silently recited her favourite Shakespeare sonnet: 'Thine eyes I love and they, as pitying me, knowing thy heart torment me with disdain have put on black and loving mourners be, looking with pretty ruth upon my pain.' Hardly a good choice to cheer her up at this moment, but she must do *something* to hold back the thought of Dan and this new betrayal until she was safely alone.

The thought nudged into her misery. Maybe the baby wasn't his? Maybe the mouse had got pregnant with someone else, someone young and penniless, and was fobbing it off on him? This made her feel better, and by the time they had arrived at her house she was in control of herself.

As the taxi went down the short street, she saw Robert just about to go into his house. Just get in your house and shut the door before you see it is me, she willed him. He was the last person—apart from Dan and his fertile mouse—she wanted to see. But Robert turned round when he saw the taxi stop outside their houses.

Christian paid the taxi then got out first and put his hand out to help her, as if she were an invalid. Sarah kept her eyes down, looking for her door key in her bag, pretending that she had not seen Robert, who was watching her with curiosity. Christian took her key from her and opened the door for her. The ping of the alarm greeted them and she went straight in to turn it off. Christian followed her in and closed the front door behind him.

'Can I do anything to help, get you some tea or something? That's meant to be good for shock.' He handed her back the key. He was watching her with concern, a slight frown puckering his brows. She felt intimidated, crowded in the corner by the alarm panel, not to mention embarrassed at him having been witness to her outburst.

'No, thank you. It's just . . . well, that was my daughter on the phone, and she said my husband is having a baby. It was such a shock.'

'That's terrible. But you're still married?' He moved away slightly and she went past him into the living-room.

'No. Well, legally we still are. Dan thought it better not to get the lawyers involved as they take so much money. I suppose he'll think differently now, and I think it would be better to divorce.' The thought made her feel sick, but she had to stop pretending. She must make sure she had enough to live on.

'The marriage is over,' she went on. 'He's found this young girl, I told you that. He wanted a more exciting life.' She forced a smile. 'I was happy as we were, but he was not.

He finds it more exciting to have a red sports car and a young woman and I suppose it is, compared to an elderly Volvo and an ageing wife.' She felt she was confessing a sin of her own.

Christian said gently, 'The male menopause.'

'I suppose so.' She sat down on the arm of a chair, her legs suddenly feeling like cotton-wool. 'Whatever it's called, it's hell for the rest of us. But some people think it's quite funny, even admire it, in a man. But if *I* had bought a sports car and dashed off with a young man, everyone would have been horrified.'

'Women are more sensible than men,' he said. 'They have more dignity.'

'I don't know that we do,' she said. 'I, too, might like a young, handsome man in my life who thinks that I'm beautiful and laughs at my jokes. But it's not worth breaking up a happy family life for.'

'True.' Christian wandered across the room and sat down on the sofa.

'Maybe this baby is not his,' she went on, 'but if it is, it throws up all sorts of problems for the children. Any money Dan might have left them will now have to be shared again. If there is any money left, after school fees and all.' She shivered. 'He is a fool. I wonder if he's thought of how much this will cost him. He'll be retired just about the time the school fees really kick in.'

'Don't torture yourself with it all, it's happened. Distance yourself from it as much as you can,' Christian said. 'After all, it is not your problem any more.'

'I just can't get used to it—my marriage ending just like that. I really didn't think there were any problems with it. We both worked hard; possibly we did not spend enough time together talking. We sat together in what I thought was comfortable companionship, reading or watching something on the box.' She sighed. 'Perhaps I was too complacent, as we rarely rowed, and then only over small things. If only he had talked about it, we could have changed things before they got so out of hand.'

'I don't suppose you did anything wrong,' Christian said. 'Life changes, people change. It's a sad fact of life.'

'Are you married?' She wondered if he had changed towards a wife and could tell her why.

'My wife died.'

'Oh, God, I'm so sorry.' She clapped her hand over her mouth as if she could pull back her question. 'That is terrible.'

'It was. Cancer, two years ago.'

'Have you children?'

'Two sons, both work in New York.'

'I'm so sorry,' she repeated. 'That is the worst. I feel ashamed now, going on about my problems, when there are so many other people worse off than me. I know I'm lucky,' she went on, trying to fill the awkward void after his news, 'I have a house and a job and enough money, if I'm careful, to live. Thousands of women are left destitute.'

'Your problems are still hard to bear,' he said. 'It's difficult when fate suddenly pulls the rug from under your feet and you have to reassess your life.'

She would have liked to tell him how she was trying to live a new life, but how things kept tripping her up, like Robert wanting her house and now this news of Dan's baby, but she did not. She had done nothing, she realized this evening, but whinge and weep. No man would want to put up with that, especially one who had lost his own wife in such tragic circumstances.

Christian was sitting on the sofa, his face serious with concern, hands clasped in front of him. She liked the feel of him sitting there in his smart suit, his blue-and-green tie. But what should she do with him? Just now she didn't feel she had the energy to be cheerful, to sing and dance for him. What if he wanted to sleep with her? She couldn't cope with that, not yet. If ever. What a nightmare it would be, undressing in front of another man, laying bare all her defects, the less than taut skin, the bulgy tummy. If they had put off her own husband, how much worse it would be in front of a stranger.

It would be impossible ever to have a love

affair now, after hearing about Dan's baby, not that she hadn't already tortured herself with visions of them in bed together. It would be worse now thinking of him, with his spasmodic back, impregnating her, listening for the heartbeat of his child inside her. But then why was she thinking of every man as a potential lover, even that Robert next door? Was it because she was afraid she would never make love again for the rest of her life?

'I don't want to hold you up, Christian,' she said, with a semblance of a smile. 'It was so kind of you to bring me home. I'm fine now. I've got to ring my daughter, and no doubt my son, and talk it over with them.'

'I thought perhaps—' Christian began, then obviously thought better of it. 'I could stay, if you would like me to,' he said tentatively.

They heard Robert's front door slam behind him. He was going out again. She did not want to open her front door and come face to face with him outside.

She said, 'That's really kind, but I'm not much company tonight.' She wondered whether she could ask him to dinner, or to the theatre, to make up for this dismal evening. But she didn't know how to. He might not want to come, and there would be cringing embarrassment as he made his excuses. She fought to hide her feeling of rejection and disappointment. He was a kind man, and in other circumstances they might have got on well together. It would be safer not to suggest another meeting at all.

'If you're sure I can't do anything . . .' He got up from the sofa. She studied him covetously, his slightly square face, his thick grey hair. Was he relieved or disappointed? She couldn't tell.

'I hope to see—' he began, and the telephone rang.

'I'll be off,' he said awkwardly, and made for the door.

Sarah hovered between answering the strident phone and saying goodbye to him. Seeing this he said,

'I'll see myself out. Goodbye.'

'Goodbye, and thank you so much, Christian.' She reached for the phone, about to tell the person on the other end to wait a moment so she could go to the door with him.

'Mum, are you all right? It's awful news, isn't it? Dad took Tim and me out to lunch today and told us. We were nearly sick.'

'Darling, I'll talk in a second.' She tried to wedge the words into Polly's tirade, but she heard the front door open and close. Christian probably thought he'd had a lucky escape. No man in his right mind would want to get involved with a hysterical middle-aged woman. And why should they, when there were all those thirty-somethings, starving themselves to stick-insect proportions while yearning for a man?

In her eagerness to tell her story, Polly did not hear her words. 'I just think it's disgusting, a man Dad's age having babies. He'll be seventy when it's a teenager.'

So he would, Sarah thought; would he have the stamina for it? To her intense annoyance, she felt sorry for him. Perhaps he had been tricked into this, but surely he must have known she might get pregnant?

'We both walked out, said we didn't want to see him again,' Polly went on. 'How could he, Mum? How could he?' She began to wail with all the pain of a selfish adolescent.

'I don't know,' Sarah said, when Polly paused for breath. 'But he is your father and . . .'

'He's not the father we knew! He's changed into someone completely different,' she cried.

What could she say to comfort her, comfort herself? The old Dan would never have behaved like this. Had this different man been lurking inside the old one all along, waiting for the moment to break loose? He could not have talked about it to her, for she would not have understood. She would have laughed, told him not to be such a fool, that fantasies seldom translated well into reality, and this would have upset him more. Deep down he must know he was being a fool, but he did not want her to confirm it.

Polly went on describing the lunch. Dan had managed to find a day when they both could make it from the holiday jobs they were doing in Cambridge.

It killed Sarah to know, but she had to ask.

'Was he pleased at the news?'

'Not really; more ashamed, I'd say,' Polly said tartly. 'He didn't bring her, said she was visiting her father. Tim said he was more embarrassed than when he asked him if he knew the facts of life. I mean, Mum, do you think Dad knows about contraception?'

Sarah could not help smiling at the irony of her remark. She recalled some fearful fumbles when she and Dan started to discover sex together. The irony was, they had both done all they could to warn their children not to have babies outside marriage. Now Dan, their own father, had fallen into the trap.

The next morning, she was greeted by a cream vellum envelope addressed to her lying on the mat. She opened it, and with cramping horror saw it was from Robert's solicitor. It was written in the usual legal jargon, so complicated she could not make much sense of it. She hid it under the papers on her desk. She could not, would not, cope with it. She would pretend that she had never seen it.

CHAPTER EIGHT

'Going away?' To her horror, Robert appeared from his house and saw her putting her suitcase into the taxi. Ever since receiving that letter from his solicitor she had managed to avoid him. She didn't want him to know she was going away in case he got up to something that forced her to leave her house. What if he trained his orchids to grow their sinister way through the floorboards, or infested her garden with something nasty?

'Only for a few days. My daughter is house-sitting with her boyfriend,' she said archly, getting into the taxi.

She had jokingly told Tim and Polly about Robert's insistence that the house had been promised to him, but she played it down so as not to alarm them.

'Joe and I will watch out for any sabotage,' Polly promised, becoming quite animated at the challenge.

Robert came up to the taxi to shut the door after her. 'Have a good time. I wanted to talk to you about that letter I put through your letterbox, but we'll leave it until you get back. I won't hold you up now.' He threw her a curt smile and shut the door, leaving her tingling with anxiety.

When she picked up Celine at her flat—

they were going to Victoria to take the train to Gatwick—she was so excited about the trip she didn't want to say anything to spoil it. There was nothing she could do anyway, unless she cancelled the trip and stayed at home to guard the house, and that would be giving in to him. She might as well enjoy this week, get up strength for the battle when she returned.

She experienced that old excitement as the plane took off, the thrill of throwing off the cares of her life for a while, being someone different in a new environment. But as the taxi took them to the Fieldings' place, old memories reared up and hit her. She and Dan had once come here for a romantic weekend. Her mother was alive then, and they had left the children with her. They'd hired a car at the airport and driven to Sienna. How golden was that place and golden their love. How could it all have gone so dreadfully wrong?

Flora and Patrick Fielding were in their early sixties and lived here most of the year. They welcomed people to their converted farmhouse: their children, children's friends, friends of their own and, in her case, their friends' friends. They left them to their own devices, the only house rule being everyone had to take it in turns to provide and cook dinner. A local woman who came in to clean washed up their efforts in the morning.

Celine had been a friend of theirs for a long time. To pay them back for their hospitality, she always brought over some of her clothes for Flora.

'I'm so thrilled to meet the designer of my favourite clothes!' Flora greeted Sarah, her round, tanned face lighting up with a smile. Sarah liked her at once, and Patrick too, though he was much quieter and alternated his time between reading and communing with his beloved plants.

It was a beautiful house, once expensively decorated but now fading elegantly and gently into sun-washed mellowness. Sarah loved it, but the ache in her heart lay in wait in the shadows of her mind, pouncing like a physical pain. The sight of Patrick in his battered straw hat bringing Flora flowers from the garden, or fetching her jacket in the cool of the evening. The small, familiar, almost instinctive things between a couple long used to each other and content with each other's company smote her heart with the yearning pain of loss. Would a man ever love her again, and what would she become if none did? A dried-out empty vessel with its heart torn out?

Christian had not got in touch with her again, but that was hardly surprising. What man in his right mind wanted to go out with a hysterical old bat who cried in fashionable glass wine bars right there for everyone to see? Five weeks had passed since that disastrous evening, and she had not heard a squeak out of him since.

She'd heard more than a few squeaks from Robert, though. Living beside him, hearing the sounds from his side of the house, unnerved her. It was like living together, and yet they did not. His water ran, early morning, as did hers, as they both bathed before work. She dismissed pictures in her mind of them both naked in the bath side by side on either side of the wall. Sometimes she could hear the mumble from his radio, which convinced her that he listened to the same programme as she did. Did he, too, think of her getting on with her life beside him as he thought up devious plans to get rid of her so he could have both houses to himself?

She kept out of his way. If she saw his broad-shouldered figure ahead of her going into his house, she would drop back and wait until he was safely inside. Through the wall she could hear the long buzz as he set his alarm, so if she was also going out she would wait until he had left the street. The worst time was when they were both in their respective gardens: she could sense him on the other side of the wall and this distracted her.

It was such a relief to be here with people she had never met before, who did not know her history. Apart from the Fieldings, there were two male friends of Patrick's, Marcus Benson and Julian Gilmore. Marcus had his wife Ruth with him. Julian, who had recently divorced, had brought a young French girl he had picked up somewhere. Flora's much younger stepsister Alexia and her partner Jeff were also there.

They were nice, easy people, and to Sarah's relief not the sort you had to make an effort with. The only 'single' man was Julian. He was tall, with a lean, pointed face, sparse greying hair and wore glasses. He was the chairman of some prestigious firm in the City.

Yvette, the girlfriend, lay almost nude in the sun all day long. Her body and rather sturdy legs were the colour of toffee. She barely spoke to anyone, even to the Fieldings, who were fluent in French. She was *'toujours fatiguée'*. She ate enormously, and lay about and did nothing for anyone. The Fieldings didn't say anything, but Sarah suspected that they were very bored with her and rather despised Julian for bringing her.

Julian reminded Sarah of a turkey cock strutting about doing his best to impress her, regaling her with stories of his sporting exploits and his prowess in the boardroom.

Yvette shrugged and pouted and grunted while he boasted of his life, telling of deals he had pulled off, scams he had unearthed. He saw himself as her mentor, explaining things patiently to her, how the garden was planted in an English style, the etiquette of bridge, which he would call out to her while he was playing, much to the annoyance of the Fieldings and Ruth.

Leave it, Sarah said silently to him. Would you really jump through all these hoops with a woman nearer your own age? She wondered if Dan behaved like this. Did he boast so nauseously to his mouse? She suspected Julian was on some power kick, behaving as if he knew he was superior to Yvette socially and in the ways of the world, and had taken it upon himself to instruct her about it.

'Do you think he instructs her in the bedroom?' Celine commented, when they were alone reading by the pool one afternoon.

'I don't think they sleep in the same room,' Sarah said. 'She's in that little room over the garage.'

'Flora always puts her least favourite people there,' Celine said. 'Silly man can't see what a fool he is making of himself. Is it really worth it for a bit of fun in bed? Or maybe there is no fun in bed.' She stretched out luxuriously on the sun-lounger. 'If there's no chemistry between two people, why bother to go to all that trouble? Life is too short.'

The next day was so hot no one moved from the property. In the evening, they congregated outside on the terrace for drinks before dinner. Ruth and Marcus were cooking dinner, or rather, making a large salad as it was too hot to cook. Sarah noticed that Julian was walking oddly, his legs apart, his bottom sticking out awkwardly.

'Caught the sun?' she joked, knowing that

he and Yvette had spent some of the day hidden in the garden.

'Y . . . yes.' He looked embarrassed, his eyes skittering away from her.

Throughout dinner he seemed to find it painful to sit still, and rocked gently back and forth, his face creased with discomfort. 'Ants in your pants, Julian?' Patrick remarked with a laugh.

Julian bushed. 'Just burnt,' he muttered.

'May we ask what part of you is burnt?' Jeff enquired, his eyes shining with mischievous amusement.

Everyone laughed but Julian and Yvette. She was too busy eating the shellfish salad.

'I'd keep it out of the sun, mate; might shrivel it up for all time,' Jeff said, with the arrogance of a young man with a good sex life.

Julian tried to join in the banter, but Sarah could see it was an effort for him. She suspected they were ribbing him to punish him for bringing this tiresome girl with him, who'd made no attempt to fit in with the rest of them.

At the end of the evening, Sarah went for a walk in the garden before going to bed. Celine was playing bridge, the others were reading inside. It was hot and still, with a sort of electric feeling as if before long there would be a terrible storm. They certainly needed one, to freshen everywhere up and lighten the air. She crossed the terrace and went on to the lawn. As she passed the huge tree near the pool, someone moved in the shadows.

She walked on, keeping her gaze ahead in case it was a couple having a romantic interlude in the open air. But Julian stepped out alone.

'Oh, hello,' she said. 'It's so hot isn't it?'

He did not answer, and she could see in the dim light of the beacons dotted about the garden that he looked terrible. No doubt Yvette had dumped him. Perhaps she was at this moment in bed with one of the two Fielding boys who had turned up at the farmhouse during dinner. They were good-looking young men, and she'd seen how Yvette had eyed them up.

'Are you all right?' she asked, while inwardly praying he would not start on about his misery at losing Yvette. She did not want to listen. She did not have any sympathy for any middle-aged man who threw away a perfectly nice wife—though she'd no idea if his wife had been perfectly nice—for some little bit like that. Her feelings must have shown in her expression, for he backed off, looking even more miserable.

'I . . .' He gave a hoarse laugh. 'Well, something very embarrassing has happened.'

'Oh?'

'I . . .' He squirmed with embarrassment. 'Well, you know how it is, trouble with the old hydraulics.'

'Hydraulics, you mean something in the

swimming-pool?' Had he broken the filter, or the cover that was put back every night to stop the birds from drowning, and was dreading having to own up?

'No, you know . . .' He glanced down at his groin, and even in the dark she could see an enormous mound there. She blushed. What was she meant to do about it? She certainly didn't want it anywhere near her.

'I'll find Yvette for you,' she said, with the shrillness of a maiden aunt.

'No, you don't understand,' he said desperately. 'You see, I've had some problems, so I brought out some Viagra.'

'Don't tell me you've overdosed?' She bit her lips to stop the giggle that bubbled up in her. He was enormous, like an elephant. She could not help looking again.

'No. It just happened, everything has swollen up. I don't know what to do.'

'A cold shower?' she said feebly, fighting to keep the laugher from her voice. Then she controlled herself. He was in agony; she really must not laugh.

'You'd better ring a doctor,' she said. 'I've never heard of such a thing before.' She didn't know anything about Viagra at all except what she had read in the newspapers. The thought of it caused another surge of panic in her. If she ever had a sex life again, would Viagra be the main feature? Did you have to wait for it to work, like dough rising? She cringed inwardly; it was all too embarrassing to contemplate.

'Look, Sarah, I hate to ask you this, but would you drive me to the doctor in the village? I can't have him here; you know how . . . well, how people . . .' He fidgeted in misery.

'How people will think what a fool you are?' she said tartly. 'Tell me, Julian, why do you do it? Are these young women worth all this agony and embarrassment? Wouldn't you be happier with someone nearer your age who might be more sympathetic to,' . . . she swallowed a giggle, ' "trouble with your "hydraulics"?'

'You mean *you*, Sarah?'

'No, I do not mean me!' The thought appalled her. 'But you seem to be torturing yourself—for what? Just to prove you can pull a young girl like you could when you were twenty?'

He looked miserable, and she felt ashamed of herself. She really must not become the scourge of all middle-aged men just because her own husband had hurt her so. But here was this man, some hotshot in the City, with goodness knows how many employees under him, humiliating himself with some greedy girl who did not care a toss for him.

'I'll take you to the doctor.' Her sympathy for him got the better of her. 'Come on, we'll walk through the garden to the car.'

102

'You're so kind, I really appreciate it, Sarah,' he said, wading behind her as if he was ploughing through deep water.

They took his car, but she had to drive it. On the way to the village, he asked her if she was married.

'No, not any more. My husband is playing the fool with some young woman, too. That's why your sort of behaviour irritates me so.' She kept her eyes on the road as they drove down the narrow lane to the village.

'I see.'

'I understand you are divorced?' she said.

'That's right. Our marriage just ended, there was nothing there any more.'

'You take the best years of a woman; she does everything for you, brings up your children, helps you up the ladder of your career, loves you, and then you dump her for some young bit. What would you have done if your wife had done that to you? Dumped you for a younger man?' She almost said 'more virile' man, but stopped herself in time.

'Put like that . . .' he said, shifting uncomfortably in his seat. 'But we hadn't been happy for years.'

'That's what they all say,' she said darkly.

He pointed out the doctor's house in the square. She stopped the car outside.

'I'll wait for you in the car.'

'Thank you.' He struggled out and she watched him hover by the front door before ringing the bell. The door finally opened and he was ushered inside. Sarah wondered how good his Italian was, and how he would explain his predicament.

Some time later he reappeared, looking rather sheepish.

'Better now?' Sarah asked brightly.

'Yes, thank you, it will wear off. At least, I *think* that's what he said,' Julian said mournfully.

'As long as it doesn't fall off!' Sarah quipped. She remembered Linda saying what fools men were over those few inches of gristle.

'That's not very kind,' he said plaintively as she turned the car and started back down the lane.

The storm broke just before they reached the farmhouse; the rain teemed down as if it was being poured from a gigantic jug. They both agreed that it would clear the air. She parked the car in the drive as near to the front door as she could and they both ran into the house, but even in those few yards they were drenched through. Sarah's thin dress clung to her like a second skin. In the hall she said good-night to him and started up the stairs to her room.

'You 'ave taken my man!' Yvette came at her, hands outstretched as if she would claw her eyes out.

Patrick was behind her. He caught Yvette

and held her.

'Steady on,' he said, but as he caught sight of Sarah with her dress plastered tight against her body, she saw a flash of desire in his expression. The rest of the house party with the exception of the young Fieldings, followed him, staring at her with some disapproval.

With sickening horror, she realized that they thought she and Julian had gone off together for some passionate encounter and had only come in to escape from the storm.

CHAPTER NINE

'You didn't did you?' Celine came into Sarah's bedroom.

'What do you think?' Sarah stared at her reflection in the mirror on the dressing-table, a towel tied like a turban over her wet hair. 'Do I appear that desperate?'

Celine laughed, sat down on the bed. 'No, but both of you suddenly disappearing like that caused quite a commotion. That silly bitch made more noise than she's done all week. Her English improved by the second. So, what happened?'

Sarah couldn't suppress a giggle, though inside she was screaming with insecurity. It was the expression on everyone else's faces that had stunned her, not Yvette's hysteria. In their accusing eyes she'd seen that, except for Celine, they'd all reached the same conclusion. She had kidnapped Julian to seduce him. Coming in like that, her dress riding up, clinging to her body after running in the rain, only confirmed it. The women were the worst, hostility pinching all their faces as they concluded that she was not safe near their men.

She'd kept silent as she stood dripping on the stairs. Never explain, never complain, her father used to say, and this was the perfect time to take his advice. Anything she might have said would only dig her in deeper. She'd glanced at Julian. He was desperately trying to calm Yvette down. She had promised not to tell anyone about the real reason they had gone off together. Seduce him? The very thought brought on a fit of hysterical mirth. Sarah had gone upstairs to her room, leaving Julian to explain.

'I promised I wouldn't tell what happened,' Sarah said, the scene in the garden making the laughter rise in her again. 'Would it do if I said he needed to go to the doctor urgently?'

Seeing her suppressed amusement, Celine said drily, 'Chest pains?'

'Lower down,' Sarah giggled.

Celene lifted an eyebrow, 'Not the clap?'

'No. But...'

'Look, people are dreadful how they jump to conclusions. Yvette stirred it all up by

106

saying she'd seen you making eyes at Julian.'

'What rubbish!' Sarah was indignant.

'I know. I stood up for you, but the others don't know you . . . and . . .' She shrugged. 'Well, you know what people are like, recently separated woman and all. They seem to think that makes you rampant for sex.'

'Only With Dan! Mad, isn't it? Especially as it would be torture sleeping with him again and thinking of what he did in bed with that dratted mouse,' Sarah said sadly.

Celine smiled sympathetically. 'I told Flora and Patrick that it was impossible. He's not even your type is he?'

'Absolutely not.'

'But as Yvette is after his money, she probably imagines you are, too.'

'So, by being kind to him, I've blackened my character irredeemably?'

'No, not in Flora and Patrick's eyes, anyway. They'll be fine about it. It will blow over. No one even likes Yvette. Everyone would be far more comfortable if you two did pair up! It's just causing such unpleasantness that upsets everyone, while they are here chilling out on holiday.'

The old guilt and shame accosted her. Just as she had begun to feel on top of things, something else had happened to knock her down once more. If she'd had her old confidence she'd have laughed it off, protested at once and she would have been believed. If

Dan had been with her, no one would have accused her of anything. But single women, as she was discovering—especially those who had recently lost their husbands—were seen as predators. This episode would upset the cheerful balance of the people staying here, and she would be blamed for it.

'I wonder what Julian's explanation will be?' she said, remembering his embarrassment. To keep his dignity, would he pretend that they *had* gone off together?

'He asked me to take him to the doctor in the village and not tell anyone about it. I hope he explains that, and doesn't make up some nonsense of us having a passionate affair.'

'They'll want to know why he went to the doctor,' Celine said.

'Promise you won't tell anyone if I tell you?' She knew she could confide in Celine.

'Of course, though I may have to tell Flora, but she won't say anything.'

Sarah told her what had happened. Celine burst out laughing incredulously.

'I've never heard of *that* before! In fact, I don't know of anyone who has actually taken Viagra. But what a nightmare.' Her eyes gleamed with horrified amusement. 'Like mumps, making everything swell up, or elephantiasis. I do hope that never happens to a man I am with. I mean, imagine!' She shook with giggles. 'At least that might curb some of them. As it is, I have frightful visions of all those geriatrics clutching bottles of Viagra, behaving like oversexed adolescents. Not that I've been bothered by any; I suppose they go after the younger women.'

'I took him to the doctor, and I assume he's coped with it. It's rather humiliating for Julian. I asked him why he had put himself in such a position and—Oh God,' she remembered in horror. 'I said something to him like "why do you middle-aged men make such fools of yourselves over young girls, can't you cope with grown-up women", and he *did* think I was referring to myself.'

'So he does fancy you?'

'I don't think so. I certainly don't fancy him, especially not after the elephantiasis incident. If he did try to seduce me now, I'd get the giggles.'

Celine's face creased with amusement. 'So would I. Even looking at him now will make me laugh, and to think he practically runs the City. Imagine if his competitors found out!' She howled with laughter.

'He's probably not the only one. It is rather depressing that sex is counted so highly these days, that any other achievements in life seem to come second place.' As always, she thought of Dan. Was it only sex with a younger woman that made him leave her, or had he disliked her for some time?

'It may be unkind of me to ridicule him, but it's time we had something to laugh about, concerning men. Normally it's us poor women who suffer all these hideous embarrassments,' Celine pointed out.

They could still hear Yvette's screaming downstairs. Celine said, 'Forget it, she's just hysterical, thinking she's lost out on her free holiday. Tomorrow, just behave as though nothing has happened. It will soon blow over.'

'I do hope so, I was enjoying myself.'

'And you will again.' Celine hugged her.

All night, Sarah was plagued by dreams. She was in a mysterious garden with endless twisting paths bordered by trees that kept bending down and pulling at her. A man was following her; vainly she tried to escape him. Running round one corner, she bumped straight into him—and it was Robert.

When she awoke, she had the impression that he was there in the room, close to her. The sun pushed its way through the chinks in the curtains and she felt his presence recede to be replaced by a faint sense of regret. What nonsense her mind was playing. She felt quite hot and embarrassed, as if Robert would somehow know he had disturbed her dreams.

More immediate worries took over her mind. She lay in bed, fretting. Should she go down early and have her breakfast before most of the others got up, then make herself scarce for the day, or should she just brazen it out and go down later, when the others did?

In the end she went down to breakfast late,

hoping that Celine would be there to bolster her up.

She went out on to the terrace. Pia, the domestic help, came early with newly baked rolls. There was fruit, coffee and orange juice laid out on the long table covered with a blue-chequered cloth. It was Sarah's favourite time of the day, before the searing heat took over, when the light was sharp picking out the colours with precision. The Fieldings kept their garden well watered, so it was iridescent green compared with the toasted earth in the rest of the region. Julian was sitting alone at the end of the table; she hadn't seen him at first.

She moved to go back inside but he caught sight of her.

'Don't go away,' he said. 'Look, Sarah . . .' His face was pasty, his eyes sunken as if he hadn't slept in weeks. 'I'm so sorry about last night.'

'It's OK.' She helped herself to coffee and sat down beside him. 'I suppose, people being what they are, it was not surprising that they all jumped to the wrong conclusions. I hope Yvette realized that.'

'She's gone,' he said mournfully. 'She made me call her a taxi and she's gone.'

'Not because of me, I hope?'

'No.' He hung his head, his face miserable. 'I had to tell her what had happened. She . . .' He was close to tears. 'She was disgusted, there's no other word for it. How I hate old age!' He thumped his fist on the table. 'I was never lacking in that department before.'

Sarah watched him crucifying himself. Here was this man, with a remarkable financial brain, a top job in the City, often hobnobbing with the Treasury, reduced to a blithering idiot because of, as he put it, 'hydraulic problems'.

He said at last, 'You were right, Sarah. I was a fool to go after such a girl. I've learnt my lesson. Women my age have far more to them, and some are still attractive.'

'Thanks a lot,' Sarah said darkly. If he hadn't looked so miserable, she would have added, 'Some of you are still attractive, but like us your skin is sagging, your hair thinning and greying, and your joints are creaking, so we might as well make the best of it and be kind to each other.'

'I didn't mean it like that,' he said.

'You know,' she said firmly, 'we should stick together, enjoy ourselves before real old age takes over. Leave the young ones to pair up among themselves. I certainly wouldn't have wanted to sleep with a middle-aged man when I was younger.'

'Wouldn't you?' he asked with disappointment.

'No. Nor would my daughter.' She thought of Polly's disgust at Dan fathering another child.

'I've had quite a few successes with younger

women,' Julian said, with a hint of bravado.

She did not say that it was probably his money and his position that was the aphrodisiac here. She spread some apricot jam on a roll and bit into it. If only someone else would come and join them; seeing them breakfasting together might fuel the others' imaginations further.

They sat in silence for a while. She became aware that he was studying her; this made her feel awkward, aware that she had tiny flakes of the crusty roll on her chin. She was about to ask him what he was staring at when he said in an oily voice,

'You may be right.' He put his hand on hers. 'You are frightfully attractive, Sarah. Right under my nose, and I didn't notice until now.'

She whipped her hand away. 'Julian, I didn't mean me. What's the matter with you? I'd have thought that after last night . . .'

'I'm fine now.' To her horror, she saw a glint of lust in his eyes.

'I don't want a relationship with anyone at the moment.' She moved away from him, fighting not to laugh as she thought of his hydraulics. 'Please let me finish my breakfast in peace.'

He smirked. 'We needn't have a relationship. Here we are, the two of us on our own. I call it a perfect arrangement. Here, in the sun, we could . . .'

'No!' she said sternly. 'You must look

elsewhere, or just remain celibate for the rest of the week, enjoying this lovely place.'

'You see,' his face drooped with sulkiness, his voice was bitter, 'you middle-aged women are all the same. I'd have thought you'd be happy to have some interest taken in you. But no, I suppose you don't like sex any more, *if* you ever did.'

His remark infuriated her. He was insufferable. 'I *do* like sex, but not with you, and not just as a pastime. I want it to *mean* something, is that so difficult?' She sprang up from the table and hurried inside, her face hot with anger. She bumped into Celine and Flora, who were just coming out.

Celine, seeing her face and seeing Julian sitting at the table, took her arm and went back into the house with her.

'Everything is all right. I had to tell Flora the truth, but she won't tell anyone, well, except for Patrick. But it's fine, Yvette has left and everyone's pleased about that.'

'I don't care who knows about it.' Sarah was trembling with anger. She told Celine what Julian had said.

'I can't stand the arrogance of these men who seem to think one should be grateful to put up with their lovemaking. I'd far rather be celibate and go to bed with a good book than a creep like that.'

'Especially one with elephantiasis!' Celine giggled. 'Look, let's go out for the day. There are so many lovely places to see.'

They heard the telephone ringing, further inside the farmhouse. In a moment, Patrick came to tell Sarah it was Polly.

Fear stalked her as she went in to the small study to talk to her.

'Hi, Mum, hope you're having a great time,' Polly greeted her.

'Yes, I am, darling. Is there anything wrong?'

'No, why should there be? But I'm just ringing to ask if it's all right for Robert next door to come into our garden to do something to his creeper. It seems to prefer us to him, and he wants to train it back. He's been quite friendly, I think he's all right.'

'*No*, absolutely not until I get back. Push his wretched creeper back to his side, but don't let him in.'

Her dream had been right; Robert was chasing her in a garden, spoiling her time out here. By being nice to Polly, he was trying to get into her house. She did not trust his motives at all.

CHAPTER TEN

London seemed drab and airless after the glowing brilliance of Tuscany. Sarah let herself in to her house—which to her relief seemed the same as she had left it—and felt the mantle of depression settling round her shoulders.

Although the Julian incident and his ongoing behaviour had been difficult, they were nothing compared to her problems back home, namely Dan's forthcoming baby and Robert.

Julian's attempts to persuade her into bed with him only made her laugh, imagining all sorts of grotesque images of Viagra-driven lusts. At least while she was in Italy she had been able to keep her problems back home at arm's length, but now they crowded back round her like noisy, demanding children.

The lights were on, so Polly and Joe must be there, unless they had gone out and left the lights blazing—a typical occurrence. The thought that they were at home cheered her at once. She'd got used to the constant companionship at the Fieldings', and realized that she dreaded the endless quiet and empty rooms when she got back home.

She had bought a pretty bag for Polly and some wine for Joe; she foresaw a good evening ahead.

Polly was slumped on the sofa, her eyes red with weeping, a balled-up handkerchief in her hand. At the sight of her, Sarah's heart fell, the mantle of depression almost choking her.

'What is it, darling?' Images first of Tim dead, then Dan, then various other dramas flashed like quicksilver through her mind.

'Joe's gone. We had a row,' Polly wailed, tears pouring down her face.

'What happened?' Sarah swallowed down her irritation and relief that it was only that. She was tired after travelling, and was looking forward to a bath, a drink and a cheerful gossip to catch up on the news, not another emotional drama to add to her own.

'He said I was too intense,' Polly sniffed. 'He doesn't want to be tied down, he wants more freedom.'

What's new in that? Sarah said to herself. Some men do it now; others, like Dan, do it later. She sat down beside Polly and took her in her arms.

'Welcome to the real world.' She muffled her words in Polly's abundance of golden hair.

After what seemed like hours of tearful explanations—Joe had apparently come to this decision only a few hours ago—Polly said, 'Oh, and Robert next door kept asking when you were back.'

'What business is it of his?' Sarah felt as if she hadn't been away at all, hadn't spent time lying in the sun with her book and a glass of wine, with no decisions to make but which novel to read next.

'He wouldn't say what he wanted. He just said he had to speak to you and would you ring him or bang on his door when you got back. I wrote his number down somewhere.' She looked frantically round the untidy room in the hopes of locating it.

'Don't worry about it tonight. I'm exhausted. The plane was delayed, we hung about the airport for ages. I'm going to have a bath and get into bed, and I suggest you do, too.' Sarah hugged her again. 'Things might seem better in the morning,' she said, with a cheerfulness she didn't feel.

'They never will be better again,' Polly moaned. 'Do you think not being able to keep a man is hereditary, in our genes?'

'Whatever do you mean?' Polly's remark hurt. 'I kept your father for twenty-four years.'

'But they go off us.' Polly humped up on the sofa with her chin on her knees, looking balefully ahead.

'Joe is far too young for the male menopause,' Sarah snapped. 'Your father is suffering from severe delusions, imagining he is a young stud, which is pathetic when you see his ageing body.' She remembered painfully that he had managed to father a child—if it *was* his. But she'd had enough of the subject, enough of wondering on the vagaries of men. She kissed Polly, suggested she had a relaxing bath as she was going to do.

She was half-way up the stairs when there was a brisk rap on the door. She wouldn't have answered it, but Polly jumped up and ran to open it, frantically wiping her eyes as she went, no doubt expecting the return of a chastened Joe.

'Hello, Polly, is your mother in?' Sarah heard Robert's voice.

She was stuck half-way on the stairs and he could not help but see her legs from where he stood. She could hear Polly sniffing, obviously with disappointment that it was not Joe.

'I think . . . she's in the bath,' Polly managed.

'Perhaps I could see her before she gets in the bath?'

Sarah heard him come into the hall and, afraid that he would join her on the stairs before she could lock herself in the bathroom, she reluctantly and with bad grace came down again.

'I've just got back from holiday and I'm very tired. I don't want to speak to you right now,' she said, barely looking at him.

'I won't keep you a moment, but I do want to know if you have received my letter and what you are going to do about it. You should have received it, as I put it through your letterbox myself.'

His voice was reasonable, but it did not stop the flutter of fear in her heart. Polly had slunk off back to her position of misery on the sofa. Robert did not look threatening as he stood there in her hall. In other circumstances he would have looked very nice indeed. He was dressed in well-cut jeans that somehow suited him, unlike Dan who sort of bulged out of his

119

jeans in an ungainly way, and a cobalt-blue shirt. His skin was touched with a slight tan. It was a nuisance that he was an attractive man, as it made it harder for her to hate him.

'I have got it, but I put it away.' She stared at him defiantly.

'I meant for you to read it, take some action.' His mouth tightened with annoyance.

'I've already asked my solicitor about my rights, and she said that unless there was some legal document saying the Blakes gave you this house, it is mine. So,' anxiety made her voice hard, 'please can you leave me alone? Take it up with the Blakes, not me, or I'll have to have you up for . . .' she searched her mind for something she could have him up for, 'trespass or harassment.' She grabbed at the words. She wanted to get to the front door to usher him out, but it meant pushing past him in the tiny hall and she did not want to touch him.

'I have found you another house,' he said, with a little pride. 'It's only in the next street. It's really pretty. Beautifully done up, you can move straight in, and I'll pay your removal charges.'

She gasped at his audacity. 'I think that my house is already really pretty and beautifully done up, by *me* to *my* taste. I do not want to move, and I will not. Now, go away and leave me in peace.'

'Sarah,' his voice was like honey; honey and chocolate and double Jersey cream all rolled into one, 'you know I want this house.'

So, he was now trying to use seduction and charm to get his way.

'You're not going to get it, so save your charms for your orchids.' She pushed past him, yanking open the front door. 'It's late and I want you gone. Leave me alone.'

Anger replaced the softness in his eyes, but his voice was controlled as he spoke. 'How long do you hope to live here? Maybe you will want to move at a future date, to the country or somewhere, near your parents perhaps?'

'How dare you try to rule my life! My parents are dead, and don't try to patronize me by sending me out to grass in the country.'

'I'm sorry to upset you, but if you'd read the letter . . . it states that if you change your plans . . .'

'I have absolutely no idea of my plans, and if I did I wouldn't discuss them with you.' She threw the words at him, pushing him quite hard to get him out of the door.

'I wish we could be friends,' he said with an attempt at a smile as he went through the door. 'After all, we do share a wall.'

'But nothing else.' She shut the door in his face.

She leant against the door, exhausted. Robert might not have any legal rights over her, but his bullying could make her life hell. Every time she came home she would feel threatened by his presence next door, thinking

121

him spying on her. He could smoke her out just by intimidation. A wave of self-pity engulfed her. Had she and perhaps Polly really got some defect that urged men to be unkind to them?

She went into the living-room. Polly had heard every word of their exchange, but her misery at losing Joe had caused a great apathy in her.

She said wearily, 'You're not going to move, are you, Mum? Just when I've got my room all together as I want it?'

How selfish the young are, she thought, but perhaps it is their only weapon to get on in this world.

'No, I'm not planning to, but if he makes things too difficult . . .' Her words trailed off; she was tired, she must not even think that he could make her change her mind. 'I just want a quiet life. When I was away I had time to think about things. I decided that I want to use my mind more, study something, not just wait around for some new man. It's such a waste of life. I've been married, I've got you and Tim, and any man I get now will only be dysfunctional in some way. I want to be more like Celine.'

'What, own a shop?'

'No, be happy and comfortable to be independent. Study something, have a new group of interesting friends.' She didn't say 'have perhaps the occasional affair'. Celine had had various long-term romances over the years, but now she was content to live alone the way she wanted to. Of course, Celine had had lots of practice, but there was no reason why she herself could not achieve it in time.

'Not university?' Polly became alert.

Sarah laughed, knowing that Polly was thinking she might enrol in her or Tim's university, turn up on the campus in some shaming student mode.

'How would it be if I went in for body-piercing and tattoos and grungy clothes. Became a "mature" student?' She couldn't resist teasing her.

'But, Mum, you couldn't!' The shock of such a thing jerked Polly out of her misery. 'I mean, mature is pushing thirty, not forty-something.'

'So? I don't think there is an age limit. Some people take degrees in their eighties.'

'But you wouldn't cope. I mean, there are so many things you disapprove of: drugs, sex, too much drink,' Polly went on desperately.

'There's plenty of that *outside* university,' Sarah said, thinking of her holiday.

'Yes, but you are protected here,' Polly replied.

'Look, love,' Sarah put her arm round her, 'don't worry, I'm not going to turn into the trendy-mummy trying to muscle in on your life. I've had my youth, and I thoroughly enjoyed it. I know I can't go back. I don't think

I'd want to, even if I could. But I do want to have something more to occupy my mind than worrying about your father's new baby and the man next door.'

'That's all right, then.' A small smile of relief like a thin ray of sun on a rainy day crept over Polly's face. 'But, Mum, you must fight back, not let Robert next door bully you. He was nice whenever he saw me, but he is determined to get what he wants.'

'What did he say?'

'Oh, that the Blakes had promised him the house and it was hard not to feel aggrieved that you had bought it, and he was sure that you would understand in the end.'

'I certainly *won't* understand. I'm sorry, but it's not my problem. He was away, and I assume uncontactable, and they needed to sell it quickly. He'll have to accept it.'

'I don't think he will, without a fight. What if . . .' Polly thought for a moment. 'What if you grew some plant, you know those huge fir trees or some vine that took over his entire garden? Or made something leak dreadfully in his house, did something to make him want to leave?' she said eagerly.

Sarah smiled; it was impossible, but at least the idea had cheered Polly up.

'Why don't you put mice through his letterbox, or even mink? They cause terrible damage. Or mustard and cress seeds? They'd grow like mad all over his carpets,' Polly went

124

on, getting quite excited by her ideas.

Sarah laughed with her. They vied with each other over more and more outrageous plans.

The next morning, she opened her letters as she ate breakfast before going to work. Polly was still sleeping off her heartbreak. There was a letter from Dan; his square, sturdy writing on the envelope made her heart ache.

He was reminding her that she owed him the rest of the money from the sale of the house. Fifty thousand pounds by his reckoning, but he'd let her off ten for the redecorating. Surely it was only fair, he said, as he had bought the house in the first place and prices had gone up enormously.

She threw the letter away, trying to squash the panic it induced. She had spent too much on doing up her new house, but that was his fault for leaving her like that and making her move.

She got on the bus to go up the Kings Road. She got off in the bend just past World's End and walked up to the Fulham Road. She heard someone running, and Robert flung himself on to the platform just as the bus set off. Sarah was sitting on one of the side seats, and before she could move he sat down beside her.

'I'm sorry we didn't finish our conversation last night,' he said.

'We had nothing more to say.'

'Oh, but we did. You'll never guess,' he eyed her warily as if he was sitting next to an unexploded, ticking bomb, 'but your husband rang me. Somehow, he knew I wanted the house and he asked what I would be prepared to pay for it.'

'I . . . I don't believe you,' she stuttered. How could Dan know? Then she thought of Polly and Tim—they must have told him. She had enemies in the camp without knowing it, and Dan would side with Robert to get her out, perhaps make her live somewhere far cheaper, so he could have even more cash from her. The thought of his letter, and the hideous sum of forty thousand pounds, jeered at her.

'It's true,' he said. 'He just thought you might like to move somewhere smaller, even in the country, now that the children have left home.'

She was right; no doubt Dan would feel more comfortable if she moved miles away, so there would be no more scenes in places such as Bond Street. But she did not want to, *would not*, live anywhere but here.

'Understand this,' she just stopped herself from wagging her finger at him to emphasize her point, 'I bought that house fairly and squarely. I love it, and I'm going to stay there. I'm going to divorce my husband,' she decided suddenly, 'and go to court about it, settle it once and for all.' She got up to leave, even though the bus had not reached her stop.

'That's up to you, but remember, the court

126

might side with him,' Robert said, opening his newspaper and burying his head in it.

CHAPTER ELEVEN

Polly stayed at home, nursing her broken heart. At first, Sarah was pleased that she was there, having her to do things for, to chat to in the evenings, but after a while she felt that Polly's apathetic misery was holding back both their chances of recovery.

It was hard to accept that one had to move on after suffering an emotional catastrophe. It was so tempting to hold on to the security of past memories, the way of life that was familiar. Sarah had come to realize that, hard though it was, letting the past go was the only way to recover. But the past, like a persistent film, kept rolling into her mind at the most unlikely times, triggered off by the most trivial of things, or not so trivial, if she thought of Dan and Robert ganging up on her to get the house. She tried to tell Polly this, to attempt to make sense of it herself as well as to comfort her, but Polly's pain was too raw to take heed of it.

'You don't understand, Mum,' she kept moaning. 'He was the only man I ever truly loved.'

'Your father was the only man I ever truly

loved,' she'd said.

'And you still do,' Polly threw at her.

'Only the dregs of it, but they'll go soon, especially if he tries to get me to sell this house,' she said, accepting that love took some dying and could not be cut off instantly like a fading plant.

'Look,' she changed the subject, 'I know you didn't mean it, Pol, but please tell Dad nothing about my life. I don't know why he still wants to know anyway.'

'Are you going to divorce him?' Polly asked. 'Or might Robert be right and the court make you give him more?'

'I'm going to find a good lawyer,' Sarah said, thinking that was the first step.

'He might get bored of Nina and want to come back,' Polly said, watching her reaction.

'It's too late, Pol.' She put her arm round her, guessing that her tears over losing Joe were also for the end of her happy childhood. 'Whatever happens, I will *never* take him back. Please accept that.'

*   *   *

'It's bad for you to have Polly like this,' Celine said to Sarah, when she told her of the conversation. 'When does she go back to university?'

'October. She and Joe were going to Thailand for a few weeks,' Sarah explained.

'She doesn't want to go alone, and for that I must say I am relieved, but it seems she has no motivation to do anything else. It's as if she'd earmarked that time to be with him and now that he has gone, she can't do anything else.'

'I could take her with me to India,' Celine said. She was due to go, as she did each year, to visit the fabric manufacturers. 'I could do with someone to help me. I couldn't pay her much, but I'd pay her fare and hotel.'

'Could you? She can be a tremendous help if she puts her mind to it, but now . . .' Sarah sighed, wondering if Polly would even consider going. But the trip would be good for her.

'I wouldn't have suggested it if I didn't mean it,' Celine said. 'She's a nice girl; got good taste, too—her bedroom is very · imaginative and pretty. You can but ask her, she can only turn up her toes and refuse.'

Sarah was determined that Polly would go with Celine. She could just fit in the two weeks before she had to go back to university. During the day, she toyed with various ways of how to broach the subject with her, and promptly forgot them all as she walked through the front door that night.

In a voice breathless with excitement, Sarah said, 'Guess what? Celine wants you to go to India with her to help with her fabrics. She does so hope you are free to go.'

Polly was lying aimlessly on a sun-lounger in the garden, resting after a limp session in the gym.

'Did you put her up to this, Mum?' She eyed her warily, sitting up slowly as if she was an invalid.

'No, I did not. It never occurred to me. She always goes to India at this time of year, and I didn't realize that she wanted to take anyone with her. But it seems she needs someone trustworthy and reliable to help her with things.'

'I can't, in case . . .' Polly hesitated, her eyes huge with misery. Sarah could read her thoughts. One of the reasons why Polly stayed at home so much was the hope that Joe would come back to find her. She suspected that the main reason Polly occasionally ventured out to the gym was in the hope of seeing him there.

She said firmly, 'Pol, do not waste your life waiting around for him. Accept that he might never come back, but that he is far more likely to if you're not here and he thinks you are off somewhere having fun without him.'

Polly's pretty young face looked ancient with misery. Sarah's heart ached for her. 'I wish he would come back, Mum. I really did love him.'

'I know, darling. It is hard. I really did love your father, too; no one else ever so much.' She sat down beside her and hugged her. The more you had loved someone, the worse was the pain when it ended.

'Well, then, you won't want to be left alone.'

130

Polly came up with another excuse to be able to stay at home.

'I've plans, I told you. I want to use my mind. There's an Egyptology class at a school near the Brompton Road. I thought I might enrol, it's something I've always been interested in.'

Polly frowned. 'Why not take up Italian? They so often have really sexy teachers.'

'All about twenty-five years old,' Sarah laughed.

They heard a movement from the garden next door, as if something was lurking in the shrubs. It was unnerving having Robert just behind the trellis, no doubt listening to everything they said.

One of the first things Sarah had done on her return from Italy was to push all the loose strands of his creeper through to his side so that he could train them as he wished and not have to come into her garden to do it.

She had given his letter from his solicitor to Rebecca. She had written him a formal letter thanking him for his and saying that if Sarah ever planned to move, he would be the first to know, but until then he must leave her alone and avoid harassment.

'I'm not harassing you,' he said, catching up with her in the street one morning. 'I only thought as you weren't really settled here, have only lived here a few months, you wouldn't mind moving so much.'

'You were wrong,' she said, darting into the newsagent's to escape him.

*   *   *

It did not take long to persuade Polly to go to India with Celine. Tim was wildly jealous.

'I'd love to go to India. I've always wanted to. If she'll pay my way, I won't ask for any wages at all.'

'But she doesn't want you, dolt, you don't have any taste!' Polly chaffed at him, sibling rivalry igniting her old fire.

While Polly and Celine were away, Sarah would go into the shop every day. Maggie, who was in her late sixties, but as energetic as a twenty-year-old, came to help part time. If her daughter hadn't suddenly appeared on her doorstep with a grandchild born out of wedlock, she would have worked full time.

'You can't turn away your own flesh and blood,' was her favourite saying. It was also the bane of her life.

Sarah had just arrived home the first evening after Polly had left, had not even closed the front door, when someone called her name. It was Gerry.

He looked as untidy as ever. He grinned, thrust a bunch of ready-arranged flowers at her, which he had obviously bought from the florist down the road outside the British Legion.

'Housewarming. Sorry I haven't been round before.' He took a step towards her, almost standing in the doorway.

'Oh, Gerry, how kind. Look, I'm frightfully sorry but it's not convenient at the moment.' He was the last person she wanted to see— well, the second last, counting Robert. She hadn't seen Linda for ages and had hoped after their last embarrassing meeting that Gerry would not follow her here.

He ignored her. 'How are you, Sarah? I thought you'd like to come out to dinner. We could eat locally and—'

'Where's Linda?' she asked abruptly.

He coloured slightly, emitted an awkward laugh. 'I'd like to confide in you, Sarah, we are such old friends, but here on the street . . .'

She stood firm on the doorstep. 'What's happened? Tell me quietly, no one else can hear. I don't want you inside on your own after last time.' Was he now going to say that their marriage had broken up, too?

He smiled. 'Come on, we're old friends. What have we to lose? You're alone and Linda, well, she's never been that keen on the old bed bit, you know, so I thought—'

'You thought wrong,' Sarah broke in, her anger mounting. Then from the corner of her eye, she saw Robert coming up the street. 'Please go home at once,' she hissed, 'and never come back with these disgusting requests.'

Gerry flinched but stood his ground. 'I saw Dan last week. He's such a fool, I told him so. I want to look after you, Sarah. You know, you and I, well, we won't hurt anyone,' he said reasonably.

Robert reached his front door. The three of them stood together outside the two front doors. Sarah did not look his way, but she was aware that he was watching them. If she weakened now, Gerry would be inside her house and all over her like a galloping rash, but if she told Gerry to go he might make a fuss and that would be embarrassing.

'Good evening, Sarah,' Robert said, forcing her to reply.

'Evening,' Sarah muttered, then, as he seemed to be taking rather a long time to unlock his front door, she said to Gerry, 'Why don't you take the flowers home to Linda?'

'I bought them for you,' he said, thrusting them at her. He glanced at Robert, who was still fiddling with his key in the lock.

'I'll come back another time,' Gerry said, eyeing her meaningfully. 'When you have more time.'

'Only if you bring Linda with you,' she said sternly, taking the flowers he thrust at her, then shutting the door firmly on both men.

She threw herself down on the sofa in despair, feeling used and insulted. She guessed what he'd got in mind. She was alone; Linda had gone off 'the bed bit', so he expected her to be grateful for sex sessions with him. It was too nauseating and depressing—if she wanted a sex life, would she have to make do with such offerings? Though she would never go with Gerry, it would not be fair on Linda.

A few days later, Sarah was alone in the shop tidying just before putting on the alarm and locking up, when the door opened and Christian walked in.

It was such a shock seeing him. She blushed like a girl and could not think of a single thing to say to him. He was immaculate in a dark suit, his face tanned and healthy, his brown eyes sparkling.

He smiled at her. 'I've been away. There was a crisis in the office in Australia. I've been there all this time. I didn't have your address or number and couldn't remember the name of this shop.' He lifted his hands in mock despair. 'Perhaps you've forgotten me altogether, but as I was passing . . .' He let the words fade and she saw a slight shyness in his expression, as if he was expecting her rejection.'

'No, I haven't, it's . . . good to see you again.' She would not say that once or twice she had thought of him longingly, perhaps even been guilty of building him up into something that he wasn't. How fervently she'd wished she had not disgraced herself with that scene in the glass bar.

'Good. Are you free tonight for dinner,

or Friday?'

She *was* free that night. She was free every night. But should she play the game of pretending she was so busy with such a social whirl that it would be difficult to fit him in? She had not been out on a proper date— excluding the drink she'd had with Christian— since she had married Dan. Anxieties attacked her like a swarm of bees. What did dinner mean? Gerry's eager ideas came back to her. Would she have to sleep with him? Would he feel he had to sleep with her? Would he have to take Viagra with his pudding? She couldn't think of anything to say to refuse him, but she didn't *want* to refuse him.

She said, 'Tonight will be fine. Thank you.'

'Good. I'll pick you up about eight. Tell me the address again.'

'You needn't pick me up,' she said. 'It's a bit out of your way.' He must live round here, as he always seemed to be passing the shop.

'I'm going to pick you up,' he said, taking out a slim leather diary. 'Tell me your address, and while you're at it,' he grinned at her, 'your last name again.'

'Sarah Haywood,' she said, her heart fluttering like a caged bird in her chest. He had not been put off by her hysterical behaviour. She would leave her mobile phone turned off tonight so no one could set her off again with more lurid tales of Dan's prowess in the bedroom.

'See you then!' With a wave, he had gone. She resisted the temptation to watch him going up the street.

She rushed home as hot and bothered as a young girl on her first date. What should she wear? Would it be smart or smart-casual? Thank goodness she'd washed her hair yesterday and had it cut recently. She raked through her wardrobe, discarding things in despair. Nothing she had seemed right. That safe dove-grey suit was too middle-aged, those silk trousers a little tight. She bathed, put on clean underwear, again sick with anxiety. Her underwear was hardly sexy, just pretty practical things from a chain-store. Although she designed underwear for the shop, she didn't possess any herself. Wonderful silk lingerie had to be hand-washed, and she did not have that lifestyle.

Nerves made her wish she had not accepted his invitation. It would have been so much easier to refuse and not put herself through such stress. Talk about 'Encounters', Linda's suggestion of *The Times*'s dating page, or a dating agency suggested by other friends—she wouldn't dare go near them.

The doorbell rang, making her jump. He couldn't be here already; it was only 7.45. She pulled on her dressing-gown and went downstairs to open the door. She had her hair and make-up done, and just had to decide what clothes to wear. She opened the door to welcome him with a smile. It was Robert.

When he saw her, his eyes lit up and she saw him struggle to compose his features.

'I can't see you at all now, I'm getting ready to go out,' she said, attempting to shut the door.

'I can see that, so I'll be brief. I have a business proposition to put to you.' He smiled as if he were an old friend. He slid his foot just inside the door.

'I don't want to hear it,' she said. Why was he always lurking? He must go. Christian would be here at any minute, and she wasn't dressed.

'I am going to tell you anyway,' Robert said easily. His eyes held amusement and a slight excitement, which annoyed her no end. No doubt he thought he could confuse her with some legal mumbo-jumbo that would work in his favour and not in hers, or say that Dan had consulted a divorce lawyer who agreed that this house was too big and too expensive for her needs. Without thinking, she put her bare foot with its pink lacquered nails on to his shiny black shoe. 'Please remove your foot from my door. I want you to go. I haven't time to listen to you now.'

He looked down at her foot, slim and pale-skinned against his black shoe. He was looking at it tenderly, almost covetously.

She shot it back and said roughly, 'Just go and leave me alone, Robert. You're like a stalker. You must stop this harassment, or I'll be forced to take legal advice.'

His face, darkened. She saw the small throb of a nerve against his temple. 'I think my idea is a good one. I want you to hear it,' he said, in an aggrieved tone.

'Write it down and put it through my letterbox,' she said. 'Now please go!'

He did not move. He said, 'I just wondered if you would sell me a piece of your garden?'

'No, I will not.' To her horror, she saw that Christian was behind him. One look at her in her dressing-gown and Robert half-way in her hall obviously convinced him that they shared a familiar relationship. His face tightened, he hesitated as if to go away.

In her desperation, Sarah called out to him, 'Come in, Christian! This is just my neighbour who is trying to bully me. I'll be ready in one minute.' She glared at Robert, who turned round and studied Christian. The two men eyed each other with hostility.

What a disaster. A pleasant evening had been spoilt before it had even begun. Christian would think she was an easy lay; it would start off the wrong way.

To add to her mortification, Robert introduced himself to Christian. Only a few days ago he had seen her with Gerry on the doorstep. She wondered if he thought Christian was Dan and would confirm their telephone call, or maybe he'd thought Gerry was Dan, bringing her flowers in the hopes of getting her back. Either way, she did not want Robert anywhere near her affairs.

'I live next door. I want to put a business plan to her. You may like to hear it and give her advice,' he said to Christian.

'He would not,' Sarah said, resisting an urge to go out into the street and take hold of Christian and pull him in. She was not yet well known in the street, and some of the more imaginative neighbours might misinterpret her action.

Christian said, 'If you are too busy for dinner, Sarah . . .'

'No, I am not.' She had a sudden sense that his interest in her was waning and that he was hoping for a way out of his invitation. She turned to Robert. 'I don't want to discuss business with you now or ever. I am not selling any part of my house or garden at all,' she said and put her hand firmly in the middle of Robert's chest and pushed him away.

'We will see.'

He nodded curtly at both of them, before going back into his own house. Christian hovered uncertainly on the pavement.

Sarah said, 'I'm sorry, Christian. It's a complicated story, but he thinks this house should be his and he never stops plaguing me about it.'

'Sounds intriguing,' Christian said, in a voice that implied that it did not. He followed her inside and she put him in a chair with a drink before rushing upstairs to finish dressing.

She put on her safe middle-aged suit, for that is how she felt now. All sparkle and sexiness had evaporated in the air like a soap bubble. In those few moments on the doorstep she sensed that whatever romantic feelings Christian might have held for her had faded. She remembered that he, too, had suffered a severe emotional crisis, with the death of his wife—why should he add to it? The baggage she was surrounded by was too much for him to take on—perhaps for *anyone* to take on.

CHAPTER TWELVE

Christian took Sarah to a dark, intimate restaurant. No huge glass windows inviting curious glances here. It was womb-like, painted dark red like Tim's bedroom. Had he chosen it so that any odd behaviour on her part would go unnoticed?

The conversation on the way to dinner had been polite chat: the weather, the traffic, the endless roadworks that snarled up the already too crowded roads. Back and forth the conversation went, as if they were passing relay batons to each other. There was not a spark of excitement between them.

Sarah was enveloped in a melancholy boredom. Had she imagined that Christian was attracted to her, when he'd asked her out earlier this evening? In her frantic desperation to be loved had she mistaken friendliness for something more? If only that damn Robert hadn't barged in like that, pricked the balloon of their tentative happiness so clumsily and completely.

Her anger with Robert lurked in her face, round her eyes and mouth and Christian obviously thought she was annoyed with him. As they sat opposite each other by the wall, slightly out of the body of the restaurant, she noticed a trapped look appear in his eyes as if he wished he didn't have to go through with this charade. She agreed with him. For a moment she was tempted to get up and say, 'Thanks for asking me to have dinner with you, Christian, but it's no good, is it? We've made a mistake. I'll go home.' But she was hungry, and bored of her own company, and she did not quite have the nerve to do it.

'That man next door is such a nuisance,' she said instead, and told him all about Robert wanting her house. 'The Blakes wanted to sell quickly and he wasn't there, so I bought the house in good faith. But he never leaves me alone, he even seems to have my ex-husband on his side.'

'He seems quite familiar with you,' Christian said. 'I suspect he wants to charm you into giving it up to him.'

'You don't really think that, do you?' But what had the spectacle of her in her dressing-gown on the doorstep with Robert half-way into her hall, looked like to onlookers? She regarded Christian intently, the firm mouth, the honey-brown eyes that looked at her now as if she was merely a colleague, and a dull one at that. I could have loved him, she thought, then as quickly scolded herself. Lusted after him, not loved him, turned him into some fantasy.

'I dislike him intensely,' she said. 'The house is mine. I'm pleased with myself for getting it on my own. I've done it up just as I want it and I certainly will not be giving it up to anyone, and I can't think why he won't accept that.'

A spark flared in Christian's eyes and then died. 'It must be difficult with him on your doorstep. Is he married, or does he have a girlfriend?'

'I don't know,' she said. Then, thinking the subject only seemed to bring out the worst in her, and not wanting him to label her a boring whinger, she asked him about Australia.

From then on things went quite well between them. It was as if both of them had taken a silent pledge to do their best to get through the evening. The food and wine were good, the menu different enough to provide quite a deep discussion on various methods of cooking fish.

While they talked, Sarah was aware that other women kept throwing Christian admiring glances. He was an attractive man, with that well-kept, polished look that suggested an enjoyment of the good things of life. Why had the chemistry between them so quickly been extinguished? Or had it only been there because she so desperately wanted it to be?

Christian explained to her that the restaurant had a jazz band that started playing after dinner. People came in to listen, have a drink after dinner or the theatre. They had just finished their main course and she was idly looking round the room, when to her horror she saw Dan come in with his mousy woman. He did not see her, giving her a few moments to compose herself and study him.

Her heart contracted as if it was shrivelling up in strong acid, but she could not tear her eyes away from him. He seemed to have developed a marked stoop, as if he was permanently going through low doorways. Perhaps they lived in a doll's house, she thought hysterically, him and the mouse.

They were shown to a table in the corner. Dan said something to the mousy woman, then disappeared into the shadows while a waiter held a chair for her.

The mouse looked squatter now that her pregnancy was showing. Some women glow in pregnancy, their bodies oozing fertility and beauty, but this woman did not. Her hair was lank and flat upon her head, her complexion dull. Perhaps they, too, had lost their chemistry. But the sight of her bulging stomach filled her with nausea. The birth looked imminent. Had she got pregnant before they'd started their affair? Or had it been going on for longer than she knew? Or was it someone else's baby altogether, and Dan was the fool who had got caught?

She became aware that Christian was watching her intently. She blushed. Yet again she had become distracted by another man while she was with him—Robert this evening, and twice by Dan. No wonder Christian was no longer interested in her, if her attention was always being sidetracked by other men, namely her ex-husband. Though he wasn't ex, was he, really? They were still married.

She said, 'I'm really sorry to seem distracted but that was my husband who just came in. He, or news of him, always seems to intrude when we go out.' She laughed awkwardly. Somehow the fact that she did not have to impress him made her tell the truth.

'I thought you were divorced.'

'Not divorced, but the marriage is finished. I'm sorry, Christian, I was really looking forward to this evening with you,' she said in a rush, 'but things—Robert, now Dan—seem to have spoilt it.'

'Are you still in love with your husband?' he asked.

'I don't want to be. I hate him for what he has done to me, to the family. All for a bit of sex on the side and a red sports car.'

'Is that all it was?' He watched her carefully.

She resented that look, those firm lips that seemed to utter those words with such conviction.

'You mean it was all my fault?' Her voice was harsh. Trust a man to blame someone else! That old cliché 'my wife doesn't understand me' really means 'she understands me too well, and I don't like it'.

'No, not your fault. Things change, people become irritated with each other not because they are terrible people, but perhaps because they become irritated with themselves and take it out on their other halves. They should change their own outlook on life, not their partner.'

'That may be true, but by the time people have admitted that, it is too late and there's too much pain to go back.'

'I think that happens a lot. We were going through a tricky time when Rachel was diagnosed with cancer. We became closer then, but it's sad to think that it needed that.' He trailed off. She saw the gleam of tears in his eyes. 'I still miss her dreadfully; trivial little things that were as familiar to me as breathing.'

How she understood. She reached out her hand and covered his. Was cancer easier to deal with than complete rejection from the person you thought loved you? The thought darted into her mind, making her feel instantly ashamed. People judged each other too much, searched for perfect relationships that didn't exist while conveniently forgetting their own faults.

'It's all hell,' she said. 'We all demand too much from each other without just enjoying what is there all the time.'

He gave her a brave smile that made all her caring instincts surge up to comfort him, quite taking the place of the lack of chemistry between them.

'Shall we go?' he said, calling the waiter for the bill.

She remembered Dan. She would have to get up and walk out past their table. They would see her. But she was with a man, a very presentable man, and though there was nothing between them and she recognized now there never would be, it gave her a sense of satisfaction. She resolved just to walk past them and pretend she hadn't seen them. Perhaps she would linger by the band for a moment, so that Dan sitting in his shadowy corner would see her. Perhaps—the thought was wild—he would wish he were back with her, unencumbered by that lank-haired woman and a pregnancy. That was ridiculous, she did not want him back as he was, yet perversely she wanted him to want her, and realize he had made a terrible mistake.

Christian paid the bill then got up from the table. He cupped his hand round her elbow to steer her through the few people who were milling round, waiting for a free table or drinking at the bar. She lent back against him, saying how much she had enjoyed the dinner. They moved forward and she was against the mouse's chair. She could have put out her hand and pulled that lank hair. In the dim light her eyes just caught Dan's startled face. She guessed he was bracing himself for one of her onslaughts. She stopped, turned to the lead singer, a broad-shouldered girl who was taking a breather from belting out 'Sweet Georgia Brown.'

'You have a wonderful voice,' she said with a smile. The girl flushed, looked pleased.

'Thank you. I'm glad you enjoyed it.'

Feeling Dan watching her, Sarah spoke softly in Christian's ear. Really, with the hubbub of chatter, she had no other choice if she wanted to say anything.

'Wasn't she good? I'm so glad you brought me here.'

'She is,' he agreed and they went on out into the street. When they were outside, he said, 'Where was your husband sitting?'

'I don't know,' she lied, not wanting him to know she had acted out that little scene hoping to arouse Dan's jealousy. 'I just saw him for an instant and then he disappeared. He might not have stayed here at all.' She was thankful for the darkness of the street to hide her untruth.

They drove back to her house almost in silence. She wondered what would happen when they arrived. Would he feel obliged to make a polite remark about seeing her again sometime? Or would he make some excuse about having to go back to Australia? To make it easier for him, she asked him if he would have to go back there.

'Not for a while. Someone was taken ill in the company and I had to go and hold the fort until another person could take over. Everything seems to be going swimmingly now.'

So, that was one excuse down, she thought, as they drove into her street. Through the chink in the curtains she saw the lights were still on in Robert's house. Was he waiting for her to return so he could start harassing her again?

Awkwardness took over, cramping her stomach. Now what? Did she say good-night and leave it at that? Ask Christian in for the coffee they didn't have at the restaurant? Whatever was the first-date etiquette these days? Trying to hide her confusion, she fumbled for her key in her bag.

He parked the car and got out to open her door for her.

'Thank you so much for such a good evening, Christian,' she said, hoping she sounded sincere.

'I'll come in,' he said, and took her key from her. Before she could protest, he walked smartly to her door and opened it. The ping of the alarm greeted them and she rushed in to turn it off. He followed her into the hall.

Her heart was fluttering as if it would take off and fly away. Was sex obligatory these days? She didn't want it with anyone else, she wanted *Dan*, his warm familiar body that slotted into hers so companionably. But he was gone, gone with that wretched woman. All this raced through her mind as she went to the corner and punched in the numbers to turn off the alarm.

Christian shut the front door behind him. If only Polly were here to chaperon her. She remembered all the lectures she'd given her about sexual behaviour, and wished she could find some advice for herself. She was being stupid; of course she could deal with this. She'd offer him coffee, and that was all.

'I'll make us some coffee,' she said briskly, feeling that she sounded like some hearty team-leader. She went into the kitchen, filled the kettle with water and snapped it on.

Christian followed her in. He put his arms round her and began gently kissing the back of her neck.

'Oh,' she said, 'I . . .' She half turned to tell

him to stop it, but he turned her round and kissed her lips, holding her close to him. Her senses reeled, her mind did not want him, but her body was responding to his urgent caresses. She could not breathe with his mouth on hers, and she tried to struggle away, but it was hopeless as she was trapped against the worktop.

It should not be like this, she wanted to say, might even have said it, but her body refused to listen to her mind, and then they were on the floor and making love and it was quickly over.

She felt foolish lying there half-dressed on the kitchen floor, and catching sight of his baleful expression she realized that he did, too. He kissed her hastily, as if he were thanking her for a favour, adding to her shame. She had not been raped. She could not pretend that her physical pleasure had not been as keen as his, but not her mind. She felt as if she had gorged on chocolate or drunk too much from pure greed, for that was what it was. Two people lonely for!love, having a quick fix to help them on their way.

'Shall I stay?' he said, putting down her clothes to cover her, tucking a strand of her hair behind her ear as if he was tidying away the evidence of their sudden passion.

'No, you needn't,' she said, infinitely sad that neither could love the other.

She looked away from the relief in his eyes.

He kissed her again. 'I'll ring you very soon, dear Sarah,' he said, but she knew he did not mean it.

The swell of music, some symphony she could not place seeped through the adjoining wall. They exchanged glances. Too many people had dampened down the flame of love that might have flared between them. His dead wife, her errant husband and, worst of all, that tiresome man next door.

CHAPTER THIRTEEN

If only Celine were here, so that she could discuss that frantic sexual encounter she'd had with Christian. She did not want to talk about it with anyone else and risk it being whispered about and having pitying or even disapproving glances thrown at her.

All those worries about never having sex again and showing the imperfections of her body to another man had been quite pointless—a waste of energy, as so many fears were. It had just happened, without giving her time even to pull in her stomach, let alone worry if he would think her bottom was too big. But the loneliness of sex without affection bit deeply into her. She had never had sex without love—or at least affection—before, and she didn't like it. No doubt she'd been spoilt over the loving years with Dan, but she found that momentary physical pleasure soon faded without the warm glow of commitment, leaving her aching with melancholy.

Christian was lonely and lost without Rachel, she was lonely and lost without Dan, but that did not translate into love, or even affection, between them. It would be so perfect if it did. He had said something about neither of them being able to connect with anyone else until they stopped searching for the person they really wanted. He'd said goodbye awkwardly, quickly, as if he wanted to file away the incident so that it could be forgotten.

'I'll be in touch,' he said, his fingertips brushing her cheek as he turned to leave the house. She thought she saw, or she hoped she saw, a touch of regret in his eyes.

'I'll look forward to it.' She played the game. Forcing herself to smile. Only when he had gone did she weep.

The next day, she reminded herself that she was going to enrol in the Egyptology class held at the school not far from the shop. The class started the following week, so she telephoned the centre to be told she could enrol when she came for the first class.

That first evening she was almost late, having been held up in the shop by an awkward customer. She paid for the class in the crowded entrance hall of the school and, after asking directions, rushed up the gloomy, grey-tiled stairs to the classroom. She was prickling with agitation from the rush to get here in time, tortured with the old fear left over from her school days of being late for class. She half wondered if she would be put in detention.

Catching sight of herself in a glass door, she saw that her hair was flying everywhere, her face shiny, her coat open. In short, she looked a mess. Perhaps this whole idea of learning something new was going to be too stressful after all.

Taking a deep breath to calm herself, she walked into the dingy classroom and saw Robert sitting there, close to the door amongst the other students. That decided her against it, and she turned to walk out gain.

He called out, 'Oh, Sarah, I hope you're not leaving on my account?'

'Of course I'm not,' she said curtly, seeing the eyes of the other students, five women of assorted ages, a young couple, and an old man upon her. 'I have mistaken the classroom.'

'Egyptology,' he said, his eyes on her face. 'I've always wanted to study it, but the classes are usually so far away it seemed too much of an effort to get to after a busy day.'

She had chosen the class almost for the same reason, but what a coincidence, not to mention a disaster, that he was here. She couldn't study it now. She had just paid out over a hundred pounds to do the course and there were no refunds unless the class was cancelled. Perhaps she could change to another subject? But the other classes they ran here did not appeal to her.

Before she could leave the room, a large untidy woman, her arms round a stack of books, entered.

'Hallo, everyone, sorry I'm late. I'm Martha, your tutor,' she greeted them cheerfully, taking her place in front of them. 'Now,' she eyed the men in the class, 'I need the screen put up and a table for my slides.'

Robert and the young man got up to do her bidding. Sarah hovered a second, planning to slip out and escape, but Martha fixed her with a look of authority and barked,

'Are you here for my class?' Her eyes swept round the rest of the students. She added with determination, 'I need a minimum of ten people, or it's not worth my time and they will close the class.'

The eyes of all the students turned on Sarah, silently ordering her to stay. If she did not join as the tenth person, the class would close and it would be her fault. Meekly, she sat down as far away from Robert as was possible, inwardly cursing him for yet again spoiling her life.

Sarah had imagined that the class would be a series of lectures, with a possible reading list if someone was interested in learning more.

She was shocked when Martha informed them that she expected either essays or a folder of worksheets from them. She glanced surreptitiously round at the others. They were all studiously taking notes already, even Robert, who threw her a maddeningly smug look.

Martha wrote some dates of visits to the British Museum on the blackboard, and a list of books to read. Sarah felt threatened by so much intensity. She'd never be able to keep up, as well as go to work and do her designs. Besides, she hadn't written an essay in years and had no idea how to go about it. It would be useless asking her children for help. She could already hear their voices protesting, 'Oh no, Mum, we hardly have time to do our own essays, we can't possibly help you with yours.'

Forms were handed out for them to fill in. The forms asked for their names, addresses and their racial origins. Was she Asian/British Indian, Black/British African, Mixed White and Asian, Mixed Other, or White Other, or Any Other? Whatever did it matter what colour you were to study Egyptology, or upholstery, or any other course for that matter? What colour was Any Other? She looked up, a laugh on her mouth at the ridiculousness of it, and saw everyone else intently filling it in as if their lives depended upon it. Robert caught her eye.

'I dare you to tick Any Other,' he said, his

eyes gleaming with amusement. No one else took any notice of his remark, leaving the two of them momentarily bound together. She hastily looked away from him

She did not tick any of the little boxes by the races. No doubt someone somewhere was being paid a fortune to make lists of how many people of each race studied each subject. She would not be part of it.

After the class, which involved slides and a description of the country and the importance of the Nile, Sarah got up to leave. But Robert was beside her, standing behind her chair so that she almost knocked him down.

'How strange that we should both pick the same class, especially as it is rather unusual.'

'I don't know if I shall keep it up,' she said, as casually as she could. 'I don't think I can be doing with all those essays.'

'We could help each other,' he said pleasantly. 'Something to do in the long winter evenings ahead.'

'I've more than enough to do to fill my evenings already,' she said, extricating herself from her place, pushing her chair in front of him as though he were a raging lion; and she wanted to keep her distance.

He moved out of her way. 'I've got my car outside, would you like a lift home?'

'No, thank you,' she said, though she was tired and would have liked one.

He said, 'Not even if I promise not to

mention the house?' His mouth curved slowly with a smile. Amusement creased his eyes, tiny wrinkles fanning out beside them.

She said yes reluctantly, but only because her head was throbbing with all this new information Martha had just drummed into them. 'Thank you, then, I will.'

She noticed that one of the other women was eyeing him up. She was pretty, with copper coloured hair tied back with a green scarf. She walked decisively towards him.

'Hi, I'm Amy, it's a fascinating class, don't you think? Great teacher.' She addressed her remark solely to Robert, her eyes sparkling as she looked up at him.

'Yes,' he said, 'fascinating.'

Amy went on at some length about her trip to Egypt a couple of years ago. Sarah hoped she would take him off her hands. Her friend, the other young woman, more stodgy-looking but with a pleasant smile, sidled up to them, too. Her eyes were on Robert, watching him listening to Amy.

He was, after all, the only available man in the class, the young man already being taken, the other man far too old, Sarah told herself, ignoring a pang of jealousy—though of course it wasn't really jealousy, just her empty stomach calling out for food.

She felt rather spare, waiting for him to finish talking to his fans. 'I must fly,' she said. She'd take the bus, after all. Leave Robert to them.

'Just coming, Sarah,' he said, and with a courteous smile he left the two women.

'I don't want to tear you away,' Sarah said as they went down the stairs together, their feet loud in the cubed tower that held the staircase.

'You haven't,' he said shortly.

She got into his car, a silver grey Alvis she'd often seen parked in the street. The smell of the leather interior evoked past glamour and elegance. The engine had a pleasant throb to it as he eased the car out into the traffic, so much nicer than that horrid little cough of Dan's sports car, and the line of the Alvis was so beautiful compared to that squatting frog. She wondered what Robert did for a living. She would not ask him, because that would show she was interested in him, which she most certainly was not.

'Your house seems quite busy, people always in and out.' He was looking ahead at the traffic as he said this, but she felt herself blush thinking of Gerry on the doorstep suggesting sex sessions, and Christian and her rolling around together on the kitchen floor. Had the sound of their lovemaking filtered through his walls as his music had done?

'The children come and go. Tim and a friend are coming this weekend, I think,' she said, surreptitiously looking for her front door key in her bag so she could rush straight inside when they got back.

'That will be nice for you.'

She nodded. She did not want to get involved with a conversation, feeling that he would somehow get some information out of her to use as a way to get her house, her finances being the weak point. If Dan insisted on the £40,000 that she had all but spent on doing up the house, she would either have to borrow it or sell the house and move somewhere smaller, in a less smart district. She put it to the back of her mind in case he could read her thoughts and take action against her.

Living so close to him, hearing the sounds of him in the house next door, was far too intimate for her liking. Yet they were strangers, and she was determined to keep it that way.

'I'm sorry if I disturbed you the other evening when you were going out. I do hope I didn't make you late for anything.' Then he did turn to look at her. She saw his face in the glow of the street-lights, the quick flick of his eyes assessing her expression. She guessed that he wanted to know more about Christian.

She would not fall for that. 'You *did* hold me up,' she said. 'I was late getting back from work and did not have much time to get ready.'

'I'm sorry. Did you have a nice evening?'

'Yes, very nice, thank you.' She looked out at the passing shops, cubes of light gleaming in the dark, showing off their wares. She would not become too friendly towards him; that would put her off her guard. In her struggle to make herself a new life, keeping the house was the corner-stone of that resolve. She must keep her wits and her emotions about her to be certain not to lose it.

He turned into their street and there was a parking place beside his house. He remarked upon it, as so often the street was full at night.

He said, 'Would you like to come in for a drink, or even scrambled eggs? We could have them with smoked salmon. We could talk over the course, even start on an essay?'

'No, thank you. I have so much to do this evening.' He was like a spider setting his trap; once he had lured her in, he would pounce and find her weakness.

'Another time, then,' he said, a maddening smile playing round his lips. 'This is quite a long term, we'll be seeing quite a lot of each other.'

She did not answer him.

They stood side by side beside their front doors, unlocked them and went inside their respective houses.

'Good-night,' he said.

'Good-night, and thanks for the lift.' She went inside to turn off her alarm, hearing Robert doing the same in his house then going upstairs. It was uncomfortable living in such close proximity to someone you didn't care for at all, especially if you suspected that everything they did had an ulterior motive.

CHAPTER FOURTEEN

The shop was busy the following morning when a young woman came in. Sarah was occupied with helping Mrs Bradshaw choose her annual Christmas dress, and she was grumbling because Celine was not there.

'She knows exactly what I want,' Mrs Bradshaw kept bleating, making Sarah want to tie her up like a trussed chicken in a bale of silk.

Maggie went forward to greet the young woman, her face suddenly going pink with suppressed excitement. She came over to Sarah and whispered feverishly, 'Fashion editor of *Vogue*.'

Fashion editor of *Vogue*! Oh, why had she come in when Celine was away? Sarah hustled Mrs Bradshaw into the changing-room with a couple of dresses. She must appear calm, treat her as if she was anyone else, not someone who could change their fortune.

'You have quite the most glamorous evening-wear,' the editor said after introducing herself. 'I passed the shop the other evening and had to stop and look in your window. We'd love to use some of your things for the feature we're doing for the party season.'

They had had some of their clothes featured in lesser magazines before, but to be in *Vogue* was the highest prize.

'Would you like me to show you what we have, or would you like to browse through by yourself?' Sarah asked, not wanting to appear too pushy, but not wanting to appear indifferent either.

'Show me, please, your newest designs. I haven't much time.' The woman's eyes darted all over the shop, taking in the displays on the walls, the floating scarves, the hats that toned in with the bright colours, the one set of underwear that was on show to be made to order.

'I adore the look of those jackets.' She went over to the rack and began pulling them out, exclaiming with delight at each one.

She did not take long to choose an armful of clothes that she wanted sent to the magazine for an immediate shoot.

When she heard that Sarah was the designer of most of the clothes, she said, 'I'd like to do a whole feature on you both.' She thrust her card at her. 'I'll ring you for an interview and a photograph. Thanks.' And then she was gone, whirling out to the street and a waiting taxi, leaving Sarah gaping after her.

'I really wanted a gold colour this year.' Mrs Bradshaw brought her back to earth with a jolt. Celine had been approached by the glossies in the past, even had clothes sent to the studio to be photographed, but they had not featured them. It was the Mrs Bradshaws of this world who paid the rent.

When at last the shop was empty, Maggie said, 'She obviously liked them, why else would she have come in? And she has chosen quite a few things to be photographed.'

'I know, but she'll choose other designers, too, and at the end of the day she might use *their* clothes and not ours. It's happened before.'

'It's high time your clothes were in all the top magazines,' Maggie said loyally. 'They are far more glamorous than those skimpy little numbers, all done up with safety pins, that always grab the headlines. Most women don't want to look like that. Most of us haven't the figure for a start.'

'But they *think* they have. We see it here every day. Look at Mrs Bradshaw. Every time she is convinced she is a size 12. It's all such an illusion, this preoccupation with youth and a washboard tummy.'

'You can never admit to being old,' Maggie said. 'We all go on perpetuating this ridiculous illusion, giving the young a power they haven't the experience for. Making the rest of us feel like failures if we don't dance to their tune.'

Sarah thought of Dan dashing off as fast as his spasmodic back would let him to his adolescent delights. It would be hilarious if it wasn't so destructively sad.

But if this feature came off—she hardly dared to think about it—she might be a success. Become famous in her own right as a good designer, though the thought somehow added to her anxiety.

When Celine telephoned her later, she told her all about it, keeping the excitement from her voice to ward off Celine's caution. 'She wants to do a feature on both of us.'

'It will be extraordinary if it comes off,' Celine said, rather dismissively, but knowing her as she did Sarah knew she was preparing herself for disappointment.

'How's Polly?' she asked, to change the subject.

'She's out with a young man she met. She sent her love.'

'I hope she's pulling her weight.' Sarah felt a twinge of guilt that Polly was abusing Celine's generosity by going out on the razzle.

'Oh, she's fantastic! All the silk merchants adore her. I'm sure I've got better deals just because of her. But she met this Englishman who is travelling, and I've given her the time off.'

'I'm glad her heart has mended so quickly,' Sarah said. If only hers would, but like a deep scar it still throbbed painfully if she snagged it with a scene from the past.

'Resilience of youth,' Celine said ruefully. 'Anyway see you in a couple of days. We're back Thursday evening.'

'The same night as my Egyptology class,' Sarah said, thinking that at least their coming back was an excuse not to go and suffer being in the same room as Robert.

'So, you took the plunge and found something interesting to study? Well done,' Celine said. 'We wouldn't dream of interrupting that. Ring me when you get back from it. Bye for now.' The line went dead.

All week Sarah had wondered how to get out of getting a lift home from the class with Robert. If he took his car each week and was going straight home after the class, it did seem churlish—which she didn't mind—but stupid, too, to refuse him. Although the school was not far from the shop, it was not near her bus stop home. There was quite a walk to get to it. This was fine on a summer's night, but less so in the cold and the dark. If only she had somewhere else to go afterwards, but skulking around in the dark, pretending she had somewhere else to go then coming home later, would be madness—uncomfortable madness, as well.

She timed her entrance to the class just as it started so she would not have to indulge in any conversation with him. Robert was sitting at the end, nearest to the door beside an empty place. It was obvious that she should sit there, otherwise it meant walking round the room to sit at the other end of the U-shape of narrow tables. He looked up as she came in and smiled, and she sensed he could read her uneasiness. Why was he being so nice to her?

What new trick had he up his sleeve?

He said 'Here's a place,' and moved a pile of books closer to his side.

'I don't want to sit in a draught, I have a sore throat,' she lied desperately, walking on round the room and sitting down next to one of the girls. She did not look at him again, but tried to concentrate on the lecture—the Egyptian way of death, which seemed to be more important to them than their way of life.

At the end of the class, she pretended to go on writing her notes, but he came up to her.

'I can't give you a lift home tonight as I am going out to dinner,' he said pleasantly, as if they had made a previous arrangement.

'I wasn't expecting you to,' she said, not looking at his face, but seeing his slim black leather shoes standing neatly beside her as she bent over her notepad.

'I'm getting quite a file together. I think I'll do that instead of essays,' he went on. 'What are you going to do?'

She hadn't thought. Whichever was easiest was her motto. She remembered helping the children do projects, buying postcards, looking for newspaper and magazine cuttings, sticking them in. She could do the same for this, it would be time-consuming, but not difficult.

'I'm going to do both,' Amy broke in. 'I've got a wonderful collection of postcards. I could give you some, if you like.' She addressed this remark to Robert.

'Thank you. I'll let you know if I need them,' he said cordially. Then, seeing that Sarah was resolutely taking no notice of him, he bent down and said quietly in her ear, 'I have something for you. I'll give it to you tomorrow.'

Her head shot up, her eyes wide with alarm. Did he mean some other solicitor's letter, or something from Dan to get her to give up the house?

'I don't want anything from you,' she said, fighting to keep her voice down. 'I just want to be left alone to live in peace.'

A flash of shame crossed his face, but he quickly recovered it. His full mouth tightened, he said, 'This is something very beautiful that I want you to have.' He turned and walked away.

Aware that the other students were looking at her, she packed up her papers slowly and got up to leave. She suddenly felt tired and defeated, and wished that she was being whisked home in a warm car, whoever was driving it, instead of hanging about in the cold at the bus stop.

She got home at last, hoping that Polly had arrived back. Knowing how often planes were late, she was not perturbed when she saw that the house was in darkness. She let herself in and when she had taken her coat off went into the living-room and saw the light on her answerphone winking furiously at her.

The first call was from Celine: 'I'm back safely. Polly is staying out a few more days—love, as they say, is all.'

The next message was from Polly. She could hear her breathless excitement, evoking tears of regret at the back of her own eyes: 'Mum, I'll be back on Monday. I don't want to come back at all, but Will says I must finish my degree. Love you lots, bye.'

Sarah remembered Polly's anguish when Joe had left her. How quickly she had recovered. How serious was Will? She was so engrossed in thinking of this that she did not take in much of the next message, but it suddenly dawned on her that it was Dan's voice. It was the first time it had been captured on the answerphone. The voice she had loved for so long, the voice that now whispered endearments to another woman.

'. . . so if you'll give me a ring, please, Sarah,' he finished.

Her stomach clenched in fear. He wanted the money and she didn't have it. Would she have to give it to him? She should go for a divorce and be free of him, but what if the court decided that she had got to much money from the sale of their house in the Crescent and made her give it to him? She would have to sell this house, there would be no other way.

She would not ring him. She could not bear to hear him being 'reasonable'. Behaving as if he was a nice, decent guy who could not understand why she should mind his defection so much and be so bad-tempered about it. She'd better get herself a good solicitor as soon as possible. Swallowing these new fears, she telephoned Celine to welcome her home and hear about Polly.

'They are passionately in love—if only you could bottle it and hand it out the world would be a better place,' Celine said cheerfully. 'And don't worry, he is charming. Good-looking, intelligent, and on his way home—you won't lose her to the travelling set.'

'Lucky girl,' Sarah said.

'I know, wish it were me. Still, love has its down side, too, and don't we know it? Now tell me about *Vogue*, heard anything more?'

Just before she went up to bed, Sarah remembered that she had not played back Dan's message. She'd spent the evening catching up on household chores and reading the paper. She always tried to keep busy in the evenings, trying to banish the empty lonely feeling round her heart. Her emotions were always at their worst in the dark and when she was tired. She'd be fine in the morning. But the knowledge that his voice was on the answering-machine tempted her to switch it on and listen.

It came into the room so familiar it hurt her like a physical pain, as if it was his voice from the dead. Yet it had no place here in her new life, and she mourned the change.

'I hope you are well. I wondered if we could meet? I've some things to discuss with you that I think are important. I'll be in the office tomorrow, so if you'll give me a ring please, Sarah.' The tape spun on in silence before clicking off.

She had a terrible temptation to play it again and again, just to hear his voice. But she turned off the light and went up to bed. She must not do it—that way led to madness.

CHAPTER FIFTEEN

Sarah had just dropped off to a restless sleep when she was woken by a woman's laughter. She heard Robert's voice in the street, then his front door open and close. She put on her light and glanced at her clock. It was a quarter to one. She hated being woken up the minute she had fallen asleep; she would not sleep well again tonight. Trust Robert to do that to her by bringing back a woman.

Her mouth felt dry and there was a little sickness in her stomach. Her reaction irritated her. It was not jealousy because she cared who Robert slept with, it was because she wished she had someone of her own to curl up with: Dan, back as he used to be. There was really no reason why Robert's love life should lose her any sleep. But it did. She picked up the historical novel she was reading and forced herself to read it, to stop the monstrous thoughts of Robert's sexual antics crowding into her brain.

When the alarm went off, waking her for work, she felt as if she had barely slept. Tired and scratchy, she pulled on her clothes, tried to inspire youth and vitality with make-up, and failed. She heard Robert moving on the other side of the wall. Was he cooking breakfast for his lady love?

*   *   *

She'd barely been in the shop five minutes when the telephone rang. Thinking it was probably Celine saying she was going to be late, she put on a cheerful voice. It was Dan.

'Did you get my call last night?' he said.

'Yes. What is it about?'

'Don't sound so grumpy, Sarah.' He sounded hurt.

'Why should I not?' she snapped. 'You have ruined our life by going off with a mouse. Why should I sound pleased to hear from you?'

'Sarah, don't let's quarrel.' She recognized his 'determined not to lose his temper' voice. 'I just felt we ought to meet, talk things over sensibly. I mean, time has gone by and . . .'

He wanted the money, and he was going to be caring and friendly while he tortured her for it. He earned a very good salary, and as this month he had not paid her the usual allowance—no doubt as a punishment for not giving him the rest of the money—he was hardly on the poverty line.

'I haven't time to discuss anything now. I've got masses of work on. *Vogue* wants to do an interview, and I'm studying hard. I haven't time to see you.'

'You can't be that busy, if you have time to go out to dinner.' He couldn't be jealous. Was that it? How dare he, after what he'd done to her?

She said, 'I can live my life as I please now. Choose who I have time to see. You have; I will do the same.'

There was a silence, and she was about to put down the receiver when he said, 'I just wondered what you and the children were doing at Christmas. I thought . . . well.' He emitted a short laugh. 'We are all adult, and they would enjoy it if we spent it together. It always was such a special time.'

Spend Christmas together? Had she heard right? Would they sleep in the same bed, and then would he go off to his mouse on Boxing Day? Or worse still, expect her to come for Christmas, too?

Sarah loved Christmas. They'd had such good ones when she was a child, and she'd kept up the practice. She always decorated the house, cooked wonderful traditional food and they usually had a party. It had been like that

173

last year. If she had been told then that it would be the last happy Christmas they would spend together as a family, she would not have believed it.

She said a little sadly, 'It *was* special.'

And before she could go on, he jumped in with, 'That's what I thought. We could all go somewhere together. A hotel, perhaps, do something different.'

'We are going to Edward and Mandy. They asked us ages ago.'

'That's always fun. Lots of shooting,' Dan said.

She could not believe his audacity. 'They haven't invited you,' she said. 'Not after what you did. You chose to leave us, Dan, for that mouse and a whirl in a red sports car. You can't just come back when it suits you. What's *she* doing over Christmas, and isn't that baby being born soon?' Was his affair over and this was his way of coming back to her? The thought, which a few months ago might have delighted her, now irritated her. Despite the aching loneliness in her heart, she would not take him back now—it was too late.

She heard the hesitation in his voice, his effort to sound casual. 'Oh, Nina has to go home to her elderly father. There is no room for me.'

So, that was it. Dan had loved their Christmases. His own mother disliked spending money unnecessarily, and he hadn't had a lavish one until he had married her. Sympathy for him oozed into her, as he knew it would.

He said, 'I think we should still celebrate this important time together as a family, don't you, Sarah?'

But the old, malleable Sarah had gone; she felt her new strength kick in.

'We are no longer a family, have you forgotten?' she said. She could not go through his defection again when Christmas was over. And what would the sleeping arrangements be? What would the mouse do if he tucked himself up in bed again with his wife? Maybe Sarah could get him back if she really put herself out, but she didn't want to. Apart from everything else, she didn't know where he had been. Maybe the mouse was not the only woman he had slept with. Maybe he had caught HIV.

She had willingly given him so much of herself over the years, and he had rejected it, thrown it back in her face. She had no more to give him now.

'You should have thought about that before you dumped me and rushed off,' she said tartly. 'Happy Christmases are part of a happy family. Thanks to you, we're not that any more.' She put down the receiver, feeling decidedly wobbly and tearful.

Celine came into the shop at that moment and could not help but overhear her last remark.

She said, 'Dan?'

Sarah nodded, then spewed out his request, then she felt ashamed of herself. 'I'm sorry, Celine.' She hugged her. 'Welcome back. I didn't mean to throw all this at you the minute you walked in. He just rang, caught me out.'

'Has she dumped him?' Celine asked, while she took off her coat.

'I don't think so. She's got to go home to Daddy. Maybe he disapproves of Dan. I wonder how she will explain the baby?'

'It will do him good to be alone, see what it is like for you. But maybe he'll find some friends to spend it with. Has he any family?'

'I don't know which friends would ask him. Most of our friends feel rather awkward about the breakup. I suppose Linda and Gerry might have him, though they usually go to her parents. Dan has a sister but they don't get on. I don't even know where she is living now; somewhere in Canada, I think.' The guilt that she had refused his request was eating round her heart, but she would not give in to it. Guilt was a woman's biggest enemy; it made them slaves to their families, and in turn made their chiidren into monsters who expected everything to be done for them. She was certainly guilty of that. The pleasure of looking after a family brought with it the pitfalls of indulging them too much.

Not having children, Celine did not

understand this kind of guilt. She said, 'You have made your plans to go to your brother and sister-in-law, haven't you? So, stick to them. What would Dan do after Christmas anyway? Gobble up his turkey and Christmas pud—all cooked by you—then go off back to her. You can't allow him to do that to you.'

'I won't. The children and I are going to Scotland without him. Edward won't have him after what he's done. He's furious with him.'

The telephone rang again. Celine snatched it up.

'She's not here,' she said, in her most imperious voice. 'Goodbye!' And she slapped down the receiver. 'The cheek of him,' she said disdainfully.

'Tell me about your trip and about Polly,' Sarah said, to change the subject before it overwhelmed her.

'We did very well. Bought some wonderful fabrics. I've got some samples somewhere.' She delved about in her large leather bag and pulled out some brilliant silks, the colours dancing in the electric light, cheering up the grey winter day.

'She's very good with people, your Polly. She picked things up very quickly, and as I said before, she's got a good eye.'

'I rather hoped she'd take up art or design, but she prefers her history.' Sarah was dying to know about the new man. 'So, tell me about . . . Will.'

Celina laughed. 'Oh, love, how I wish it would hit me again like that! They met in the street; it was ridiculous, really—if we'd been there a minute earlier or later, they might never have met each other. Fate, I suppose. I don't know why we Westerners don't trust it more.'

'So, they just met in the street?'

'Yes. They caught each other's eye. Hardly surprising, I suppose, two Brits standing on a street in India. They started talking, and he came with us to the shop. That was it, but he's lovely; perfect for her, I'd say.'

'I'm so glad.' Sarah remembered how much Polly had professed to love Joe, and how deeply his defection had hurt her.

*   *   *

Polly arrived back so late before term started that she hardly had time to turn round and get back to university.

'I don't want to go back at all,' she said blissfully. 'I want to stay out there with Will. Oh, Mum!' She hugged her. 'He is the one. I can't think what I saw in Joe. He was such a baby.'

Sarah had not the heart to tell her that Dan had suggested they have Christmas together and that she had refused him. Will was not coming back to Britain until February, so he would not be part of the equation. But Sarah's plans were made and she would keep to them. The three of them would fly up to Scotland on 23 December and stay there until just after the New Year.

The following week, Tim rang her at home one evening. 'Mum, Dad's going to take us skiing for Christmas. He's got us into a chalet; do you want to come?'

'But we're going to Scotland! It's all settled, I've got the tickets,' she said, aghast. How dare Dan go behind her back like that?

'Oh, Uncle Edward won't mind, he's easy like that. It's the only chance I'll get to ski this year, and Dad's paying, which is great as I'm skint.' He went on enthusing about it. 'You can come, too,' he said, 'if you want to.'

'I don't want to,' she managed to reply. This is what broken families were like. Children's loyalties split like this. If Tim had said he'd made other plans to spend Christmas with friends, she'd have been sad, but would have accepted it. Dan had quite ruthlessly engineered this because he did not want to be alone for Christmas.

'And Polly?' she said.

'Yes, Pol will come. Dad rang me the other evening, suggested it.'

'Is that woman going?' She could not stop herself from asking.

'Nina? No, she's got to go to her father. He's not well, and being pregnant she can't ski anyway. We'll only be gone a week. Then we

179

can come and join you in Scotland, have another Christmas with you,' he said cheerfully.

She put down the phone and wept. How easy it was for Dan to get what he wanted. The children loved skiing, but it was an expensive holiday and a couple of years ago Dan had told them he could no longer afford to pay for them to go. Now all he had to do was offer to pay and she had lost them.

It was no good saying that Dan was their father and it was only natural that they wanted to be with him. Skiing was more fun than Scotland, and the bait he had offered was too difficult for them to refuse.

When Polly rang a little while later, Sarah could hardly listen to her convoluted explanations.

'Why don't you come, too, Mum? We can all be together then,' she said with enthusiasm.

How simple it was for them. Tim and Polly wanted her and Dan to be together again, perhaps even imagined this holiday would fix that, but it was quite impossible for her. They would not know the agony she would suffer being with Dan, knowing he no longer loved her and wished that another woman was there in her place.

'No,' she said, controlling her misery as best as she could. 'I'll go to Uncle Edward's as planned. You go with your father.'

'But Mum!' Polly wailed knowing she had betrayed her, but unable to resist a skiing holiday with her father, especially with him being on his own, without Nina.

'Don't worry about it, Pol,' Sarah said, and rang off.

The doorbell rang, hard and strident. Crushed with this new onslaught on her happiness, she went robot-like to open it. Robert stood there, a spray of pure white orchids arching from a pot in his hand.

'For you,' he said, 'something beautiful.'

She burst into tears and tried to slam the door, but he had his foot in it.

'Heavens!' he said. 'I didn't mean for you to react like that. Don't you like them?'

'Please go,' she spluttered, embarrassed and ashamed of her constant weeping.

'Let me put this inside for you,' he said, marching into the hall and going into the living-room. 'This is so pretty,' he said admiringly, looking round the room. He put the pot of orchids on a magazine that lay on the table.

'You're surely not crying because I gave you an orchid, are you? I haven't poisoned it or anything. I just thought you'd like it.'

She had controlled herself by now. 'It's nothing to do with you, but I would like you to take the orchid away again. Nothing you say or do will ever make me change my mind over the house.'

He stood there, regarding her. His hair was blown about, giving him a raffish air; his slate-blue eyes were like deep pools, waiting, probing into her face.

His presence made her uncomfortable. She had a ridiculous urge to rest her head on that blue-shirted chest. She could almost feel the smoothness of the linen against her cheek, hear his heart beating under her ear. Perhaps he would put his arms round her, hold her to him.

She firmly banished such a ridiculous thought. 'Please take the orchids away. I don't like them.'

'Throw them in the bin then,' he said, and walked out of the house.

CHAPTER SIXTEEN

Sarah did not like orchids. She'd always thought them sinister, with their freckled throats and their luring petals that threatened some strange magic power. But this one was different. She sat and looked at the delicate arch of its stem with the cluster of pure white flowers springing like stars from it. It was beautiful in its simplicity. Although she tried quite a few times, she could not bring herself to throw it away.

She could take it to the shop or give it to Celine or any other of her friends, but the thought of explaining how she had got it and why she wanted to get rid of it wearied her. It would die soon anyway. So many indoor plants had contracted some terminal illness or early death in her hands.

She did not see Robert for a few days, though she heard him going in and out of his house. Although she treated his gift with suspicion, she felt awkward about not thanking him for his orchid. She could have put a note through his door but somehow she did not. She could not help feeling that he was ganging up with Dan against her.

Through Rebecca, she found a divorce lawyer—Hugo Pollard, a young man with a large stomach and a face like a boiled ham.

'You know that divorce is irrecoverable—there is no going back,' he said, with the air of a doctor discussing some major surgical procedure akin to amputation. 'Is there no way you could settle your differences—with marriage counselling perhaps?'

'Absolutely not.' She imagined going with Dan to some soothing counsellor who would not understand the change in him, the crippling pain that had destroyed any way back.

The more Hugo talked, the more panic-stricken she felt—putting aside their other differences, a judge might think that Dan had treated her fairly over the financial side, might not think it unreasonable for her to return the money he asked for. After all, the children were over eighteen and able to fend for themselves, and her house was worth a good bit and if she sold it she could still afford to live in comfort somewhere smaller. She struggled from his office, battered and bruised.

'The law is black or white, and most of life's events are grey,' she grumbled to Celine. 'If I go through with it, I could lose the house, be forced to move somewhere cheaper. I shouldn't have spent so much on doing it up but you know how it is if you don't do things at once you never do them at all, and it was looking very shabby.'

'You could probably get a mortgage or some sort of loan to pay Dan off,' Celine said. 'Ask Rebecca to look into that for you.'

'That's an idea.' But it added to her fears. All these lawyers cost money, and she couldn't afford it, especially now that Dan had written to her saying that if she did not return the money that was rightfully his, he could no longer afford to pay her the monthly amount. Was the mouse so expensive? Perhaps she demanded jewels and clothes from Bond Street every week.

Her financial state was beginning to be a worry. She didn't like to ask Celine for more money, she paid her well. But perhaps she'd have to find another job at weekends, or take in lodgers to make ends meet.

Robert arrived late to the Egyptology class and left early. He barely looked her way. If he

184

chose to ignore her, then that was fine. Her pride certainly wouldn't let her make the first move. She couldn't cope with any more emotional traumas. The children deserting her at Christmas to spend it with Dan was almost worse than her worries at losing the house.

She felt herself withdrawing into herself, pulling in her emotions like a snail going into its shell.

Celine noticed her mood and said,

'Cheer up, love. Welcome to the grown-up world of independence. Perhaps Dan will break his neck, and as you are still legally his wife you'll get the lot. Or perhaps he'll injure himself so badly that that woman will have to push him around in a pram with the baby.'

Sarah smiled at the picture that these words conjured up, and then she was hit by a thought. What would happen if he *did* break something and the mouse couldn't be bothered with him? Would he expect Sarah to pick up the reins and be a loving, supportive wife again? In the eyes of God and the law they were still married—the terrifying words 'for better and for worse, in sickness and in health' burnt into her soul.

*　　　*　　　*

Dan rang her again to tell her their travel plans; he did not mention the money and nor did she. She blurted out, 'If you break

185

anything, don't count on me to cope with you.'

'Of course I won't,' he said impatiently, going on about plane times. She couldn't bear it, him making plans without her.

'Why tell *me*?' she snapped. 'The children are perfectly able to cope on their own.'

'I just thought you'd like to know,' he said.

'I don't.' She rang off, wishing she'd told him how devious she thought he was. And desperate, too, the thought suddenly hit her. He didn't really like skiing any more, it hurt his back, yet the children adored it. Was paying for their skiing holiday the only way he would not be alone at Christmas? It was a sobering thought. His foolish love affair had cost him dear.

Dan had obviously not thought things through when he careered away from the tedium of family life in his squatting frog car, how he might come to miss the stable structure of the family he had so quickly dismissed.

Celine said, 'Anyway, here's something exciting for you. *Vogue* wants to do their interview on Friday. Should be in the February issue.'

One dress, coupled with two others from another designer, had made *Vogue*'s current issue. Neither of them thought the picture had done it much justice; the model's jutting hips had spoilt the line. What would the interview do to them?

Anxiety and excitement chased through

Sarah. 'Where, here or do we go to a studio?'

'Here. Eight in the morning. We hope to be through by lunchtime.'

They spent the rest of the week wondering what to wear. How should they look?

'Bared breasts and slits up to the navel are so naff,' Celine said. 'Pathetic, too, at our age. Shall we appear artistic, or just elegant?' They settled on glamorous, like their clothes.

Celine dressed in fuchsia-pink silk trousers with a dark-blue and fuchsia jacket. Sarah was in a loose peacock-blue silk trouser suit that made the most of her blonde hair.

'I think we look glamorous, yet creative.' Celine studied them both as they stood side by side in front of the mirror.

'You do the talking,' Sarah said. 'It is your shop, after all.'

'But you are the main designer.'

The interview took all morning, and when at last it was over and the hot lights and endless people connected with it had departed, Celine said rather despondently, 'I wish we hadn't done it now. They might mix up what we said and make us sound awful.'

'We didn't say anything awful, did we?' Sarah caught the panic in her voice.

'I hope not. What if they make our clients and our clothes sound old or ugly or unfashionable or whatever. Oh, Sarah, I wish we hadn't done it now. You know how journalists can twist things.'

'I'm sure it will be fine; anyway, she'll let us see it before it's published, won't she?'

'I do hope so.' Celine did not sound convinced.

* * *

As time went on, their fears receded. There was a lot of work on. Their dress in *Vogue* did produce some response, and quite a few people wanted one like it in time for Christmas. They were both worked off their feet. All Sarah seemed to do was work, struggle home and sleep; she even missed one Egyptology class, and had not used the half-term week to get her file together.

One evening in late November, when Sarah got back home she found among her post on the mat a thick white envelope with her name on. Inside, there was a flourish of writing in black ink.

Just to inform you that I will be away for the next month. I have left my keys with Diana Bentley at No. 9. Sheila, who cleans for me, will be going in, otherwise no one else should be there.
Happy Christmas.
R.M.

What a relief that he had gone. She could go about her life without the constant worry of him turning up with yet another ploy to try and persuade her to sell him her house. And yet as she went to bed that night and lay alone in the dark, she felt bereft. This was ridiculous and she scolded herself severely; she didn't even know where his bedroom was in his house, and the idea that they lay side by side in their beds with only a wall dividing them was barmy. Anyway, he had women companions in his bed, so he would hardly think of her at night unless it was to plot and plan how to get her house from her.

But she realized that she had found his presence next door strangely comforting. Just knowing that someone else—and, she admitted rather shamefacedly, a strong man in particular—was there made her feel safer. She had been used to living with a man most of her life, after all. Being scared of being on her own was stupid, too—vague feelings of worry in case someone broke in, or the ceiling fell in or the water tank burst could happen to anybody. Some disastrous things had happened to her when Dan had been away on a business trip, and she had coped perfectly well. Maybe she was joined by one wall to a man who might, in extremities, come to her aid. Though, in truth, if anything terrible did happen, Robert would no doubt use it to snatch her house from her.

She went to that week's Egyptology class, telling herself it would be much more enjoyable without having him sitting on the other side of the room, or worrying about how to avoid going home with him, not that he'd asked her these last few, times. But she found her mind wandering during the class. It wandered even more when Amy said with hardly concealed self-importance, 'Please, Martha, could I have a set of notes for Robert? I promised I'd keep him up to date on the class.'

Sarah determined to write up the most amazing file. There was a planned visit to the British Museum this weekend, which she would go to, and she would buy masses of postcards to illustrate it. Amy no doubt would buy some for Robert. She would take the work up to her brother's house to do over Christmas—she needed something to fill the void left by the absence of her children.

Tim and Polly appeared back from their universities, excited about their skiing trip. Sarah resented every demand of 'where's my ski suit?' 'I need a new jersey, it's going to be so cold', 'I've lost my passport', and all the other things concerned with an imminent trip that kept drilling into her head, fuelling her irritation and the wretched jealousy that gnawed at her heart.

Polly guessed her feelings and once or twice put her arm round her.

'Please come, Mum. It won't be the same without you.'

'I can't, Pol,' she said. 'Don't you see how

difficult it will be for me, knowing he no longer wants me and is only putting up with me out of guilt and a dread of being alone for Christmas?'

'It won't be like that.' Polly defended him and Sarah said no more. She thought it important to keep fathers special to their children; you could have as many husbands as you could bear to. It was one thing saying a few home truths about a husband, quite another about someone's father.

Tim, taking after Dan, did not want to discuss it at all.

'I can't think why you won't come. You love skiing, and we won't get another chance this season.'

It was so painful knowing that never again would they plan a holiday as a happy family together. Tim could not, or more likely *would* not, see that.

'You can have separate rooms, or double up with Pol and I'll go in with Dad,' he said, as if that would somehow solve it. Sarah could not bring herself to tell him that the pain of being with someone who no longer cared for you was worse than not being with them at all.

They left the day before she was to leave for Scotland. They planned to have a Christmas celebration when they got back, give each other their presents then. But when they begged for ski gloves and jerseys, she bought them for Christmas and gave them to them before they left.

She kissed them goodbye and walked off down the road to work, biting her lip against those dreary tears that threatened to engulf her, yet again. She was thankful that she would not be there to see them leave later this morning.

Celine said when she walked in, 'What you need is a delicious lover.'

'Find me one, then,' Sarah said, with a wry smile. 'Have you any cast-offs you can hand on?'

'I have actually, but it's too late for Christmas,' Celine said. 'As you know, I am going to one of my ex's for Christmas. He's getting on, and bits of him are wearing out, but we have a good time. I'll hand him over after New Year.'

Sarah laughed, but she did not say how she was dreading her first Christmas as a discarded wife. It was the anniversaries that were always the worst; like after a bereavement, the happy memories held such pain. The comfortable happiness of her brother and sister-in-law would make her feel worse, making her yearn for her and Dan to be together as they used to be, but she couldn't not go because of that. She'd have to get on with other people's happiness; at least she'd had some in her life, and she still had a lot to be thankful for.

They were shutting up the shop until after the New Year, and Sarah did not get back home until nearly seven. As she approached her house, she saw that someone was standing by Robert's front door. Perhaps it was the cleaner, or the neighbour with the key. She quickened her steps, worried suddenly that something might be wrong with her own house.

The person turned as she reached her door. She was a young, heavily pregnant woman.

When she saw Sarah she said, 'Are you the person who lives next door to Robert Maynard?'

'Yes.' Sarah looked at her under the streetlight. She was an attractive, well-dressed woman of about thirty years old. She felt the old prejudice jump in her. Was Robert responsible for this woman's condition? Had she come to give birth to his child on his doorstep?

'Perhaps you'd let me in, then. I don't have a key, and Diana seems to be out. I never said I was coming, but maybe he'll turn up later this evening.'

'He won't, he's gone away for a month,' Sarah told her, seeing by the woman's expression that her prejudice must be written all over her face.

'Damnation! I knew I should have rung. Anyway please could you let me in to his house?'

'I don't have a key.' Sarah now saw that she had a large bag sitting on the pavement.

'Oh.' The woman sounded surprised. 'I thought you would, being so close to him.'

'We are only close because we share a wall,' Sarah said darkly. She wanted to get into her own house, out of the cold. To sit down with a glass of wine before starting her packing for Scotland. What could she do with this woman? Maybe Diana would soon return and she could decide whether or not to let this woman into Robert's house. She glanced hopefully down the street towards No. 9 but it was still in darkness.

'I really don't know what to do. I haven't got anywhere else to go.' The woman sounded a little desperate. 'I'm sure Diana will be back soon,' she added doubtfully.

It was old and damp, and it would be churlish to go into her own house and shut the door on this woman in her present state while they waited for Diana's return. The situation irritated her. Had Robert got her pregnant and then gone off to wherever without telling her? This was surely his responsibility and he should be here to deal with it.

She said 'Surely you know where Robert is, or has he just gone off and let you down?' All the angry words and accusations against him banked up inside her head like planes ready for take-off.

She was about to let them go when the woman said, 'I'm not very good at keeping in touch with him. I feel rather ashamed of

194

myself, but I have no other choice at this moment in my life. I'm the prodigal daughter, turning up because I'm in one hell of a mess and I've no one else to turn to.'

CHAPTER SEVENTEEN

'You are Robert's daughter?' Sarah hoped she didn't sound too surprised.

'Yes. I'm Freya Maynard. I live in France, or I did until this morning. What's your name?'

'Sarah Haywood.' She squinted at this girl in the half-light. She was tall, dark hair flowing from a fur cap. She would have to ask her in. It was far too cold to go on standing here on the pavement.

'You'd better come in while we wait for Diana.' Sarah opened her front door and Freya followed her in.

Freya went into the living-room, saying as she looked around, 'It's very like Daddy's house, except he has got the dining-room-cum-kitchen this end. His living-room opens up on to the garden.'

Sarah did not care what his house was like. She thought instead of how like Robert Freya was. She didn't look particularly like him facially, but the way she moved and certainly the way she seemed to commandeer her house were just like her father. At least the house was tidy and clean; Polly and Tim, perhaps feeling guilty at leaving her behind, had done it for her.

Freya sat down on the sofa. 'You don't mind if I sit, but my back's giving in! If I'd known how uncomfortable this pregnancy lark would be I'd have thought twice about it.'

As apparently Freya had nowhere else to go but her father's house, there were perhaps more important factors she should have considered before embarking upon a pregnancy. But Sarah didn't say anything. You couldn't say anything remotely judgemental these days. People were allowed to behave however they wanted to, expecting small children to fit in with their romantic arrangements and assuming that society would pick up the pieces if anything got broken. Then they wondered why they were often so unhappy. Having and doing it all did not make for an easy life.

She felt annoyed by this girl sitting here when she wanted to relax after the last frantic day in the shop before shutting down for the Christmas break. She wanted to think about her packing for Scotland. If Freya had been anyone else but Robert's daughter, she might have felt differently. Besides, what would happen if Diana had gone away for Christmas?

She said, 'So you didn't know that your father would not be here?'

'I didn't know what he was doing. He's a law

unto himself. But it's my fault I haven't been in touch with him for ages.' She undid her coat, struggled out of it and settled herself comfortably back on the sofa.

'Mmm, so nice to sit down,' she said, closing her eyes like a contented cat. 'I've been travelling most of the day. The train was hopelessly late.'

Sarah had so many things to do before she went away, and having this girl here cramped her thoughts. She said, 'If it is not rude to ask, where is your mother?'

'Oh, she's in LA. Been living there for ever with her new man. It's too late in the pregnancy to fly that far. Anyway, it's not Mummy's scene to be a granny.' She laughed, but Sarah detected a stab of pain behind it.

'Will it be your father's scene?' Somehow she couldn't see Robert coping with disturbed nights and nappies.

'He won't mind. I'll be gone soon anyway. When it's born, I'll be off again. I just thought I'd rather have it in this country!'

Sarah wondered if she could enquire who the father was and what had happened to him. Had Freya been deserted, left alone to bring up this child? Instead of prying further, she offered tea or coffee and said she had to pack. She also informed Freya firmly of her own plans. The flight for Scotland left early tomorrow afternoon, and there was no way that she would miss it.

'Fine, go ahead, don't mind me,' Freya said, her eyes still closed.

Sarah made her some tea before going upstairs to pack. She found that Polly had snitched one of her best jerseys, which added to her feeling of being put upon. She did not want to be nice to this girl, but she had not the heart to tell her to go.

She wandered aimlessly round her bedroom, collecting things up and then discarding them and really getting nowhere. Every so often she peered out of the window into the street to see if Diana's lights had gone on and she was back, but her house stayed in darkness.

As the time went by, her agitation grew. What would happen if Diana did not get back before she left? Would she have to let Freya stay here? The enemy in the camp. If Robert came back before she did, then he would have instant access to her house.

She went firmly downstairs again. Freya was reading the newspaper. She looked up and smiled at her—Robert's smile, which was so disconcerting.

Sarah said, 'As I told you, I'm going away tomorrow until after the New Year. What will you do if Diana does not come back?'

Freya thought for a moment then said, 'We'll have to break in over the garden wall. I'm afraid you'll have to climb over it, of course—I can't in this condition—and then let me in by the front door.'

'Have you absolutely nowhere else to go?' Sarah sat down opposite her.

'No, I haven't. The few friends I've kept up with have gone away. I really thought Daddy would be here, or anyway Diana with the key. What about his cleaner? She must have a key.'

'I don't know where she lives.'

Freya regarded her, a frown creasing her brow. She said imperiously, 'It's odd that you don't have a key. The people who lived here before always did. They were constantly in and out of each other's houses.'

Sarah said sharply, 'Your father and I don't get on.'

'Oh? Why's that?'

'He seems to think he should have this house. Apparently the Blakes promised it to him, but in the event they sold it to me.'

'Did you gazump him?' Freya demanded.

'No. He was away and they needed to sell it quickly to buy something else in France. I happened to be here and bought it. I didn't know about him wanting it until he came back.'

'I see. Funny he didn't leave them his number. He was probably in Scotland, where he has recently inherited a glassworks. He spends quite a bit of his time there. I think he's got a girlfriend up there, too.' She smiled. 'He usually has one somewhere.'

'Don't you have his number there?' Sarah's

voice was sharp. 'Or his mobile?'

'I've left them behind in France. I can't even remember the name of the business. And his mobile doesn't seem to work.'

'Why doesn't he live up there permanently?'

'Maybe he will. But he's got his job here,' Freya said.

'And what's that?'

'He consults for various firms now. It gives him a bit more time to do what he wants to do.'

'Orchids?' Sarah guessed. 'But who looks after them when he's away?'

'Perhaps his cleaner does, or maybe he farms them out.' Freya glanced at the white one Robert had given Sarah. It sat on the table by the window, its pristine beauty dominating the room. 'Did he give you that?'

'Yes.'

'Then he must like you. He only gives them to people he thinks will care for them.' Freya regarded her with renewed interest.

Sarah ignored the ridiculous bubble of euphoria that rose in her. She said sharply, 'Or to bribe them.'

'Bribe? Why should he want to do that?'

'He wants this house so badly I think he might do anything.'

'He usually gets what he wants. That's something I've inherited from him,' Freya said. She moved to get up, her hand on her back as she attempted to stand. 'Do you have Diana's telephone number? I'll ring and see if she has come back.'

'I haven't got it. I don't even know her, but I'll go outside and check if she's back.' Sarah left the room, wanting suddenly to be outside, away from Freya's demanding presence.

She went up to No. 9, but it was still in darkness. Just as she turned away, a young couple came out of the house next door. Sarah asked them if they knew where Diana was.

'She's gone away, she'll be back on Boxing Day,' the man said cheerfully.

'Do you have a key for her house, because I need the key for Robert's house?'

'I don't. She leaves one with her sister, I think, but I don't know her exact address. It's somewhere in the New Kings Road.' The couple seemed impatient to be off.

It was obvious that unless Sheila, the cleaner, turned up, there would be no way until Boxing Day that Freya could get the key from Diana. She asked the couple if they knew Sheila's number.

'No,' the girl said, 'but she came today. I saw her leave at lunchtime. She wished me a Happy Christmas, so I don't suppose she'll be back until after it.'

Heavy with irritation, Sarah went back and told the news to Freya. She couldn't chuck a pregnant woman out into the street, yet she certainly could not leave a stranger in her house, either. Would Freya be able to find a

201

room in a hotel?

Freya did not look unduly worried. 'We'll just have to break in,' she said. 'We, or rather you, can get over the back into his garden. He's got a rather dodgy window-catch, and if he hasn't mended it you can open it with a knife. Then you can open the front door for me.'

'I can't possibly do that. Anyway I'll set off the alarm. We'll call the police station; they'll know what to do.' She reached for the phone book.

'No, don't do that.' Freya's face became strained. 'Not unless we have to. Please do this for me. I'll be eternally grateful.'

She couldn't say she was not sure Freya was Robert's daughter, as there was enough resemblance for her to have no doubt, but it was possible that Robert would not want her in his house. If she only wanted to contact the police as a last resort, maybe it would be wrong to let her in. Yet Freya was hugely pregnant, and the other alternative was to let her stay here until Diana returned, or Sheila, or until whoever looked after the orchids went in. Sarah did not want that.

'I don't want to do it,' she said. 'Anyway, we can't do it now in the dark.'

'You must. Please, Sarah, I've nowhere else to go. I know it is my fault I didn't call Daddy before, but I decided a few days ago that my relationship was not working, would never

202

work, so I thought it better to leave him and come here and have the child.'

'Couldn't you have waited until you had contacted your father?'

'No. I had to get here before it was born in France, and the trains are hopeless between Christmas and New Year.'

Sarah's agitation increased. Was that going to be the next thing? Freya going into labour at any moment?

'When is it due?'

'In a couple of weeks. I'm really sorry to have put you to so much trouble, but I've no one else who can help me. I'll square it up with Daddy if that's what you're worried about. Any damage you do I'll get mended. He'll understand.'

'I'm sure he won't. Anyway, I can't do anything tonight,' Sarah said again, lamely. 'We'll have to see in the morning.'

'Thank you so much, you've saved my life,' Freya said triumphantly, proving that like her father she usually got what she wanted. 'Would you mind if I slept here? I'm too tired to go and find a hotel.'

Of course she had to agree. Sarah put her in Polly's room, and Freya went straight to bed, saying she wanted no more than a banana to eat.

Sarah spent a miserable evening and night wondering how she could get rid of her. She couldn't possibly break in to Robert's house.

203

He would surely use it against her if she did.

The next morning was bright and sunny. Freya was downstairs early. She said, 'Let's do it now. Then I can get out of your way.'

'I think we ought to find a locksmith,' Sarah decided, reluctant to break in to Robert's house, but also afraid she would miss her plane if this took too long.

Freya guessed at her anxiety. She pointed out, 'That will take ages. They are bound to have to ask the police or whatever. Look, please Sarah, it won't be difficult.' She went to the French windows that led to the garden, and asked Sarah to unlock them.

Sarah could imagine Robert's anger, and the endless nasty letters coming from his solicitor, accusing her of all sorts of horrors. What if Freya, who obviously made decisions on a whim, decided to go back to France and the father of this child, and left her to face his anger alone?

But she unlocked the French windows, and Freya went out into the garden and stood by the trellis-covered wall that separated the two gardens.

She studied it carefully, then she said, 'It's quite high, isn't it? But look, you could saw through it just there, where the creeper is not very thick. Then, by standing on something, you can just pop over into his garden. That window by the door can easily be opened with a knife. I showed him once how dangerous it

204

was to leave it like that, and he probably hasn't done anything about it. You open that and then you are in. Easy!' she smiled at Sarah encouragingly.

'How do you know he hasn't mended it? And how do *you* know how to open it in the first place?' Sarah asked bossily.

Freya blushed, looked awkward. 'Well, if you must know someone showed me. Oh, a long time ago. I don't do it any more.'

'Do what?' Sarah felt anxious again. Was this girl a thief and that was why Robert hadn't kept in touch with her?

Freya said with defiance, 'When I was sixteen, I was rather wild. I was at a boarding-school; it was so boring. I met up with a man who was a burglar.' She smiled dreamily. 'He was so good-looking, and so exciting compared to the drippy boys I met through the girls at school. I went on a couple of raids with him. But I was caught.'

'So you mean you were a thief?'

'No, I just went on the raids. He showed me what to do, but I didn't do it or even go into the places. Anyway, there was a dreadful stink; I was expelled and Daddy sent me abroad. I'd never take anything that wasn't mine or smash up people's property, but this man did show me how to break in.'

'I don't like it,' Sarah said. 'I'm sorry, but there must be something else we can do. You could go to a hotel for instance. I'll lend you

205

money if you haven't any.'

'No, thank you,' Freya said firmly. 'Look, Sarah, you get me in and then I'll deal with Daddy. I promise you he'll be fine about it.' She looked at her watch. 'You said your flight is at two, you'd better get on with it.'

Despite her misgivings, Sarah fetched her light aluminium step-ladder and sawed through the trellis. It was old and damp, and split instead of cutting cleanly. She had to hack away much of the creeper, making a terrible mess of it. Then, with Freya holding on to the ladder she climbed up and over into Robert's garden.

She stood a moment and looked round it. It was full of all kinds of plants she had never seen before. Some were covered with straw to protect them from the frost.

Freya came up a few steps of the ladder and looked over the wall. 'Now for that window on the side. Take the knife and slip it under the frame; jerk it up and the catch will open. It's quite a knack, so take your time.'

The whole of Sarah's being protested against this act, but time was marching on and if she missed this flight she would not get on to another one this side of Christmas. Following Freya's instructions, she did what she said. It didn't work. She tried again, and the knife slipped and cut her hand. The scarlet blood sprang out, splashing over the white-painted windowsill.

206

'Damn,' she swore, dropping the knife and sucking her hand.

'Wait, I'll get you a handkerchief.' Freya disappeared and returned a moment later with a drying-up cloth. 'Wrap it up and have another go,' she said, looking at the wound. 'The cut doesn't look too bad; you've just bled rather a lot. You've got to open the window to get through the house, or you'll have to spend Christmas in the garden.'

'I won't, you can lift over the ladder and I can get out again,' she said angrily, inspecting her hand. The cut hurt and was still bleeding, dripping on to the stones by her feet.

'Please, Sarah, try one more time,' Freya begged.

With her hand wrapped in the towel, Sarah tried again in desperation. However had she got involved in this? She would not bear it if she missed her flight and had to spend Christmas here. Not that she would; she'd drive all the way up, if need be, though it would be hell to do on her own.

She tried again and again, and suddenly the catch flicked up and she pushed the window open.

'How am I meant to get through that?' she demanded, the window being a few feet off the ground.

'I'll push over the ladder, or better still, stand on that pot beside it,' Freya said, rather impatiently.

A huge green pot containing something shrouded in sacking stood by the window. If she put her foot on the rim of it, she could lever herself through the window. She did this, and just as she pushed off with her foot the pot cracked and a large piece of it fell and shattered on to the stone paving.

'Don't worry, I'll get him another one,' Freya said. 'You're there now. Remember the alarm code. I'll come round and be outside the front door.'

At least Freya knew the alarm code. 'It's easy, the ages of Mummy and Daddy when they finally got divorced. Daddy uses it for everything. 3638.'

'Don't lock me out of my own house!' Sarah said sharply before she heaved herself through the window and landed on the back of a chair in Robert's drawing-room.

She felt like a thief. She heard the low hum of the burglar alarm, so she hurried through the room, only briefly taking in the muted colours and elegant watercolours on her way to the alarm panel. This was situated in exactly the same place as hers was.

'3638,' she kept muttering while she keyed it in. The hum stopped.

She walked along the short passage to the front door. She passed the open-plan kitchen and dining-room. The cupboards were painted denim blue, and the curtains were white, blue and olive, giving the room a fresh, almost

208

Mediterranean feel. It surprised her. Somehow she'd imagined his taste would be more drab. But she had no time to look round; she opened the front door and Freya came in, dragging her bag behind her.

'At last!' She hugged her. 'Thank you so much, Sarah. Now, forget about me and go and catch your plane. I'll be fine. I'll get the key off Diana when she gets back.'

'But what about food?' Sarah said, unable to stop herself fussing.

'I expect, he's got some in the freezer, and I can probably get some things off the milkman if I hear him come.'

Freya opened Robert's freezer. 'Look, there are pheasants and smoked salmon, even bread. Daddy always lives well. I shall be fine.'

'You better have my milk, I've some fruit and cheese too; they won't last until I get back.' Sarah suddenly felt sorry for Freya spending Christmas here alone with her child's birth so imminent.

As if guessing her thoughts, Freya said, 'Thanks. I'll get you some more when you return. But I'll be fine, honestly. You don't know how happy I feel to have made this decision and to be safely here. I like my own company, and Christmas was never much of a thing for me anyway.'

There was no more time to go into it, if Sarah was to catch her plane. Feeling decidedly uneasy about it all, she put a dressing on her hand, finished her packing, locked her house up, got into the minicab and departed, hoping that all would be well.

CHAPTER EIGHTEEN

As her brother drove her to his house, Sarah said, 'I can't tell you, Edward, how relieved I am to be here.'

He laughed. 'You sound as if you're escaping some wild beast!'

'Almost, but it's not so much her as her father.' She explained about Robert and Freya.

'What would she have done if she'd arrived today when you had left?'

'Goodness knows. But I'm so pleased to be away from it and be here in this glorious place with you all.' She felt happy to be here with him. They had always got on, but because he lived up here and she in London they did not see that much of each other.

They had been brought up in the country, and Edward had always preferred it. Mandy came from round here, so he had been content to settle with her near her old home. They had a farm, and sold their meat and home-made pâtés and game pies to various prestigious shops around the country. They had just finished their busiest time of the year cooking and sending off the hams.

But as she sat with them in their large warm kitchen having tea, she was suddenly assailed by a terrible sensation of loneliness and despair. Here was the perfect picture of a contented family: dogs dreaming by the stove, the two boys cheerfully ribbing each other in the corner, Mandy and Edward happily sitting side by side pouring each other tea from the old brown teapot, with a plate of freshly baked scones and a Christmas cake on the table.

Her marriage had been like this once. If an onlooker had come upon them, they would have thought how happy they were. Had the very ordinariness of it all bored Dan rigid?

So many advertisements were full of attractive young people having a wonderful time because they ate a certain food or drank a certain drink. People were fed this picture day after day. 'Other people' were younger, sexier, slimmer, all having a wonderful time, leaving the boring people out. No one wanted to be thought boring and past it today. Had this happened to Dan? Had the drip-drip effect of other lives, golden fantasy lives, dazzled him from the security of his own?

These days it was probably politically incorrect to show an ordinary happy family, just sitting together round the table of a shabby kitchen, with home-made cake and scones for tea. It would be seen as being offensive to those who did not have such a family.

Edward, glancing up from buttering his scone, seemed to guess her mood. He said gently, 'Missing the children?'

She smiled at him, she was not going to be a wet rag and spoil Christmas for them. 'I suppose I am. This is the first Christmas I've had without them, but they've got to that age now. Next year, they might easily be off somewhere with friends.'

Mandy leant over and squeezed her hand. 'We'll have a great time, you'll see. We've quite a few parties on while you are here. You might meet someone lovely.'

Sarah laughed. 'I doubt it, but I shall enjoy myself anyway,' she said determinedly.

On Christmas Day, Polly rang at teatime.

'Happy Christmas, Mum. Are you having a good time?'

'Wonderful,' Sarah said, feeling replete and sleepy with contentment. 'We've just finished the most amazing lunch. As you know, both Edward and Mandy are exceptional cooks.'

'I know,' Polly said grumpily. 'We've just had the most dreadful lunch. The turkey wasn't even defrosted properly, so we'll probably all die of salmonella. The chalet girl hasn't a clue how to cook, or even how to get it all ready at the same time.'

'I'm sorry, but is it fun otherwise? Snow good?' Sarah hoped she did not sound smug. She wondered how much they were grumbling at Dan.

'It's so cold. And yesterday there was a complete white-out and we couldn't ski at all,' Polly went on indignantly.

'Well, maybe tomorrow will be better. How's Tim?'

'He's fine, sends his love. He's met some girl and gone off with her. I wish Will was here.' Polly went on to tell Sarah about the girl Tim had become enamoured with. She was obviously feeling left out. What was Dan doing? Why were they not having a happy father and daughter relationship together?

Sarah said, 'Are you skiing with Daddy?'

'He can hardly ski. His back and knee hurt. He goes so slowly that we might as well walk down. He thinks he needs a new knee joint.'

'What's wrong with his knee?'

'I don't know. It just doesn't seem to work as well as it used to. I expect it will be all right if he doesn't ski again,' Polly said wearily.

Perhaps very low sports cars were not good for ageing knees, Sarah thought. How would the mouse cope with helping him over such an operation—if he needed one—while looking after a new baby? When Tim and Polly were babies—there was just over a year between them—it had been dreadfully hard work. But she and Dan had been young and fit, and had got on with it. Was having babies really compatible with new knee joints and goodness knows what other repair jobs an ageing body might need?

213

On Boxing Day, they were invited to a party given by some friends of Edward and Mandy's who lived a good hour's drive away. No one round here thought anything of driving miles for a party.

'The McNairs give these marvellous parties,' Mandy explained. 'They always invite masses of people on Boxing Day, and again at New Year. I don't know how they do it.'

'They just love entertaining,' Edward said, 'and this is their big time.'

They arrived at the McNairs at about 7.30, having dropped the boys off at their friends' house on the way.

A vast Christmas tree, smothered in tartan silk bows, and gold and silver decorations, stood in the hall. There was an enticing scent of pine needles, wood-smoke and mulled wine. The babble of voices heralded a good evening ahead.

Sarah was introduced and made welcome. She remembered one or two friends of Edward and Mandy's from other times she'd stayed with them, and so she did not feel too much of a stranger. She suspected that Edward had told them about her and Dan's split, and for that she was grateful, as no one mentioned him. That was one of the worst things about socializing, having to explain her new position and endure the sympathetic or intrusive remarks.

She was busy talking to a local artist she

knew, when she glanced across the room—and there was Robert Maynard watching her.

She was so surprised to see him there that she stopped mid-sentence. The woman she was talking to followed her gaze, but as Robert was standing in a group she did not know whom Sarah was looking at. Sarah stared at him again, to make sure that it really was him and she wasn't experiencing some dreadful hallucination.

'Sarah,' he said, leaving the group and coming over to her, 'how strange to see you here.'

She stared at him in disbelief, managed to gulp, 'Even stranger to see *you.*'

He said, 'I have a business up here now. Besides, I like to have Christmas in Scotland. Why are you here?' He was dressed in a dark-green velvet smoking jacket. His skin glowed as if he had been spending time in the fresh air. His brown hair, flashed with silver, was thick and gleaming.

'My brother and sister-in-law live here. I am staying with them.'

Another couple came up who obviously knew Robert, and for a few moments the three of them were engaged in a lively conversation about a new hotel and health club that had opened locally.

Then she remembered Freya. She did not like to say anything in front of his friends. He might not even know that his daughter was pregnant, and it would surely be better to break such news to him in private.

The other couple, perhaps thinking she was with Robert, asked if she would join them for dinner. A huge buffet was laid out in the other room and they were all starving.

'Margaret's food is not to be missed,' the round-faced man informed her with a merry smile, moving towards the other room.

Sarah hung back and eyed Robert. She must tell him about Freya as soon as possible. She said, 'I'd love to, but . . . I just need to say something to Robert in private first, if you don't mind.'

'Ah-ha, so it's like that, is it?' The man guffawed and slapped Robert on the back. 'Lucky chap, come on Liz,' he took his partner's arm, 'let's make ourselves scarce.'

She saw the irritation in Robert's eyes, saw it increase as the couple laughingly said something to another couple who looked their way. Too late she remembered how Mandy had told her that nice as their neighbours were, they were dreadful gossips and one had to be very careful about what one said and what one got up to. This couple obviously thought that she and Robert were romantically involved. Nothing could be further from the truth.

Robert's mouth was now set in a hard line. He said, 'Look, we are away from the problems of London now, can't we enjoy this

216

party without talking about our differences?'

'Certainly we can,' she said. 'I just thought I ought to tell you that . . .'

'Listen.' He put his hand on her arm, as if he was warding off her words. 'It is obvious that you haven't understood that letter from my solicitors yourself or got your own solicitor to explain it to you. It's not so very threatening. When we get back, I'll come over and we'll discuss it, but not here, not now.'

He made to move away, but two men came up and started to talk to him about some shooting. At the same time, Mandy and a man came up to Sarah and spirited her away to the dining-room.

'Mandy, that is Robert, you know, whose daughter I had to break in to his house for,' Sarah whispered, fearful of being overheard lest the news be passed round quicker than the huge plates of cold ham and beef that were being carved by their host.

'Oh, *him.*' Mandy glanced his way. 'He's very popular. He's fast turning the Kettlewell Glassworks away from bankruptcy. Tell him later. This is Philip Macpherson. He has recently come to work up here, and is dying to meet you and catch up on what's happening in London.'

She nodded to Philip, who said cheerfully, 'I moved up here six months ago and I love it, but I miss London. I want to hear all about what art exhibitions are on and what's on at the theatre. I went to all the shows when I lived there.'

He had a plain but kindly face, and looked good in his kilt. He took her arm and said confidentially, 'Let's go and sit over there. This house can be awfully draughty.'

Other people joined them and the evening passed pleasantly. She only glimpsed Robert from time to time. Each time, he was surrounded by people, often attractive women, and she remembered that Freya had said that she thought he had a girlfriend up here. By the look of him, he had quite a few girlfriends up here.

It got late and people began to leave on their long journeys home. She had to tell Robert about Freya before he disappeared.

She had drunk a few glasses of wine throughout the evening, so she felt braver than she might have done if she'd been cold sober. She went over to him where he sat by the fire in its huge grate with his group of friends, and said,

'Robert, I simply must talk to you before we go. I've something really important to tell you.'

She was aware of the interest, and in some cases resentment, of the others in the group.

Robert eyed her carefully, said firmly, 'Let it go, Sarah. I'll be back home next week, you can talk to me all you want then.'

Someone asked if they knew each other

from London, and Robert explained that they lived side by side. All the time he explained this, he watched her defiantly and she could read his mind. Why was she bothering him now, when she barely spoke to him in London? She wondered if she should just leave it and let him return to London to find Freya and possibly a new baby ensconced in his house. She turned to go, but he got up from his chair and came over to her.

'Is it really that important, Sarah? Has the house fallen down or something? I haven't heard any dire news from Sheila or Diana.'

By his expression, she could see he was irritated. Irritated, no doubt, by her being here, appearing from his other life like the ghost at a feast. Perhaps he was afraid she would tell tales that would tarnish the reputation he was building up here.

He stood over her, his eyes skimming her face in a way that made her feel he was assessing her, waiting to slap her down should she let out one word against him.

She said coldly, 'I don't know how important it is to you, but I had to break in to your house to let in your daughter.'

219

CHAPTER NINETEEN

'*Freya.*' He dropped his hand on her arm as if for support. The annoyed arrogance she'd seen in his eyes was replaced by panic, quickly followed by pain.

Sarah saw both emotions and said more sympathetically, 'I don't know how many daughters you have.'

'Only one, only Freya.' His fingers tightened on her arm, his eyes implored her. 'Is she all right? Tell me what happened, tell me everything.'

'Robert, it's time we went, or we'll be swept out with the dust.' A slim woman with brilliant-blue eyes and pale hair came up to them, smiling. She gave Sarah a hard suspicious look, but kept the smile locked on her subtly made-up face. When she saw Robert's hand on Sarah's arm, she linked her hand through his other arm and gave him a little playful tug.

'Bedtime,' she crooned in an intimate way, throwing Sarah a triumphant look of possession.

'Just a minute, Helen.' He barely looked at her, almost shook her off. 'I'll come in a minute, but this is very important.'

'I'm sure it can wait until the morning,' Helen said, her voice still soft and gentle, but

Sarah saw her dislike for her in those wide blue eyes

'It can't, I'm sorry, Helen. Give me five minutes.' He sounded impatient for her to be gone, and she knew it.

She threw one last look of dislike in Sarah's direction before she left them, calling out brightly to some people who stood by the door, 'He'll be with us in a minute. It seems he has some business here. Some people never miss a chance to muscle in, do they?'

If Robert heard Helen's remark—intended, Sarah knew, for herself—he showed no interest. He slipped his hand under Sarah's elbow and led her firmly away from the crowd that lingered by the door to the end of the room by the dying fire and the debris of the party.

'Tell me everything,' he commanded, leaning against the mantelpiece, his eyes never leaving her face.

'I'll just tell you what happened. It may come as a shock, but—'

'Just tell it, Sarah. Don't go round the houses first.' His panic was making him angry. He took hold of her again, both his hands gripping her arms. Any moment she was expecting him to shake the story out of her.

She took a step back from him and he loosened his hold. 'I came home the other night and saw a woman outside your house. She told me she was your daughter and that

221

she had hoped you or Diana would be there to let her in.'

'Why didn't she ring or write?' he demanded. 'I have my mobile, she can get me anywhere.'

'Apparently your mobile didn't work.'

'Damn, I had it stolen a couple of months ago and I had to change the number. I'm sure I gave it to her, though.' He looked uncertain, raking his fingers through his hair.

Sarah said impatiently, 'Anyway, I had to put her up for the night. Diana's gone away until Boxing Day, and I couldn't wait to see if your cleaner turned up—not that she would at night—though, according to a neighbour, she'd already been that day and wouldn't be back until after Christmas.'

'So how did she get into my house if she didn't have a key?'

'I was coming up here and had to leave the following day, so Freya suggested that . . .' Sarah paused, prepared herself for his anger, 'well, that we break in.'

'Break in?' his expression changed to horror. 'You broke in? Couldn't you call the police or a locksmith?'

'I suggested that, but she didn't want to.' It was surely not the time to mention what Freya had told her about her teenage romance with a burglar.

'How did you get in?' His eyes drilled into her as if he was a policeman interrogating her for some major crime.

It was just as she had thought. He was going to be furious with her when it was really his daughter's fault. Or perhaps it was *his* fault for not having a closer relationship with Freya.

She said defiantly, 'I had to cut the trellis—it's so high—to enable me to climb over the wall. She told me how to wiggle the catch on the window. I got in, turned off the alarm, and opened the front door to her. That's all there is to it.'

'Which side of the trellis did you cut?' She could see he was fighting to hold his temper. Little tight muscles worked like drawstrings beside his mouth. His eyes were cold as he studied her face.

'The one furthest away from the house, where the creeper was less thick.' Really, what did it matter? It was winter, and the plants were virtially dormant. They'd be resurrected in the spring, and a good pruning would probably do them good.

'The trelis was rotten. You could do with a new piece.'

'But it has to be done carefully. Did you hurt my *Epipremnum aureum*?'

'Your what?'

He had his hand on his chest now, as if she had cut a major artery.

'My *Epipremnum*. That creeper is very tricky to grow. It's taken me years of careful nurturing. It hates to be disturbed or

223

cut savagely.'

She *had* cut it savagely, and some of the stems had split and broken when she'd climbed over. Then she remembered that shrouded plant in the green pot. She'd broken off the side of the pot when she'd stood on it, exposing some of the roots. No doubt that was a valuable, sensitive plant too. It was now left wide open for some insect to eat it or the frost to freeze its delicate root system.

'Look, Robert,' she said firmly, 'I don't know that much about the specialist sort of gardening you go in for, but it had to be done.'

'But why did *you* do it?' His look suggested that she had done it on purpose, determined to inflict the most damage she could. 'Freya knows about plants. She would have been careful.'

His anger annoyed her further. 'Your daughter is pregnant. In fact, she may have had the baby already. I had no alternative; she could hardly get over the wall in her condition.'

His face went white. 'What did you say?'

Sarah was aware that more people, her brother among them, were coming towards them. The party was obviously over. The room, which had a few moments before been so alive with dancing and chatting, now seemed as tired and dishevelled as the guests.

'Look, it is difficult to talk here. Perhaps I should have broken the news to you more

224

gently,' she said, sympathy for him again rearing up in her. 'I don't know much about it. She seems very well, very determined to do what she wants to do.' She did not add that Freya had obviously got this characteristic straight from him. 'She just happens to be eight and a half months pregnant, and she came over here to have the child.'

'Sarah, sorry to butt in, but shall we go? We've a long drive ahead.' Edward came up to them.

'I'm coming. This is Robert Maynard, Edward Talbot, my brother.' She hoped Edward would remember what she had told him about Freya. To her relief he did.

He said, 'Give Robert our telephone number so he can ring us if he should need to. Hang on, I've got a card here.' He took one out of his wallet and handed it over.

'Thank you.' Robert rocked back and forth on his heels, looking shell-shocked. He put the card in his pocket. 'I just want to ask Sarah one more thing.' He looked apologetically at Edward, who nodded and left them, saying he would fetch the car.

Sarah said, 'There's not much more I can tell you. You can ring her in the morning, get the whole story from her. There was nothing else I could do. I didn't want to leave her in my house.' Seeing his face, she added with a touch of defiance, 'I have to guard my house from; you and your family.'

'You're exaggerating,' he said. 'But I still think you took drastic action.'

'We didn't know where you were. What else could we have done? She really wanted to be in your house, seemed relieved to be away from her boyfriend.'

'She should have known where I was,' he said. 'She knew I inherited this business and have a house here.'

'She'd left the number in France. I think she was expecting you to be at home in London.' Seeing the flash of guilt in his eyes, she felt that her remark had been a little unfair. She was tired and hit with that flat, empty feeling that sometimes comes after a good party. She wanted to go home. It was hardly her fault that Robert and his daughter couldn't keep in touch with each other. Would this happen to *her* children? Would they go off on their own lives and lose track of Dan? Of her? She could not bear it if something like this happened to Polly. Alone and hugely pregnant at Christmas-time.

'You know, when you are pregnant you often become forgetful; it's part of the condition.' Thinking of Polly, she felt she had to stand up for Freya. This is what happened with broken families, mothers gone off, fathers unavailable.

Robert noticed her expression, said more gently, 'I'm sorry I sounded so ungrateful and bad-tempered. It is just such a shock. Freya is a very independent person, but I wish she'd told me about this coming child. She lives in France with her boyfriend, or did, by the sound of it. We do ring each other and meet up from time to time, but we haven't for some months.'

'Don't you call her at Christmas-time?' Sarah couldn't help asking.

'Yes, I do. I tried this Christmas, but there was no answer from her place in France. I wasn't unduly worried as I thought she was away. They often go to the mountains at this time. I knew we'd catch up soon.'

'She's caught you now.' She resisted making a dig at him becoming a grandfather. 'We must go. The McNairs look exhausted. Ring me if you need to, though once you've talked to Freya you'll know it all.'

She turned to go and find the others. He took her arm again, gently, just to detain her. He said quietly, 'Thank you for what you did, Sarah. I do appreciate it; it's all too much to digest at once. Thank goodness you were there.' He smiled, and she had the crazy feeling that he was looking at her for the first time and seeing something different in her that he had not noticed before.

She felt suffused in a warm glow at the tenderness in his eyes, and for a second she basked in it. Then she muttered a goodbye and walked away. Once he'd seen what she had done to his plants, he would only hate her again.

As they drove home in the all-enveloping darkness, Mandy said, 'Well, Sarah, you've certainly put the gossips here into overdrive! "Pushing herself in and taking him over" was how I heard Helen Donaldson describe it.' She laughed. 'Robert is certainly very attractive, single and such a catch as the new heir to the Kettlewell Glassworks.'

Panic fluttered through Sarah like a swarm of bees.

'It's not like that at all,' she protested. 'He lives in the next house to me in London and ...'

'You mean he's the frightful man who swears that your house is his?' Sarah had told Mandy all about it.

'Yes, and had to break into his house through his garden to let his hugely pregnant daughter in.'

'Now I've clicked!' Mandy exclaimed. 'You were telling him about that and the local gossips thought you were pulling him.' She laughed. 'That's what living in a tight community does for you. Most of the people around here are lovely, but they do jump to conclusions, especially from outsiders. Oh dear,' she sighed, 'I'm afraid that by tomorrow they will have married you off, or at the very least imagined you are having a torrid affair.'

'But that's terrible!' Sarah wailed. 'Nothing could be further from the truth. We *hate* each other.'

'You knew what they say about hate and love,' Mandy said brightly. 'Do take up with him then you can live up here, closer to us.'

'Oh, come on, Mandy, don't be silly!' Sarah protested.

Mandy laughed, and leant over from the back seat and touched Sarah's shoulder. 'I don't know anything about it, but that last look he gave you was hardly one of hate.'

'Nonsense. You're as bad as the rest of them,' Sarah retorted, but she could not forget that sudden glow his last look had provoked in her.

CHAPTER TWENTY

The following day, Polly rang.

'Dad's baby's been born and he can't get back to see it,' she announced with no preamble, her voice breathless as if she could not wait to expel the words.

Sarah's heart felt as if it was somebody's punch-bag. Yet underneath she felt a pang of—was it *relief*, that Dan had missed that most intimate of moments? Her mind raced back to the birth of their own children, the magical moment when they both saw for the first time the tiny being they had created together. It was these special, intimate times that he was now sharing with someone else which she found so hard to accept.

'We can't change our plane tickets, so he can't leave until 30 December, unless he pays full fare on another flight,' Polly went on. 'He's in a state; well, so is she, crying down the phone.' She sounded disgusted. 'She shouldn't have got herself pregnant in the first place, if she can't cope with it.'

Sarah silently agreed with her, but it would not do to start on a hate campaign against that pathetic mouse—she wasn't the only woman to want a child from the man she loved. It would have been tough for her to have had to go through childbirth on her own, especially if it was her first time. But what havoc and pain she had caused them all, though Dan had been to blame, too. Now there was a new baby in the middle of it all. Poor little thing; it was hardly its fault.

Dan hated wasting money. Would he ditch his ticket and pay over the odds to get back to her three days earlier? It would be interesting to see.

'It's up to him what he does. You two enjoy yourselves—while you can.' The pain at the news seared through Sarah's heart.

'It's just so cold, and the chalet girl can't cook,' Polly complained, listing a string of grievances until Sarah said sharply,

'Look, Pol, you *chose* to go skiing with your father. We all know it can be very cold out there at Christmas time, and that chalet girls can't always cook.' All the hurt she was feeling surged towards Polly. She'd known about the coming baby and yet somehow she had been living in some sort of denial. Now the baby had been born, it was living proof that Dan had ditched her, had slept with and set up home with someone else.

'I can't talk any more now, Polly. I'll see you in a few days anyway. Bye.' She put down the receiver, blew her nose firmly and went to the other end of the kitchen, where Edward and Mandy were just serving up lunch,

Seeing her face, Edward said, 'Bad news?'

Her nephews were not in the room; Sarah could hear them scrapping in the playroom off the kitchen. She fought to stop the tears that sprang up in her throat, failed, and when Mandy put her arms round her, she sobbed on her shoulder.

After a moment, she said, 'I wish I could get over Dan. He's gone, doesn't love me any more, but his baby has been born and I feel terrible. Betrayed all over again.'

The telephone rang once more. Edward answered it. He looked over towards Sarah and mouthed: 'It's Robert. Do you want to talk to him?'

Robert. He was surely only ringing her to complain about her massacre of his beloved plants, which Freya must have told him about by now. She imagined him questioning her in minute detail on the state of every leaf and

231

curling tendril. She could not face any more unpleasantness today.

She shook her head and Edward said, 'Sorry she can't come to the phone right now. Could I take a message?'

Robert's answer was obviously no, and Edward put down the receiver.

This diversion stopped her tears. She said, 'Sorry. I really must come to terms with this.'

Mandy told her, 'Like with a bereavement you have to take your time. Dan's a real louse to behave like this. I must say, though, it did surprise me. I always thought he adored you. You don't think he had some sort of a breakdown, do you? Or has he been put on tranquillizers? They say they can change your moods and your very character. I've read that some people even commit suicide while on them, or kill other people.'

'Oh, Mandy, don't go overboard!' Edward said. 'I think he's behaved appallingly, but some people do that without any interference from pills, booze or anything else.'

Shouts, cries, a crash and more scuffles came from the playroom. As Mandy left to investigate, she said, 'Small babies are a doddle compared with hyped-up teenagers. How is Dan going to cope when the baby is this age? He'll be seventy. I find it all I can do to cope with it now, and I'm only forty-three. I wonder if he's thought of that?'

They heard her shout at the boys and

demand that they wash their hands and quietly come to lunch.

Edward said, 'Poor Sarah. I don't know what to say. I suppose it *is* his child?'

'I think it probably is. I do wish I understood why he suddenly upped and left. From a male point of view, do you know why?'

'I suppose it is sex. Although you love each other, it does get a bit dull when you've been together for ages. Other things seem to take over. The children, work, running the house, just getting on with life. I admit, I've been tempted from time to time, but it's not worth breaking up all *this*,' he gestured round the cheerful, lived-in family room, 'for a few bouts of frenetic sexual activity.'

'I hoped Dan would feel the same. Do you think we *were* happy, or was I just deluding myself?'

'You always looked happy together. I liked Dan a lot. Unless you can think of any other reason, I can only think it's the dreaded male menopause, if that exists. But whatever name it comes under, it is very destructive.'

'What's so destructive?' Mandy came into the room, followed by the two boys.

'The male menopause,' Edward said.

'What's that, Dad?' Simon the younger boy asked.

'When you have a brainstorm and think you're twenty again, only you aren't,' Henry, the older one, explained.

'That's about it.' Edward hastily changed the subject, in case the boys hurt Sarah by their crass remarks.

Sarah knew it was pointless, reflecting on what she and Dan had had and why it had ended. That part of her life was over and she must move on. It was no good wishing she were like Edward and Mandy.

Mandy later admitted that occasionally—very occasionally, she said, seeing Edward's eye on her—she fancied some hunk, but they both seemed to be able to put their sexual dreams into perspective.

'I'm all for fantasies,' she enthused. 'They work out as you want them to. In reality, one would be tortured with guilt and self-obsession, wondering if one was slim enough, pretty enough, sexy enough for the new man. Far less trouble to stay with the old devil you know.' She'd laughed and pinched Edward's bottom affectionately.

Sarah laughed too, but the pain that she had lost that easy, warm relationship with Dan was difficult to bear. Like good wine, a relationship took years to mature. But if she wasn't careful, she would become a bitter old bag whose jealousy for happy couples would ruin all her relationships with the people she most cared for.

That evening, as they sat in the snug little study by the fire, she remembered Robert's call and asked Edward what he had wanted.

'Just to speak to you.'

'Did he sound cross? I have ruined his garden, and as he seems to prefer plants to people, even his own daughter, I suppose he was ringing to complain.'

Edward thought back. 'I don't know how he sounded. Perhaps a bit miffed that you wouldn't talk to him.'

'No doubt he'd worked himself up with all his grievances against me and was frustrated that he couldn't offload them,' Sarah said.

Mandy put down the magazine she was reading and said, 'We don't know him, but everyone around here likes him enormously. Apart from the fact that he is attractive and not too old. Early to mid-fifties, wouldn't you say?'

She glanced at Edward, who nodded and said, 'More important than his effect on female hearts, he saved the glass factory. It was on its last legs; his uncle, or whoever left it to him, had been ill for some time and it was in a bad way. When he inherited it, his accountant advised him to close it.'

'There was quite a fuss, as so many local jobs would have been lost,' Mandy explained. 'He didn't live up here, knew little about the life, but when some of the workers wrote to him pleading for their jobs, he had the decency to come up and see it all for himself. Against the advice of his accountant, he decided to give them a year and see if they could turn it round. He's lost quite a bit of money over it, I believe, but I think he's saved it, and it's beginning to break even.'

'It needed some new ideas, a bit of modernization,' Edward went on.

'It's quite a fun place, we should go and see it,' Mandy suggested. 'There's a showroom now, a shop and a coffee place. It's attracting quite a lot of attention.'

Edward and Mandy went on, building up Robert's qualities. Sarah suspected that they were building him up because they wanted her to have a new man in her life. Well, he might be venerated up here, but she knew the real man.

She said, 'He has a girlfriend, doesn't he? That Helen I saw at the McNairs.'

'Oh, Helen Donaldson. I think she likes to *think* that she is his girlfriend. I'm afraid she has a reputation of taking over men. She's never married, and I suppose she is getting desperate.'

Edward laughed. 'Oh, Mandy, I don't think she's *that* bad.'

'Some men love bossy women,' Mandy said.

'Dominating, you mean,' Edward corrected. 'All whips and spanked bottoms.'

Mandy giggled. 'I don't think she's like that, do you? Anyway, Sarah, just you talking to Robert alone and so intensely that evening is bound to add more drama to his life, and when people find out that you live next door to each other in London . . .' she rolled her eyes with exaggeration, 'the mind boggles. It will generate enough gossip to liven up the whole winter!'

'He is the most difficult man,' Sarah said, with irritation. 'He is determined to buy my house for his orchids, and unfortunately he's in league with Dan.'

'Dan? Is he a friend of his?' Edward asked.

'Maybe they are now, I wouldn't know.' She told them about the money, and how Dan, having heard from Tim and Polly that Robert wanted her house, had contacted him.

'So you might have to sell it, after all?' Mandy asked.

'I'm sure there's a way round it,' Edward said. 'I'll think about it for you, a mortgage or a loan or something. I'm sure Robert wouldn't steal it from under your nose.'

'I don't share your confidence,' Sarah sighed. 'But he's in for a rude shock when his daughter gives birth to her baby. She said she had nowhere to go, so he might have to put her up for ages.'

'What hell for you,' Mandy said. 'You say you can hear him lumbering about next door, so you'll hear the baby crying, too.' She frowned, glanced round the room in their large, detached manor house. 'I've never lived next door to anyone. I can't imagine hearing every move they make through the wall. It must be rather eerie.'

'It's quite comforting, actually,' Sarah said, before she could stop herself.

'So, how much more comforting would it be if the wall came down?' Mandy asked jokingly.

'That would be terrible, Mandy. Just terrible,' Sarah protested vehemently. Too vehemently, Mandy thought, and she smiled a tiresome knowing smile that irritated Sarah no end.

Mandy guessed this and retreated behind her *Country Life*, though Sarah could see that her smile took some time to fade. She curbed her irritation with difficulty. She was fond of Mandy, and knew her sister-in-law wanted to see her happy again, but if she thought she'd be happy with Robert, Mandy was hopelessly wrong. That was just one of her fantasies, written to her own desires.

*   *   *

Polly rang again that evening.

'Daddy can't get home until he comes with us on the thirtieth,' she informed her. 'Nina is furious.'

Can't, Sarah thought, or won't spend the extra money? She did not want to talk about Dan and his baby, though she suddenly realized she didn't know what sex the baby was. She asked Polly.

'A girl; Annabel, I think Nina wants to call her. I can't believe that I have a half-sister. It's

238

weird, isn't it, Mum?'

'It is, rather.' Then, to get off the subject, she told her about Robert, his daughter and the coming baby.

'When you get home, don't be surprised if you hear a baby crying next door.'

'At least that is normal. I mean, being a grandfather at his age,' Polly said. 'Imagine when I have children. Supposing I had one soon, it would be almost the same age as my half-sister. Dad would be a grandfather and a new father, all at the same time. That really is creepy, isn't it?'

CHAPTER TWENTY-ONE

Sarah arrived back home from Scotland on the evening of 2nd January. She was feeling tired and hung-over after another good party given by Edward and Mandy's nearest neighbours. To her relief, the guests were more local and no one mentioned Robert.

Tim and a girl were in the hall on their way out.

'Hi, Mum.' Tim kissed her somewhere round her ear. 'Had a good time?' He did not give her time to answer. 'We're just out. Oh, this is Jessica.' He gestured towards the skinny girl who hovered behind him, holding on to his other hand as if her life depended upon it.

Sarah smiled, said hello. She supposed this was the girl Tim had met while skiing, but it was better not to make any reference to it in case it wasn't. She said instead, 'Is Polly here?'

'No. She'll be back later.' He dropped Jessica's hand and took her suitcase from her and put it by the stairs. 'Must dash. See you tomorrow.' He rushed out, Jessica scuttling out behind him.

Sarah tried to ignore the heavy emptiness that threatened to envelop her. On her first evening back, she'd have liked to have had her children here around her. The house seemed drearily silent after being with Edward and Mandy. There was never a moment's peace in their house. Boys fighting, playing loud music, dogs joining in. A noisy, rumbustious family house, like hers had once been.

She went into the living-room and saw the overflowing pile of post that had been put on a chair. She'd pour herself a glass of wine, put on some music and go through them. Polly might be home soon.

The smooth, haunting sound of Beethoven's 'Moonlight Sonata' lifted her spirits; she let herself sink into it, only to be disturbed by a baby's cry piercing the wall. So, Freya's baby had been born. How was Robert coping with that?

She sat on, reading late Christmas cards, smiling over messages from friends, sorting the bills, throwing out the junk; but the baby's cry seeped in under the music, urgent, demanding, pitiful. The unwelcome figure of Dan appeared in her thoughts, looming up so close he could have been here with her in this room, bringing with him memories of their past.

She tried to push them away. Hadn't she promised herself that her New Year's resolution would be to forget Dan? Padlock their life together into the recesses of her mind and throw away the key? But the memories marched on and stood to attention before her, willing her to think of them. That was the trouble with having children, she thought weakly, they were the past *and* the future. Their conception, birth and childhood bound one for ever to the other parent.

When they'd arrived back from the hospital after giving birth to Tim, she and Dan didn't know what to do when he cried. Her own mother came to help, though she seemed to have forgotten what to do with newborn babies, and kept escaping to Harrods instead. They rocked him, fed him, worried over him, and even drove him round the silent streets at three in the morning, hoping he would sleep. When he was silent they were afraid he had died, and they crept into his room, half fearful of waking him, half fearful of never waking him again.

Would Dan remember those times now as his new child cried? The mouse, according to Polly, had never had children. Would she worry while he, an old hand at fatherhood, reassured her?

She must not imagine things that might not be happening. She must put her life with Dan behind her and get on with her life. But the baby's cries kept throwing up pictures of Dan when he was the proud young father of Tim and Polly, and her heart thudded with pain. If only that child would stop its crying, she could get her mind off it. She turned up the music, but still underneath the soft tones the cry went on.

There was a long ring on the bell. It must be Polly, who had forgotten her key yet again. Lucky for her she was here. She opened the door with an exasperated smile of welcome, and Robert, pale and dishevelled, stood there.

'I'm really sorry to disturb you, Sarah, but there's no one else.' His voice came out slightly awkwardly. 'If there was anyone else I could call on, I would; but you're a mother, you must know about babies.'

He looked so distraught—his immaculate hair on end, his face pouchy under the eyes—she had to laugh.

He said grumpily, 'It's not at all funny. We can't sleep; this child never stops crying.'

Sarah said, 'It's a long time since I had a baby.'

'You must know *something*,' he said desperately. 'More than us, anyway. Please come, if only for a minute. We are at our wits end.'

Freya looked exhausted. She was dressed in a grey tracksuit that drained even more colour from her face; her hair lank, and unwashed, was looped behind her ears. In her arms was a furious red-faced baby, screaming its lungs out.

Freya said, 'He was all right in the hospital, but ever since we got him home he won't stop crying. The health visitor says there is nothing wrong with him, but . . .' She had to shout over his screams. The noise was beginning to give Sarah a headache.

'Are you feeding him enough?' she asked.

'I'm trying to, but he won't take it, and this breastfeeding is so painful. I can't think why. It's meant to be natural, isn't it?' Freya sounded as if she was on the verge of tears herself.

Sarah remembered the betrayal she had felt over the same subject. 'Childbirth is also natural, and, as I remember well, jolly painful,' she said. 'Have you any baby milk? You know, in a packet?'

'They gave me a sample pack. But I shouldn't give it to him, should I? It's not so good as breast milk, it will get him off to a bad start.' Freya implied that giving him baby milk would poison him at once.

Sarah sighed. Oh, the guilt of parenthood. From the moment of conception, even *before* conception, one was advised to eat certain foods, play music, talk to the growing foetus to provide it with the maximum chances before it was born, as if it should emerge as a ready-made genius, tutored before birth. You were made to feel guilty if you wanted a pain-free birth, in case the drugs hurt the child, or if you couldn't or didn't want to breastfeed. On it went, through school and adolescence and even on to adulthood. When would someone have the courage to shout *stop*—why add further difficulties to the hundreds already there?

'If you haven't got enough milk yourself, you should give him some baby formula,' she said. 'It's all very well waiting for your milk to come in, but in the meantime the baby needs to be fed. It might not be that, but let's start there.'

Freya looked unsure, but Robert said loudly over the baby's cries, 'Then please do it. The milk's in the kitchen, I'll show you.'

Sarah followed him into his denim kitchen. He opened a cupboard and produced a small packet of milk formula and a new bottle. Of course, there were no sterilizing tablets.

'Have you a clean saucepan?' she asked.

'Of course it's clean,' he said. 'What do you think?'

She took it, filled it with water, and when it was boiling put in the bottle and teat, and boiled them up. He watched her in amazement.

'It's got to be sterilized. It's easier to do with special liquid or tablets. You can buy some tomorrow.'

She made up the formula and thought of Dan. Would he remember what to do if his baby needed feeding? Robert interpreted her grim expression as being against him. He said coldly, 'I repeat, I am sorry to have bothered you, but I didn't have a lot to do with Freya when she was born.'

'It might not be the reason he is crying; it's just the most obvious suggestion.' His coldness added more weight to her feeling of rejection.

'I do hope it is,' he said fervently. He stood with his back against one of the worktops and watched her mix up the formula. Dan would have done that, watched her doing it while somehow thinking he was doing it himself.

For weeks she had not mourned Dan as much as she was now. This baby coupled with Robert who was about Dan's age, made her think of him too much—though Robert was playing the correct role of a grandfather not a father. Was Dan pacing around even now with a screaming child in his arms?

The silence between them stretched on. Robert broke it. 'Thank you again for helping Freya when she turned up before Christmas. It's all been rather a shock. I can't quite come to grips with it.'

No doubt this was a prelude to complaints about the damage she had done to his beloved garden.

She said quickly, 'It's all worked out in the end. When was he born?'

'Four days ago. I came down the day after I saw you at the McNairs'. Through my GP, I found her a private gynaecologist. He thought it better to induce her, so there was none of that dashing in to hospital in the night. It was all very civilized.' His expression indicated that it was after the birth that the civilization had stopped. It would get worse.

'Now you are on your own, it's not so easy.' She shook the filled bottle and tested the heat of the milk on her inside wrist. She did it unconsciously. The skill must be embedded in her. She was too busy fighting her demons about Dan to notice the admiration in Robert's eyes.

'Let's see if this is what he wants.' She went past him into the living-room to Freya.

She handed her the bottle. Freya tried to get it in to the baby's open mouth, but he screamed louder, twisting away from it. She burst into tears.

'I can't cope, I never thought it would be like this. I feel as though I'm sitting on barbed wire, and my boobs hurt—it's all so awful!' She howled.

Sarah remembered it well. She, too, had howled the first time. Her mother had told her it would get better, and then went off to Harrods. Dan had held her, looking fearful, out of his depth as Tim had lain between them, screaming and kicking his minuscule legs like a furious beetle upturned on its back. Firmly dismissing these thoughts, Sarah sat down beside Freya and took the baby from her. She gently ran the teat over his screaming mouth. He gulped, screamed some more, then grabbed it between his lips and started sucking. There was a glorious silence.

Sarah could feel the tension relax in the room. Robert was looking at her in awe, as if she had achieved one of the greatest miracles of all time. He had one hand on Freya's shoulder. Freya blew her nose fiercely and apologized for her tears.

'Don't worry about it,' Sarah said, 'we all went through it. Especially the first time.'

The weight of the baby and his rhythmic sucking soothed her. Sarah sat there, looking out into the lighted garden. The curtains were not drawn, and she could see the plants and the broken trellis from where she sat. She wondered if she had killed the plants and tensed herself for his accusation.

Freya said, 'Would you mind if I had a quick bath and washed my hair? I feel so grubby; I haven't had a moment, and when I have I just collapse and try to sleep.'

'Go ahead,' Sarah said. The almost transparent eyelids of the child, threaded with tiny veins, flickered then closed as he continued to suck.

Robert sat down in a chair opposite her, blocking her view from the garden.

'You have been most awfully kind,' he started again. 'Freya never let on either to me or her mother that she was having a baby. She's so independent, you see, but now . . .' He shrugged helplessly. 'Well, you can't always be independent, can you?'

'No. Having your first baby is one of the greatest changes to anyone's life.'

'I remember it,' he said.

Sarah wondered what his wife had been like; tried to imagine him as the supporting young father, as Dan had been.

Robert said brusquely, 'I can see this is the most awful bore for you. Shall I take over and let you get back to your house?'

There was an irritation, verging on a dislike of her, in his voice that stung her. Her face must have been showing all the anger she felt for Dan.

Before she could stop herself, she heard herself saying, 'It's not a bore at all, it's just that my ex-husband has just had a baby with another woman and I can't stop thinking about it. Hearing this baby cry makes his baby seem suddenly more real.'

'I am so sorry.' He made a move towards her, then obviously thought better of it and leant back in his chair. 'If I had known, I wouldn't have asked you, but . . . there's no one else around at the moment.'

248

'It's fine.' Her confession embarrassed her. 'I will get used to it. I'll have to.'

'I must say, fatherhood is not something I'd want to take on again,' Robert said. 'I think there is a time for everything, and I'd rather be a grandfather than a new father now. I'd hate to say I felt too old, but I've got my life sorted as I want it to be, and another child would just ruin it.'

'I don't know if he planned it.' She did not say she wondered if it was his at all.

'Is the woman much younger? Has she had children?' he asked.

'She hasn't had children. I suppose I can't blame her for wanting one, but if only she'd chosen someone else to have it with.' She remembered Dan and Robert were in league together over the house. She must be careful what she said, in case he used it against her.

He watched her, studying her face as if wondering how much he could ask her. He said at last, 'Do you still love him?'

His question troubled her. She glanced down at the baby, enjoying the warm weight of him in her arms. Were all women programmed like this, feeling complete when they held a child in their arms?

He said, 'Sorry, that was intrusive. I had no right to ask you.'

She said, 'Old habits die hard. For twenty-four years I thought I was happily married to a man I loved and who loved me. It seems I was mistaken. Although my mind tells me that it is over, my emotions haven't yet got the message.'

'I am sure you were not mistaken. Perhaps his perceptions changed. Maybe he felt time was passing him by, or just got caught up with this new woman and it went too far.'

'If only he had talked about it! We could have got through it, instead of him just rushing off in a red sports car with this mousy woman.' Her anger rose and spilt over. 'If she'd been beautiful or clever or something better than me, I might understand. But she's so *plain*!' she burst out, then immediately felt ashamed of her outburst. 'I'm sorry,' she muttered, 'I suppose it's her youth—I don't have *that*. Look, he's quiet now.' She moved to give him the child. 'I'll go.'

'Don't be afraid to say what you feel, not in front of me anyway. My own father did the same, devastated my mother all for some tart in the village. Once she'd got his money, she dumped him and ran off with someone her own age.' He smiled ruefully. 'If ever I feel tempted to go after some young thing I remember that time, not that I've a wife to destroy, but it can look so ridiculous somehow.' He blushed slightly. 'I hate to be laughed at, made fun of, you know.'

The baby had finished the milk. He lay asleep in her arms, his even breath punctuated from time to time with tiny, shivering sobs.

250

There was an atmosphere of contentment, of ease, between them.

'Dan doesn't think he looks ridiculous, even though he can hardly get in and out of his low-slung car. He must have wanted something more, something I couldn't give him.' She wished she hadn't said that. It sounded like she'd refused him sex, had a headache every bedtime. Most men would feel sympathy for a man in that situation.

Robert smiled. 'Don't beat yourself up over it. You probably just reached the end of the relationship. We all live so long now. Maybe he didn't feel comfortable without the children?'

She hadn't thought of it that way, running out of time with a relationship. Though maybe that was true—marriage and people changed as life went on; having babies, pursuing careers, children growing and leaving. Dan obviously didn't like the phase of their life when they were back alone again.

Robert said, 'We are all fools, imagining others see us as we see ourselves. We may still feel young inside, even if it is obvious we are not. Anyway,' he leant forward in his chair, as if to get closer to her, 'another reason I try not to get involved with younger women is they *do* seem to want children. I don't think I'm that great a father anyway.'

'But Freya came to you.'

'But she didn't tell me she was pregnant until the end. She didn't feel she could confide in me when things began to go wrong with her relationship. Now she insists she'll be all right on her own, or at least she said that before the baby was born. She wants to return to France. She has a high-powered job there, but she'll have to find somewhere different to live, and child-care.' He shrugged. 'I'm worried about her, but what can I do? She'll only think I'm interfering with her life.'

'Whatever you do as a parent, and possibly a wife, seems to be wrong.'

She caught his glance and momentarily there was a strong bond between them. Then she inadvertently ruined it.

'Will her mother help out?' Even as the words left her mouth, she realizad she should not have asked him. His face changed to one of annoyance, the expression she'd become so familiar with.

He said 'She can't even look after herself, and the idea of being a grandmother appals her. Talk about delusions. She thinks she is still thirty-five years old.'

'I see.' This was fascinating. How ever had he got involved with such a woman?

As if he guessed her thoughts he said, 'She was very beautiful, and we were very much in love in the beginning. We stayed married for twelve years, but then she left me for another man.'

Freya came into the room; she looked polished and pretty in a blue jersey and grey trousers. She heard her father's remark.

'And I went to boarding-school and spent my holidays between each parent. But I don't think I suffered too much.' She smiled at Robert. 'You had some pretty nice girlfriends, who were extra nice to me so they could impress you!' she laughed.

Robert looked slightly uncomfortable. 'I'm sure it wasn't like that, Freya.'

'It certainly was,' Freya retorted. 'Caroline was the easiest. She bought me all sorts of forbidden things to take back to school. Jane was quite good, though she insisted on buying me healthy stuff when all I wanted was chocolate bars and crisps.'

To her immense annoyance, Sarah felt excluded. Robert was an attractive man; extremely attractive, she conceded ruefully. Why would he stay on his own when his wife had left him?

Sarah gave the baby back to Freya and explained how to make up the baby milk.

'Don't feel guilty about not feeding him yourself straight away. Do both for a while until you have enough.'

'I will, thanks so much.' Freya smiled at her, Robert's smile. 'I've got a few months off work, then I'll have to stop feeding him anyway.' She sighed. 'It's odd, but since I've had him I don't know if I want to go back to work or not. Perhaps I should stay here with you, Daddy?' She grinned at him.

Sarah saw Robert's face blanch. He had told her he did not like his life being disturbed.

He replied, 'Think how bored you'd be after a while, how you'd miss your friends and your life in France.'

Freya laughed, agreed with him. 'If you'd bought Sarah's house, I could have lived there with the orchids.' Her voice was light. It was probably meant as a joke, but Sarah felt threatened by it. She did not look at Robert, but jumped up to leave.

'Wouldn't you like to see my orchids?' he asked. 'I have them all upstairs.'

'They have a whole room to themselves,' Freya said. 'No wonder there's not much room for me and Jack.'

'I must go home now.' Sarah went to the door.

'I can't thank you enough, Sarah.' Robert came so close to her, she wondered if he would kiss her, but from the look in his eyes she felt that he was accusing her of causing homelessness to orchids. Because she would not fall in with his plans, the orchids might even be forced to camp out in the street.

She must not forget how much he wanted her house. Whatever he said or did, that was his ultimate aim.

CHAPTER TWENTY-TWO

When Sarah arrived at the shop one morning, Celine was bursting with excitement. The first bus had been too crowded and Sarah had had to wait for the next one so she was a little late.

'Guess what?' Celine grabbed her the minute she walked in, and held on to her, her eyes shining. 'We're going to be millionaires!'

Sarah laughed incredulously. 'You've won the lottery?'

'No. *We* have! That article that's coming out in *Vogue*.' She picked up the magazine from the desk. 'This is a preview, well, it may be out already in the shops, I don't know, but two shops in New York—Saks and Bloomingdales —and somewhere on the West Coast, want to buy our clothes!' Her voice shook with excitement as her finger stabbed at the glossy photograph on the page.

Sarah took the magazine from her. There was a rather contrived picture of her on a chair with some of her clothes draped around. Celine stood behind, looking very important.

'We don't look too bad, do we? At least our cellulite is hidden,' Celine went on cheerfully. 'I've received orders from these buyers. We must shut up shop and do a tour of America.'

Sarah stared at her, still unable to grasp what she was saying. 'Shut up shop?'

255

'Well, not literally; we'll get someone else to manage it while we are away. I've one or two contacts in America, and I faxed them the article and they came back with these orders. Someone I know out there can set it all up for us.' She laughed almost hysterically. 'Darling, we are made!'

Sarah skimmed through the article.

'Are you sure about this, Celine? It's not some hoax?'

'Of course I am.' She showed her a fax from the buyer at Saks, suggesting a meeting. 'I know her—not well, but this is real. We must pack up suitcases of samples and go out there. We can fund it from the firm. I've some money put by, and anyway you have to spend some to make some.'

'When do we go?' Sarah asked, a string of objections quickly lining up in her mind. How long would it be? What if the children needed her? What about the house? Would Robert have somehow turned it into an orchid sanctuary before she came back?

Celine folded up the fax, put it back on the desk. The laughter in her eyes was replaced by a glint of determination. 'You know what they say about every cloud? Your silver lining is Dan leaving you while you are still young enough to enjoy it. You are a free woman, Sarah. Your children are at university and with their lovers, and we can go off on this trip and make our fortunes.'

256

Sarah swallowed the negative thoughts rising in her, fuelled by insecurity. 'Can I?' she wondered doubtfully.

'Look, love,' Celine gave her a little shake, 'you are the main designer behind these clothes. It is *your* designs that sell them. You have to come with me. This is your golden chance, *our* golden chance. I will not let you ignore it.'

A small bubble of euphoria gurgled its way through her. Why shouldn't she? Why shouldn't they? Even if nothing came of it, it would be an adventure.

Celine said briskly, 'That's settled, then. I'll put everything in motion. Pity Polly isn't free to run the shop, but we'll find someone else. Maybe Maggie can be persuaded to leave her grandchild for a few weeks. Now,' she seemed almost manic in her energy, 'you must get together a smart-looking portfolio of your designs. You can have time off if you like, and we must get some more things made up. Maria better bring in her sister, her mother too, to get them made in time.' She reached for the telephone.

The morning whirled on, and then the days. Sarah redid almost all her designs on clean new paper. She spent long hours in the sewing-room, telling the girls what she wanted, checking and double-checking the cut, the seams, the placing of the embroidery, the silk and velvet trimmings. She worked half the

257

night, hardly realizing what time of the day it was, let alone what day of the week.

Polly, who had some job waitressing, which seemed to involve an enormous amount of time getting ready and an enormous amount of time resting afterwards, said, 'You'll kill yourself before you get there.'

But she was grudgingly proud of her mother, and showed everyone the *Vogue* article when it came out in the shops.

Sarah noticed that Polly and Freya had become friends. Once or twice, Freya and the now better-tempered baby came round and gossiped in Polly's room.

One evening when she came back from the shop, so tired she was almost hallucinating, there was a note from Polly on the stairs: 'Freya and I are cooking, come next door for dinner.'

Did that mean that Robert was not there? It must do, and the girls were doing their own thing. She had not seen him for a couple of weeks, or at least she had not noticed if he was there or not. She was very hungry. She'd hardly eaten all day, and she had been hoping that Polly could be persuaded to cook something if she was home. Well, she had, but it was next door.

She stared at herself in the hall mirror. She looked almost transparent with exhaustion. Her eyes seemed larger, and there were violet smudges underneath them. At least she'd had

258

the energy to wash her hair last night, but she must try and catch up on some sleep before she collapsed. She would eat dinner next door, but she would not stay late. She hoped they had got it ready and she would not have to wait half the night before she could eat it. She rang their bell. Freya let her in.

'I am so glad you've come, Sarah. I've wanted to say thank you for so long. In fact, I've bought you a case of wine.' She indicated a cardboard box that stood in the narrow hall. 'I should have given it to you sooner, but it's only just arrived. Polly will bring it round.'

'Oh, Freya, you needn't have done that,' Sarah said, touched by her action.

'You saved our lives that evening,' Freya said. 'Once I got the feeding going, both Daddy and I slept far better.'

She led the way down the narrow hall towards the living-room. As she passed the kitchen, she saw Polly stirring something on the stove.

'Hi, Mum,' she said, her face flushed, her hair falling over it. 'I'm not quite sure about your sauce,' she said to Freya. 'How spicy should it be?'

Sarah resisted the temptation to ask if she could help.

Freya said, 'I'll see to it. Have a glass of wine Sarah and make yourself comfortable in the living-room. We'll be there in a minute.' Freya poured her out a glass of white wine.

The curtains to the garden were open, even the door to the garden was ajar but the room was very warm with a blazing fire in the grate. She'd seen the room before, but because of the dramas going on at the time she had not taken much notice of it. It was simple, yet expensively done. The walls were covered with heavy slub-silk wallpaper in a creamy colour that set off the bright watercolours in their pale wood frames. Each piece of furniture was a jewel in its own right; the room had a feeling of comfort and good taste.

The scent of sweet applewood burning in the fireplace permeated the room, and there was music playing. It must be some collection of pieces; the one that had just ended was Latin American, and this one reminded her of the slow, smoochy dancing of her youth. She felt soothed and relaxed. Grateful to the girls for asking her here and cooking her dinner.

The pictures were fabulous. Bright and vibrant, without the wishy-washiness of some watercolours. She especially liked one of a market scene in some old provincial town, the glowing fruits and vegetables piled high on the stall, the bunches of flowers thrust in buckets, the gleam of fishes on the fish stall.

She heard the garden door slide open and Robert say, 'I'm so glad you came, Sarah.'

She'd thought he was not here. The relaxed feeling disappeared at once. Freya came into the room, carrying a bottle of wine.

'Sorry I was so long, just finishing off the dinner.' She refilled Sarah's glass before she could refuse. Had she really drunk one already?

The three of them stood rather awkwardly in the middle of the room. Then Polly came in and the two girls began discussing the dinner. Sarah feigned a great interest in their discussion, but all the time she was aware of Robert standing a few feet away from her. She felt that he was watching her, though she would not look to see if he was.

A waltz began to play. Polly laughed.

'This CD is so dated, I love it! Can you do this, Mum?' she giggled. 'I suppose you can.'

'Well, we did it at school, two girls dancing together. It was pretty awful,' Sarah admitted.

'Did you and Dad never dance a waltz together?' Polly asked, twirling round the room, laughing.

'I think we may have done, just occasionally.' She remembered some rather old-fashioned hunt balls they'd gone to in their youth, where they had waltzed together. In fact, they had done all sorts of dances in their time: rumbas, tangos, the twist, of course, and rock-'n'-roll.

'*You* must have done them, Daddy,' Freya challenged Robert.

'I suppose I did, years ago,' he said.

'Do show us.' Polly stopped her twirling. 'I'd love to see if you could still do it. Come

261

dancing.' She twirled again, holding out her arms to an imaginary partner.

'Oh, go on, let's see if you can still do it!' Freya cried, and put the CD back to the beginning of the waltz. 'You start, we'll follow,' she said to Robert. 'Right, Polly, shall I be the man or the woman?'

'I can't remember it at all,' Sarah said, inwardly cringing with embarrassment. She could not possibly dance with Robert, not as intimately as for a waltz. She felt as affronted as a Victorian matron, but the girls laughed, assured her she could. Freya pushed Robert towards her.

'Come on,' she said, 'we want to know how to do it.'

Robert, looking as if this was a difficult task he had to do, so he might as well get it over with, put down his glass and took Sarah into his arms. She did not know where to look. The feel of his arms round her, the scent of him was sending her heart into overdrive. She would probably have a heart attack any moment and then she wouldn't get to America. He turned her round and she found her body responding to his, to the music, as if she had been waltzing all her life. The two girls tried to copy them, holding on to each other, giggling hysterically, as if they could not believe that their parents came from such a dinosaur age. It was the most ridiculous thing she had ever done, dancing a waltz with a man she did not like.

Yet the music, cloying and sweet as some luscious confection, held a compelling magic, stirring memories long gone. Not, strangely, memories of Dan, just of dancing, the sheer pleasure of letting go, being free to give oneself up to the will of the music. She tried to keep her face averted from Robert's, but she could feel his breath on her cheek, the warmth of his body close to hers. The scent of the applewood dulled her brain, the exhaustion of too much work and the wine she'd drunk lowered her resistance. She had to hold on to him so as not to lose her balance.

As the music finished, another piece started up, rich and melodious, insisting that they went on dancing.

She heard Polly shriek, 'God, the dinner!' There was a scuffle as both girls ran from the room.

Sarah slowed down, willing her legs to stop dancing, her arms to go back to her sides, but Robert held her close, waltzing her round and round, and they were in the garden, dancing together under the moon. She wanted to stop, she *must* stop; this was so ridiculous, dancing a waltz as if she were in another time. She faced him to tell him this, but he bent his head and kissed her on her mouth.

She opened her mouth to protest, tried to drag herself away from him, but he went on kissing her, his arms holding her like a vice.

Then he stopped, quite suddenly, and she felt bereft.

'I'm sorry,' he said, still holding her. 'I couldn't resist it. I've been wanting to kiss you for ages.'

'Well, now you've done it, you can let me go,' she said, fighting the ludicrous desire that spun through her body. How could she possibly desire him? Perhaps the drink had been spiked.

He smiled, but he would not let her go. 'I can't help myself. I wanted to dislike you, it would be so much easier to fight for what I want, but I cannot.'

'I don't trust you,' she said, 'and you should hate me for killing your plants.' She could see the tangled creeper from the corner of her eye; even by the dim lights in the garden she could see that it looked very ill.

'I do dislike you for that. And all that blood on my white paint, as if a murder had been committed,' he said. 'You must pay for it.'

'Give me the bill and I will.' She struggled to free herself.

'Here it is,' he said, and kissed her mouth again. To her horror, she found she was kissing him back. Her lips would not obey her, nor indeed would her body. It was straining towards his as if it wanted to belong to him. Then she thought of the children.

She could not, would not, be seen kissing this man. With superhuman effort, she sprang

264

free and stood away from him. He laughed.

'I might be in love with you,' he said. 'What do you think of that?'

Freya came to the door. 'It's ready,' she said. 'We just saved it in time from burning.' She turned to Sarah. 'Is Daddy moaning about his plants? You killed at least two of them, apparently, when you let me in that night.'

'We've discussed it. She'll pay me back.' Robert gestured to her to go inside. 'Have you killed that orchid, too? That was very expensive.'

She saw the tender amusement in his eyes as she turned to go inside. His hand brushed the small of her back. To her intense mortification—for she knew that he knew— her desire matched his. But it could not be, not in front of their children. He was no doubt taking advantage of her lonely, sexless state, thinking a woman with no man in her life was easy, grateful prey, as Gerry had done. She must beware of him. It was only another ploy, the oldest one in the book, to get access to her house.

*   *   *

The dinner, pork tenderloin in a spicy tomato sauce, was good, if a little burnt at the edges. Polly, who seemed quite at home in this house, talked proudly of Sarah's achievement.

'So, Mom's a jet-setter at last,' she said

affectionately. 'Do get one of those outrageous houses in Los Angeles and invite us all to stay,' she egged.

Robert said, 'Freya showed me the article. Well done. I must say, it was a very glamorous picture.'

'Airbrushed.' Sarah concentrated on spearing the string beans with her fork.

'I don't think so,' he said. 'So, when will you go?'

His question was loaded. Once he knew when the house was to be empty, he would make plans. Perhaps aided and abetted by Dan to take it over. The thought of what he might do when she had gone had ruined her excitement.

She said, 'It hasn't been settled. I'll be back and forth all the time anyway.'

'I'm off the day after tomorrow,' Freya said. 'A friend has found me a flat and hopefully someone to look after Jack, so I can go back to work.'

Sarah suddenly wondered why Polly was still at home. 'Aren't you meant to be back at uni, Pol?' she questioned her. 'I've been so busy I've lost track of the date.'

'I've got essays,' Polly answered vaguely, 'but I'll go back in a day or two. Will is coming back very soon. I'll have to be here for him.'

Her children had their own lives, and anyway they should be working hard at their studies—she could not expect them to guard the house for her. Robert's eyes were on her, but she would not look at him. She felt his leg push gently against hers. He might as well have shouted it from the rooftops—when the girls had gone they would be alone, each in their own house, side by side. It was an intoxicating yet terrifying thought.

The girls began to clear the plates. Sarah moved to help, to escape Robert, get into the safety of the kitchen.

'Please don't, thanks all the same,' Freya said, whisking the plates away from her and carrying them out.

Robert said, 'And *your* essays, Sarah? Have you done one on the Egyptian way of death? Or,' he paused and like tossing a coin into a pool of water, causing circles of ripples, he added, 'or way of love? Have we learnt about that? Perhaps you did when I was away.'

'No, we have not. I won't have time to go any more. I won't be here, will I?'

'I suppose you won't.' Then he said more softly, 'I'm glad I don't have to go any more, either; she was such a bad tutor, so dull. I'd rather go to the lectures they have at the British Museum.'

She looked at him sharply. 'Why did you keep going, then?'

His eyes held an amused tenderness that she found disturbing. 'I heard you telling Polly, when you were both in the garden, that you were going to take up Egyptology. I thought it was the only way we could meet in a civilized fashion.'

He was lying, surely he was, yet why did her heart insist on doing these cartwheels? Poor, sad woman that she was, she was letting herself be drawn in to his trap. He was spinning a web round her, and when he had caught her he would kill her with his derision.

To her relief, the girls came back into the room with the pudding. Freya took over the conversation, and she and Polly with their youth and high spirits carried the rest of the evening.

Soon after the coffee, Sarah got up to go home. She had a design to finish before bed, and she was almost falling asleep in her chair by the fire. Robert said he'd walk her home.

'It's one step,' she said. 'Please don't.'

She thanked the girls for the dinner and praised their cooking. Robert came with her to the door.

'I want to make love to you,' he said in her ear. 'We can't with our daughters here . . . but when they have gone.'

'Good-night,' she said, as firmly as an elderly virgin. 'Thank you so much for having me.'

'I wish I had.' He laughed. 'Oh, how I wish I had.'

She blushed furiously. Her words had been automatically dredged up from some reserves of manners taught at home long ago. Trust him to exploit them. She ran out of his house and across to her own door, his laughter chasing her all the way.

She hardly slept that night, tortured by the feel of his body, his soft yet urgent kisses burning her mouth. When the girls both went their sepatate ways, perhaps she should move—in any case sleep in Celine's house until they went to America and she got over this ridiculous craving for him.

It was only her being alone and feeling so lost and rejected after Dan's desertion that made her feel this way. But she didn't tell Celine about Robert—somehow it never seemed to be the right time.

CHAPTER TWENTY-THREE

Freya hugged Sarah warmly as she left to go back to France. 'You saved my life, how can I ever thank you?' she said dramatically. 'I'll keep in touch through Daddy—see you keep him in order.' She laughed as she said this, but Sarah felt she meant it seriously. To her relief Robert was not there to witness her remark.

Obviouly bored after her new friend's departure, and with Sarah's total immersion in her work, Polly left soon after Freya to go back to university.

Now she and Robert were alone, living here

side by side. She would not allow herself to be enticed by his flattery into giving him his own way. He wanted her house more than her; she must never forget that. She would maintain a friendly but distant relationship with him, as she would with any other man who lived in the street.

Yet sometimes the memory of his lips on hers, his arms around her as they danced that ridiculous waltz, reared up to taunt her.

But such thoughts were sentimental madness. She spent the first evening after Polly had gone back with Celine, the next with another girlfriend, coming back late and creeping into her house so as not to disturb him. She felt rather foolish doing it on the second night, as he was obviously not there at all. She realized that she was letting Robert rule her life just as if he had insisted that she behave like this. What a relief that she was going away soon and could forget all about him.

She was woken up early on the Saturday morning by the sound of a lorry arriving and men's voices in the street. A minute later, she heard a strident ring on Robert's doorbell and he answered the door. There was further clattering and voices, then all was quiet.

Damn him for waking her up so early on a Saturday, she fumed, snuggling back into bed and pulling the bedcovers over her as if to shut him out. But however hard she tried to go back to sleep, she could not, and in a thoroughly bad humour she got up and went downstairs in her dressing-gown. She went into the kitchen and put on the kettle for some coffee, and heard men's voices in her garden.

She shrank back by the door. She had not drawn the curtains, and peering round, she saw to her horror a workman in her garden, pulling down the trellis. How dare they intrude on her privacy? What if she'd had nothing on? She flew back upstairs and pulled on her jeans and a jersey, then ran outside.

'What are you doing? You have no right to be in my garden!' she cried at the startled man, who, armed with a screwdriver, was fiddling about with her wall.

'Ooh, sorry, love, just obeying orders. Got to come round this side to take the trellis off, like.'

'I don't want it taken off; you are to leave it alone!' she barked at him. 'Now, go back over that ladder and stay in Mr Maynard's garden.'

Another man popped his head up. Then Robert, obviously alerted by the commotion, appeared from inside the house. He smiled at her through the leaf-encrusted squares of trellis. He smiled in the way one might smile at a raging bull.

'Sarah, I'm so sorry to disturb you, but they came far earlier than I thought. I was expecting them at lunchtime. I was going to tell you about it, but you're never here. We

271

need to replace the trellis after you broke it,'
he said reasonably, yet making her feel that he
was blaming the whole thing on her.

'But not standing in my garden, invading my
privacy!' She stormed up to the wall and faced
him through the trellis. 'You have no right to
have people in my garden without my
permission.'

Her instincts had been right. Just because
he'd kissed her, sensed her desire for him, he
now thought he could take advantage of her.
It hadn't taken him long. Next thing there
would be a conservatory filled with orchids
encroaching on her garden.

'I was just about to come and tell you, but
they arrived a couple of hours before I thought
they would,' he said, with extreme patience, as
though she were simple-minded. 'Look, come
round and have a coffee, and I'll explain. I'm
only replacing the trellis, nothing more, but as
you can see, half the bracket is screwed on
your side; it needs to be unscrewed from
there.'

'I want you to leave it,' she said firmly. 'I
don't want it changed.' Perhaps once it was
down he would leave it down, getting one step
nearer to taking over her garden. The thought
of her coming trip to Americ' filled her with
disquiet. He knew she was going away. What
would he get up to when she was gone and her
house was empty?

She saw his mouth harden in that defiant

manner he had when he wanted his own way. The two workmen looked on with interest. The one in her garden had gone back over the ladder, and the three men stood like spectators at a show, watching her keenly.

'These men have another job to go to, they want to get on with this quickly. They will not be long and I will have the new trellis fixed to my side of the wall so you will not be bothered again. It is hardly my fault you are never here to ask.' His eyes glittered with impatience.

'Why couldn't you have put a note through my letterbox?' He was insufferable. Perhaps he'd thought she'd gone away already and was losing no time in getting what he wanted?

'Because you don't seem to read things that you don't like. If you'd read that solicitor's letter properly, you'd have seen I was asking for first refusal should you want to sell or to reduce your garden. Please, Sarah.' He was fighting with his irritation. 'Just let them unscrew it, then you won't be bothered again.'

The two other men smiled at her encouragingly and she felt outnumbered by them, but furious too.

'I will not be taken advantage of,' she said defiantly.

One of the workmen smirked, which added to her anger.

'It is surely plain good manners to wait until your neighbour agrees to your plans before you embark on them,' she said icily. She

273

wanted to go back inside her house and shut the door on the lot of them, but she knew she'd have no peace. What a fool she'd been to let him kiss her, to kiss him back. She felt hot with embarrassment, as though the image of the two of them kissing was held up for all to see.

Robert said, 'Look, it's ridiculous talking through the trellis like this. I'll come over and supervise the whole thing. Make quite sure nothing is disturbed on your side.'

'No, thank you.' She would not give him a single chance to try and get round her by any form of seduction. 'I will stand here now while it is done. I am very unhappy about it, and I want you to know that this is the very last time you carry out any work that involves my property without my written permission.'

'Thank you, Sarah.' Robert gave her a maddening little bow, increasing her anger further. 'Right, Len,' he addressed one of the men, 'let's get on with it.' He retreated back into his house, leaving Sarah fuming in her own garden.

'It will be all right, lady,' Len said brightly. 'I won't hurt anything.' He gave her a kindly smile, as though to humour her.

*   *   *

Later that day, Robert went away and Sarah felt relieved that she had the weekend to

274

herself. With any luck he would have gone back to Scotland and she need not see him again. The new trellis was up; it was not as high as the last lot, and although the creepers had been wound through it, there were a lot of gaps that she did not like. He should have asked her what she wanted, as it was on her wall too. She wished it was higher—even fencing, to block him out completely—but now it was done she could not face him starting all over again.

The plans to go to America were taking a bit of time. Some of the people they needed to see there were away, or going to be away, but slowly it came together and the date for their departure was set for the end of February.

Sarah found it easier to work on her designs in the shop, staying late after the sewing-girls had gone. She sat in the back, in the sewing-room. She told Celine she'd rather work here with the fabrics around her, but she knew she was doing it so she would not have to see Robert. She had heard him return home a few nights ago.

One evening, she worked until after midnight. It was a wild night, the wind lashing the rain against the windows. She had not realized the weather was so bad, or that it was so late, she'd been so engrossed in her work. She closed the shop and wished she had rung for a taxi, then she saw to her relief the number 14 bus trundling down the road.

Ideas went on spinning in her exhausted brain. She must stay awake so as not to miss her stop. Once or twice she dozed off, then jerked awake. At last she arrived at her stop and got off the bus, pushing her way through the wind and the rain. She'd forgotten her umbrella, but the teeming rain made her feel fresh, washing away the confines of the day. Though the wind was cold, it seemed to blow away her tension.

She reached her front door, her key in her hand and Robert's door opened.

'You look simply dreadful.' He was standing beside her, getting wet too.

'Thank you,' she said. 'Good-night.'

He took her arm and pulled her towards his door. 'You need to dry out, have a drink to warm you,' he said firmly.

'It's so late. I want to go to bed.' She jerked away from him.

'Good,' he said, 'so do I.' He picked her up and carried her into his house, shutting the door firmly behind him. Then he kissed her.

It was sheer exhaustion, she told herself later, that had so undermined her senses. It was not her fault that he had carried her straight upstairs to his bed, pulled off her wet clothes and made love to her. Her body was very odd the way it had responded to his, as if it had been waiting for him and fitted so perfectly with his. He'd no doubt spiked her drink; only she hadn't had a drink. But she

276

wasn't meant to make love to him, not like this, and enjoy it.

Later, they shared a shower, and they stood tightly together—well, there wasn't much room if both of them wanted to get under the warm, streaming water.

'You mustn't catch cold after being out in that wind,' he said, rubbing soap all over her and then himself, so their bodies slid together, making the soap foam like whipped cream between them.

She woke late the next morning. When she realized where she was, she sprang up in horror. What had she done? How could she get out of here without the neighbours seeing? Or his cleaner—they were the worst gossips, and he might use this aberration as emotional blackmail against her. What had he made her say last night? Had she signed over the house or garden to him?

Robert came into the room. He was fully dressed, she was not, and she hastily pulled the sheet round her. He laughed.

'Why are you covering yourself up? You have the most beautiful body.'

She blushed, thinking of her bulgy tummy, the sagging breasts. Perhaps lying down on her back in the dark, she didn't look so bad. 'Hardly,' she said.

'It *is* beautiful,' he said, and came to sit on the bed. He bent to kiss her.

'I've got to go home,' she said. 'I'll have to

go back through the garden, in case anyone sees us.'

He laughed again. 'Perhaps you are right. No one will mind, but they might gossip.' His eyes crinkled with amusement. 'As you are now so famous, in *Vogue* and all.'

'Please go and let me get dressed. Then help me back over the fence. I must get to work, and you . . . shouldn't you be at work?'

'Not on a Saturday,' he said. 'Have you forgotten the days?'

She regarded him intently. 'I have. I've been working so hard.' She frowned. 'Is it really Saturday?'

'I'll show you the newspaper, if you don't believe me.'

'I must go, anyway. I've lots to do.'

'I thought we'd spend the day together,' he said. 'In fact, the whole weekend.'

'I can't,' she said, and wondered why she couldn't.

'You can,' he said. 'You can work here if you want to.'

'I've got things in my house I need, and I want clean clothes.'

He smiled. 'I have a stepladder that I'll put against the wall. The trellis is not so high; you can step over on to your side of the wall and jump down, or even put a ladder your side, too. We can go back and forth, and no one will know.'

So that was it, she told herself sadly. He had

278

put in a lower trellis to give him easy access to her garden.

'No,' she said. 'We can't disturb your creeper again, climbing over it. It will never get better. Besides, the children will see and . . .' He stopped her protestations with kisses, and even as she responded to his lovemaking, part of her mind warned her to keep guard.

In the end she agreed to put a ladder on each side, so they could visit each other without anyone else knowing.

'You still don't trust me?' His eyes held defiance.

'I want to keep my independence,' she said, thinking that was where self-preservation lay. If they each kept their own space, there would be less chance of him tiring of her.

He showed her his orchid room upstairs. He had put in large windows in the back to give the plants more light; blinds on them, so he could control the levels. He reeled off some of their names—*Phalaenopsis Follet, Miltoniopsis St Helier*—with a tenderness as if they were his children. To her surprise, she thought them beautiful; she had never really thought about them much before. He did not have any of the ones she thought sinister, with odd markings and long tendrils hanging down as if to ensnare. There was a glorious blue one that hung on the wall, its bare roots getting its nutrients from the air, and wonderful pink ones like huge pansies; others had such

279

intricate markings, it was as if an artist had painted them on.

'They take seven years to grow.' He showed her one that he had grafted himself, which was about to flower.

'They are your most favourite things, are they not?' she asked, studying some small flasks on the bench, containing yet more growing orchids.

'They are. I was about to make an expedition with a group to Thailand to look for some, when I inherited the glass factory. So that was put on hold, but yes, they are a bit of an obsession.' He took her in his arms, resting his chin on the top of her head. 'But I can have other obsessions, too.'

She knew how much he wanted his conservatory for them, but she said nothing. Her life had changed so completely, and she had learnt from Dan's defection not to give everything away. To her relief, Robert did not mention it.

*   *   *

Dan rang, to remind her about the money.

'I think we should divorce, let the courts decide,' she said. 'And you should marry that woman.'

'We've talked about that, Sarah, how much money lawyers take.'

'I know, but I think we should, now you

have a child.' She rang off before she got further embroiled with him and he renewed his demand for the money. She didn't have it now, perhaps she would in the future if Celine's dream came off, but she was reluctant to give it to him. He'd made his decision; if he'd stayed with her, this would not have arisen.

The time ticked on closer to her trip to America. They would be gone for at least a month, and her feelings were confused. She longed to go, and yet that meant leaving Robert behind. No one, not their children, not even Celine, knew about their love, though Celine had remarked on her looks, her radiant face.

'Your talent has paid off at last. You see how fulfilled it has made you feel? How much confidence it has given you? You look fantastic. It's better than love, isn't it?'

Sarah smiled. There would be plenty of time to tell Celine about Robert. It was still so new, so magical, she did not want to discuss it. She could imagine Celine saying, 'Not that man next door? Whatever are you thinking of? He'll make you sell the house for his blessed orchids, or move them in and make you adapt your life to accommodate them.' She had to admit that thought was at the back of her own mind.

And once people knew about it, they would throw up questions, questions that might have awkward answers, and she did not want to think about that just now.

* * *

Robert was unusually quiet one evening. They were sitting together In her house after dinner.

He said at last, 'If it's not intrusive, can I ask why, if your husband left you and has a child with someone else, you are not divorced?'

She was surprised at his question. They hardly ever discussed Dan at all. She didn't want to, in case he mentioned any deal he and Dan had made over the house.

'Dan said he'd have more money to give me if we didn't involve lawyers, but I do want to divorce him now. Only, I'm afraid I'll have to give him some of the money from the last house.' She didn't say any more, concerned that he would guess that if she had to pay him she would have to sell her house. She wondered if Robert knew that, had discussed it with Dan.

'I see.' He watched her intently, his eyes inscrutable.

She felt a pang of unease and said a little sharply, 'Why do you want to know?'

'I want to know if you still love him, if you are holding on in case he wants to come back. Some men do, you know, they realize the foolish mistake they have made; and you obviously have some feelings for him.' He

282

glanced over to a photograph on the table. A laughing group—Dan, Sarah and the children. A picture she'd kept to remind herself of the happier times.

She did not jump up and go to Robert, kiss away his fears, swear she loved only him. She sat there and thought over his words. Why did she still hold on to Dan, why did she not let him go? He had hurt her more than anyone had ever hurt her before, but love could not be turned off as easily as that. Twenty-four years and two children did not vanish in a moment.

'I understand your feelings,' Robert said gently, 'but ask yourself this, if he knocked on that door now and wanted to come back, what would you do?'

'He has a new baby now,' she said, to stall for time.

He shrugged. 'So? That might not stop him wanting to come back to you. What would you do?' His question lay heavy in the air between them. No one had asked her so pointedly before; no one had needed to.

She could not look at him, because she wanted to be honest with him. She knew what he was asking; he was not a man to give his love lightly. If he gave his love to her, would she give hers unequivocally to him, or would she wish that he was Dan as he used to be? There must be no half-measures.

'I wouldn't take him back,' she said at last. 'Not as he is now. We had a very happy marriage, or I thought we did. I became part of him and him me. Losing him is . . .' she laughed awkwardly, 'as they say, like cutting off a limb. But it is foolish to go on clinging to the past. He has changed, I have changed, and I do love you.'

'Do you trust me?'

She almost cried out 'Of course', but she did not. She did not completely trust him, not if she thought of the house. Dan's defection had broken her trust in men. Did Robert love her more than his orchids?

She turned to him to explain this. He'd been watching her intently. He smiled, but it was a sad smile. He got up.

'Lay the ghost to rest, darling, once and for all; without that we have no future together.' He blew her a kiss and left the room. She heard him climb back over the ladder into his garden, and then she heard him pull the ladder in her garden back over to his side of the wall.

She sat there a long time, thinking over his words. It was not fair to give a man only half your love because the rest of it was still stuck in the past with someone else. Now the thought of going away and leaving it unresolved bothered her. Would the love they'd shared wilt and die as his tender plants had when she had broken them? But this trip to America was a gift, an amazing chance at independence and success. She could not let it go.

The following day, she went to the travel agent to pick up the tickets. Celine was giving her new staff in the shop one last lecture.

She waited by the traffic lights to cross the road. Just up the road, a woman was feeding the meter in front of a rather battered four door BMW. A man with a pushchair came towards her.

'Sarah.'

It could not be, this strained ageing man could not possibly be Dan. Her shock must have shown on her face, for he said rather grumpily, 'I saw you in *Vogue*. Polly showed me.'

'Yes. I'm off to America on Thursday with Celine.' She wondered where the red frog of a sports car was, then realized that a baby and all its paraphernalia would not fit into a sports car. Even if it did, it would somehow spoil the image he had destroyed so much in order to achieve. His life had gone round in a circle, and he was back to a less glamorous family car as before.

The mouse quickly joined them. She stood close to Dan, her hand on his on the handle of the pram. She stared at Sarah defiantly. Sarah made herself look into the pushchair, expecting to see a miniature Tim or Polly, but the pale, dribbling baby hardly resembled Dan at all. Tim and Polly had been such lovely babies, glowing and happy, but this one looked miserable. She waited for the pain of Dan's betrayal to hit her, crush her heart in its savage teeth, but it did not.

The baby opened its mouth and screamed. The mouse leant over it. Dan's face became agitated. The lights changed. Sarah felt him looking at her, studying her as if he had not seen her before.

'Oh, Dan,' she said quietly, so that the mouse would not hear. 'Tell me, was it worth it?'

He did not answer her, but she sensed from his manner that it was not. But he was a loyal man—for a while, anyway—he knew it was too late and there was no going back. Sarah crossed the road quickly, leaving them behind her.

Dan had gone backwards while she was charging forwards to so many new and wonderful things. Her heart was suddenly free, soaring like a bird, flying into an endless sky.

CHAPTER TWENTY-FOUR

Sarah raced back to the shop, bubbling with euphoria, a new lightness round her heart. She was over Dan. He had changed from the man she knew and loved when he had left her, but she had stubbornly clung on to the person he used to be, harbouring a secret thought that he would suddenly reappear and their life would go on again, happy and tranquil. But seeing him today, tied up in his new life, bound irrevocably with the ties of recent fatherhood, she accepted that he would never again be the man she once loved.

She must tell Robert—quickly, now, before she got bogged down in the last-minute preparations for going to the States. She dialled his home number as she sat on the bus; after four rings he didn't answer it and she rang off. Of course he wasn't there at this time, he was working. She'd have to wait until she got home tonight to tell him. Her heart and body sang at the thought of it.

There was so much to do at the shop that she did not manage to leave until seven. It was a cold night, but she barely felt it in her agitation to get to Robert and tell him she was free of her emotional ties to Dan. The bus journey seemed interminable, stopping and starting like something in pain. Many times she almost jumped off to run up the road, but then the bus would start up again, lumbering on quite hopefully before juddering to another stop.

She turned round the corner into their street, her heart beating with excitement. Robert's house was in darkness. He was still at work, consulting somewhere or someone, she told herself, to soothe the slap of bitter disappointment. But looking at his house again, her heart stopped. There, standing proudly by the gate, was a FOR SALE sign. For one second she thought it had been put up outside her own house, but as she hurried onwards she saw by the light of the streetlamp that it was fixed firmly on to Robert's side.

It could not be true. Only two days ago they had been lovers. Had he had enough of her, and decided to escape to Scotland and sell his house here?

Panic and despair chased through her, leaving her staggering and weak. All the old pain of rejection and the terrible ache of loneliness, which his love for her had healed, now seized her again in a vice.

Had he just gone, left her without a word? Perhaps he'd left her one of his famous letters. She fumbled with her key and pushed open the door. A pile of letters and various flyers lay on the mat. She sifted through them quickly, but there was nothing from him. She ran into the living-room; he must have left her a message on the answerphone, but there was no red button flashing at her.

It was over. She slumped down on a chair. There was no commitment today; why should there be, when modern morals almost encouraged people to perfect their lovemaking skills with many partners, as they might perfect their golf swing? Why settle for one, when there was a whole host of choices out there?

But why hadn't he told her he was leaving? And why so suddenly? Had he known all along that he was going? Perhaps his glass business made it necessary that he live in Scotland. Perhaps he'd thought Helen Donaldson, free of encumbrances, would be a more peaceful partner.

But despite her prejudices, her distrust of him, that he might use any means he could to get her house, she had loved him. Did still love him, she admitted, as the pain tore through her. She'd have given him anything, the whole house for his orchids, just to please him. Well, now she wouldn't have to. She must not let this grind her down. It was just another setback, as all the others had been on her difficult path to her new independent life. But she had, after all, achieved something more lasting, something she could not have done if she was still married to Dan. She was a professional now, on her way to important and lucrative deals in the States. She might not spend much time here if it went well, and a love affair would only hold her back.

The telephone rang, and she jumped up as eager as Polly to answer it. It was Celine.

'My, you sound eager. It can't be for me. Who did you hope it was?'

'Oh . . . no one, I mean one of the children. But how are you, got home all right?'

'Of course, Sarah. I only had to walk ten

minutes down the road. Why wouldn't I? There's something up, isn't there? You're not waiting for a lover, are you?' There was laughter in her voice, and Sarah resisted the urge to pour out the whole sorry tale.

'Me? No such luck. What's up?' She hoped she sounded carefree.

'I just wanted to go over the travel plans again. We didn't have much time in the shop. Afternoon plane on Thursday, from Heathrow. I'll book a minicab to take us, put it down to the business.'

'Why not a limo, while you're at it?' Sarah tried to joke.

'Next time.' Celine laughed. 'But something's up, I know it. You're not getting cold feet and running out, are you?'

'Goodness, no. It's just I got back to find a "for sale" sign on Robert's house. It's quite a surprise. He didn't tell me.'

'Well done, you've won!' Celine enthused. 'Don't you see? As he failed in his devious tricks to get your house, he's decided to move on. Perhaps he didn't really want it at all, but was just trying to wield some sort of power over you. I'm so glad. Everything is coming right for you, Sarah, and about time, too. You deserve it after what you've been through. This trip, your talent as a designer being recognized, and now your house safe from that scheming man.'

She'd burst into tears in a minute, those

stupid tears that threatened to engulf her at every point. She couldn't tell Celine that she longed for Robert, wanted him to stay on, whatever his terms. Celine would not stand for it; she would tell her in no uncertain fashion that she was a fool for being controlled by her emotions, and having just been freed from loving Dan for preparing to jump straight back in to the quicksand again with another man.

'Got something cooking,' she said. 'See you tomorrow. I'll be there by lunchtime.' She rang off. She had a few more designs to polish up and she was staying at home to do them.

She hardly slept that night, listening for Robert to return, but he did not. She struggled out of bed in the morning and forced herself to work. But half of her was straining to hear him return or at least to ring her. If only she had his mobile number, but she had not asked for it. But even if she had it, was she going to be the one to ring? No, if he had sneaked off like that without telling her, her pride would not let her call him first.

Some people passed her window and stopped by Robert's house. She tensed; she heard his front door open, the ping as his alarm kicked in, then silence as it was turned off.

Had he come back with some friends? It was nearly time for her to leave to go to the shop. She packed up her designs, she'd take them with her. She'd work on them better in

291

the shop with Celine and the girls around, making her feel she must get on, not sit dreaming and brooding. She got ready quickly, hearing from time to time the sounds of people moving round his house. She hovered in the hall, thinking to ring his bell with some simple enquiry before she left for work. But she heard his front door open, and she opened her door and went out on her way to work.

A young man with a middle-aged couple stood on the pavement looking up at the structure of the house. The woman was dowdy, her face apathetic with exhaustion. The man turned to her; his face lit up, a sickly smirk on his pudgy face.

'Good Morning! We might be your new neighbours,' he said with a leer, his pink hands darting like fish in her direction.

She ran down the street and up the New Kings Road to the bus stop. If that man moved in, she would leave. Horrific images of him leering over her fence and those hideous little hands trying to catch her as they passed in the street loomed up to torture her.

Celine was out most of the day, seeing to various financial details, but Sarah felt too dispirited to confide in her. She got home again after seven, dawdling on her way, dreading to see Robert's empty house. As she feared, it was still in darkness, but she forced herself to put in a load of washing and think about her packing for her trip.

Glancing out at her garden from the kitchen, she saw that the light was on in Robert's garden. It hadn't been on last night. Had an estate agent left it on? She opened the door to her garden and slipped out. It was cold, the wind nipping at her like a terrier. She heard a movement from the other side of the wall, and she went over to the fence that divided them.

'Robert?' She said his name quietly, wondering what she would do if it *was* some intruder.

'Yes.'

One word. Was it his voice? She tried to peer through the trellis, but it was difficult to see among the shadows.

'Is it you or some thief?' she said loudly, her heart lifting just a little.

'It's me.' He was close to the wall, and though she could not see him, she could feel him there.

'Why didn't you tell me you were going to put your house on the market?' she asked. 'I might have wanted to buy it myself.'

'You can't afford it,' he said. 'I want a quick sale.'

'Are you going to live in Scotland?' The pain was back again twisting in her like poison, but she would not let him know.

'I don't know, here or there, it doesn't matter.'

'But your orchids—where will they go?'

There was a silence. For a moment she thought he had gone back inside, then he said, 'While I have this house, I know you will never trust me. You'll suspect everything I do as trying in some devious way to possess your house. By selling mine, I thought it might show you that I love you more than this house, more than my orchids.'

His words crept through the trellis, curling into her, lifting her. She could not speak. Had she heard him right? He loved her enough to sell his house?

'There is a couple who saw it today, who have made an offer already,' he went on. 'I could be homeless very soon.'

'Oh, no!' she cried out. 'Not that horrid little man with his darting hands and downtrodden wife!'

He laughed. 'I don't know what they look like. But they seem very keen.'

'You can't,' she said. 'I won't let you. You mustn't sell your house. I don't want you to.'

'Are you sure?' His voice held an edge of severity. 'I don't much care for these separate relationships, Sarah. I want all or nothing. I want you to marry me.'

Marry? Here they stood, each in their own garden, unable to see each other through the plant-encrusted trellis, and he was asking her to marry him. She wanted to see his face, to see if he was just being sarcastic.

'I don't trust marriage,' she blurted.

'I'm not asking you to trust marriage. I'm asking you to trust me,' he said. 'Come over here. We can't go on talking through a wall like Pyramus and Thisbe. Come on, I'll open the door for you.'

'You come here to me,' she said.

She heard him leave the garden, and she ran to her front door and opened it. He stood there, looking at her, his expression a little apprehensive under his smile. He came in to the hall, and she fell into his arms.

*   *   *

'I thought you had gone without telling me,' she said, as they lay on the sofa, replete with lovemaking.

'I thought shock tactics were needed,' he said, glancing over to the photograph of Dan, Sarah and the children, which still stood on the table. His eyes studied her, his hand stroked her hair. 'I know how much you have been hurt. I've been through it, too, and it took me a long time to get over it. I really admire you for your courage in picking yourself up and getting on with a new life. I know I added to your struggle, and I'm sorry.' He pulled her down to him and kissed her.

'Yes, you did, but I'll forgive you. Well, I will only if you take your house off the market.'

'Because you want me to stay, or because you don't want that lecher to live next door to you?'

She saw the flash of insecurity behind the teasing in his eyes. We are all insecure she thought, all afraid to give too much of ourselves, in case we get burnt.

'What do you think?' She shifted her weight, sat up and looked down on him.

He cupped her face in his hand as if it was something priceless. 'You need just that extra bit of courage to put the past behind you and start again.'

'I'd better get some brochures on conservatories, then,' she said, lying down beside him as he laughed and covered her with kisses.

No one knew what life held, what the passing of time would do to a relationship. Would she really rather stay on the sidelines in case it turned sour like it had with Dan?

She got up and went over to the photograph of the four of them—a happy family, laughing out at her. She was lucky she had had that, but it was over now, though she still had the children. She put the frame face-down in the drawer and closed it firmly. That part of her life was over. Her new life was with Robert.

*   *   *

'Smile, look happy.' The photographer gave a broad grin, his white teeth flashing with delight against his dark skin.

Sarah laughed out loud; she was so happy, standing with Robert on the steps of the Register Office. Tim, Polly and Freya surrounded them, arms round each other, laughing also. Even little Jack—her step-grandson—now firmly on his feet, caught the mood and grinned and waved at the camera.